'Don't you e— — — —
Remy murm— —
her hair aro— —
and bringing — —

She didn't like w— — — —ation was
heading. How much honesty did she want to
allow herself? Yes, she got lonely. Damn right
she got lonely. Why else would she be lying
here beside a convicted killer, wishing she
could believe this whole crazy charade they
were playing?

'Dana?'

'Sometimes,' she admitted.

'I think the nights are the worst,' he said.
'Don't you wish you had someone beside you
then, to talk to?' He stroked her cheek with
the ends of her hair. 'Or just to hold in the
dark?'

She moistened her lips. 'Sometimes.'

He leaned closer.

Was he going to kiss her? What would she do
if he did? How could she stand it if he
didn't…?

Dear Reader,

Welcome to Silhouette Sensation—the best in romantic suspense.

Paula Detmer Riggs leads off the line-up with *Born a Hero*, the first book in a special six-book set of linked novels that we've called FIRST-BORN SONS. It's a fascinating set of books, running once a month from July to December, about six first-born sons who are bound by a powerful legacy. Following that comes Ingrid Weaver with *Fugitive Hearts*, where a mysterious stranger collapses at the heroine's doorstep and turns out to be a fugitive from justice!

The Seduction of Goody Two-Shoes comes from the award-winning pen of Kathleen Creighton whose wonderful cynical, protective hero McCall just doesn't realise the kind of trouble Ellie Lanagan is about to get him into! There's another protective man in Marilyn Pappano's latest, *The Sheriff's Surrender*, where a sexy sheriff ends up protecting his former flame, holding her life—and their future—in his hands.

Harper Allen, who you might know from Intrigue, is writing her first Silhouette Sensation in *Protector with a Past*, where a couple reunite to find a killer and save a child. And our last book for the month is *Moonglow, Texas* by Mary McBride with another trademark Sensation lawman who's protecting a witness, but also falling in love…

Enjoy them all!

The Editors

Fugitive Hearts

INGRID WEAVER

™ SILHOUETTE®
SENSATION™

First published in Great Britain 2002
Silhouette Books, Eton House, 18-24 Paradise Road,
Richmond, Surrey TW9 1SR

© Ingrid Caris 2001

ISBN 0 373 27171 9

18-0702

Printed and bound in Spain
by Litografía Rosés S.A., Barcelona

INGRID WEAVER

admits to being a compulsive reader who loves a book that can make her cry. A former teacher, now a homemaker and mother, she delights in creating stories that reflect the wonder and adventure of falling in love. When she isn't writing or reading, she enjoys old *Star Trek* reruns, going on sweater-knitting binges, taking long walks with her husband and waking up early to canoe after camera-shy loons.

Ingrid is the recipient of the Romance Writers of America's RITA Award for Best Romantic Suspense Novel for her book, *On the Way to a Wedding...*

To Katie O'Toole,
Realtor Extraordinaire,
Forty-seven acres of thanks!

Chapter 1

At first Dana didn't realize the lump on her doorstep was human.

She assumed the snow that had been piling up on the roof of the caretaker's cabin all day must have slid off, a mini avalanche triggered by the wind. Or else the storm had swirled the snow into a freak drift. If the wood box beside the fireplace hadn't been getting empty, she would have waited until the morning to dig herself out, but she didn't want to risk having Morty catch another chill at his age. So instead of going back inside when she saw her way was blocked by the lump, Dana plunged ahead.

The snow wasn't the powdery mass she had expected. Her left boot came down on something firm and rounded. And the snowdrift groaned.

Dana shrieked and jumped backward, windmilling her arms to keep her balance. Her elbow smacked into the door frame. Her flashlight flew from her grasp and hit the underside of the eaves. With a tinkle of breaking glass, the beam winked out.

"Oh, my God!" She fell to her knees and reached in front of her. "Who's there? Are you hurt?"

Nothing. No more groans, no sound at all apart from the hiss of the wind and the pounding of her own pulse in her ears. In the dim glow from the window there was no trace of movement.

Dana inched forward, thrusting her arms into the tracks she had made. Immediately her hand connected with the form she had stepped on. She pulled her hand back and removed her mitten with her teeth, then extended her fingers. She touched fabric and pressed harder, running her fingertips along what it took her only a split second to realize was…an arm.

She put her mitten back on and started to dig, scooping the snow away as quickly as she could. "Hang on," she said. "Hang on, I'll help you."

It seemed to take forever, but it couldn't have been more than a minute later that Dana uncovered a figure that was definitely human. And, judging by the size, undoubtedly male. Wrapped in an overcoat, curled into a fetal position, the stranger remained silent and ominously motionless, except for the shivering that shook his large frame.

Stories her grandfather had told her in her childhood, tales of unwary trappers who had frozen to death mere yards from shelter in storms like this, popped unbidden into her head. Half Moon Bay Resort was only three hours north of Toronto, but it was like a different world up here—just last year there had been those snowmobilers who had gotten lost in a blizzard and hadn't been found until the spring thaw….

"Oh, God," she muttered. "Don't die, mister. You can't die."

Scrambling to her feet, she reached behind her to open the door. The wind shoved it inward, smacking it against the wall in a vicious gust. Snow streamed giddily over the threshold as Dana turned back to grasp the stranger under the arms.

Her boots slipped on the ice that coated the doorstep, sending her back to her knees. Her hands rapidly grew too numb to maintain a grip on the limp form. In desperation, she hooked her arm around the stranger's neck and dragged the dead weight backward like a swimmer, crawling and sliding until his body cleared the threshold. Unable to do more, she shoved his long, denim-clad legs to the side so that she could swing the door closed.

In the sudden stillness after the storm was shut out, Dana's rasping breaths seemed unnaturally loud. The fire on the hearth crackled, the clock on the mantel ticked and the snow hissed distantly against the windows. Everything was just as she'd left it mere minutes ago. Cozy and quiet, exactly as she wanted it.

Except for the body on her floor.

No, not a *dead* body kind of body. He had groaned, and he was still shivering enough to knock puffs of snow onto the floor around him, so he couldn't be dead.

Yet.

Dana toed off her boots and ran for the phone. Snatching up the receiver, she dialed 911. Surely the emergency services would still be working, despite the storm. And even if the ambulance couldn't get here immediately, at least she could talk to a doctor and find out what to do....

It took her a moment to realize the call wasn't going through. Nothing was. The line was dead.

"Oh, no." She jiggled the button. She dialed again. She checked to make sure the phone was plugged into the jack. Still nothing. The storm must have knocked out the phone lines.

Now what? They were miles from the highway. The resort pickup truck was four-wheel drive and might have had a chance with the snow, but it was standard transmission, and she didn't know how to handle a stick shift. And until the snowplow cleared the roads, there was no way she could risk driving her car anywhere. Not that she'd be capable of loading someone this man's size into her subcompact by herself even if the roads were clear.

Panic that she hadn't had the time to feel before now knotted her stomach as she went back to the stranger's side. At least she had assumed this was a stranger. No one she knew had been planning to make the trip up here—her family knew better than to disturb her when she was on a deadline. That's why she had come here in the first place, wasn't it? For peace and quiet and a complete lack of distractions.

Distractions? she thought wildly, feeling a bubble of hysteria tickle her throat. Hoo, boy, when it came to distractions, this one was a doozy.

Taking a deep breath to regain her control, Dana tore off her coat, then peered at the man's face. Snow clung in a wet shroud to his hair and had solidified into beads of ice on his eyebrows. His hawk-sharp nose, his prominent cheekbones, his square jaw all looked as if they could have been carved from a glacier. Beneath the frost-tipped edges of his mustache, his lips were blue.

Dana's stomach did a quick lurch. She was right. He was a stranger. She had never seen this man's face before. If she had, she definitely would have remembered.

"Mister?" she said. She gently shook his shoulder. "Hey, mister, can you hear me?"

No reply. But she hadn't really expected one. If her clumsy efforts to get him into the cabin hadn't roused him, it was doubtful her voice would.

She glanced at the coat he wore. It was long and navy-blue, made of wool that was fashionable but not very practical in weather like this, even with the collar turned up to shield his neck. His leather gloves wouldn't provide much protection from the cold, either. Nor would his jeans or his sneakers.

Why would anyone set off through a snowstorm with no hat or boots? What kind of man wore jeans and sneakers with an expensive overcoat and kidskin gloves?

And what on earth did it matter? Whoever he was, whatever he was, he had to get warmed up. Now. She didn't need a doctor or a paramedic to tell her that much.

Dana dropped to her knees at his side and tugged off his gloves, grimacing at the coldness of his hands. She spared a few seconds to breathe on them, chafing each one in turn between her palms before she turned to his other clothes.

Getting his damp coat off was a challenge. He was a tall man, and despite the complete laxness of his limbs, he was rock solid and outweighed her by at least eighty pounds. By the time she managed to extract his arms from his sleeves, she realized she would have no hope of getting him to the couch or the bed. Leaving him lying on his coat, she grasped his ankles and dragged him closer to the fireplace.

When she saw the dying blaze on the hearth she remembered why she had ventured outside in the first place.

"Oh, great," she muttered. She threw on the last of the wood, then sprinted to her bedroom and returned with an armful of blankets.

Was his shivering getting worse? Yes, it was, she realized. Taking off his coat was a good start, but she still needed to get him out of his wet clothes, or whatever body heat he still retained would drain away. She dumped the blankets on the floor and pulled off his shoes and socks, then looked at his jeans. The denim was thick, but it was as encrusted with snow as his overcoat. There was no way around it, the jeans would have to come off.

To her credit, Dana didn't hesitate. Much. This was no time to worry about proprieties. Under the circumstances she had no choice. Kneeling at his side, she unfastened the stud at the waistband of his jeans. When she grasped the tab of the zipper, she paused to glance at his face.

"Mister?" she said loudly. "Can you hear me?"

The snow and ice crystals that frosted his hair and mustache were beginning to thaw, revealing their color to be as dark as the charred logs in the fireplace. Water drops trickled over the ridge of his jaw, down his neck and into the collar of the blue chambray shirt he wore. Apart from his shivering, he still didn't move.

"Sorry," she continued, lowering the zipper. "But I have to do this. For your own good." She slipped her fingers under his waistband and tried to tug the jeans down. Her knuckles rubbed over his hipbones, and she was startled by the warmth she felt...both the warmth of his skin and the warmth of the ridiculous blush that sprang to her cheeks.

But she wouldn't permit herself to be embarrassed, not even when the jeans slid neatly past the top of his plain white briefs and bunched just inches from the junction of his legs, refusing to slide any lower. Dana studiously ignored the large, masculine bulge that had stopped the descent of the denim. She struggled unsuccessfully to ease the garment down for another awkward, blush-inducing minute.

"This isn't working," she muttered. "Maybe it isn't really necessary." But she knew it was. The melting snow was already seeping through the denim in dark patches of dampness.

Finally she got to her feet and straddled his legs, gaining enough leverage to yank his jeans the rest of the way off. She tossed them aside and went to work on his shirt. She didn't want to think about the silky black hair that feathered his chest and trailed down his flat abdomen, or the muscles that ridged his arms. She couldn't regard him as a man, not at a time like this.

But he was too large and heavy to be anything else. It took all her strength to roll him off his shirt and coat and onto the thick quilt she positioned beside him. By the time she had tucked the last blanket carefully around his shoulders, she was out of breath. "There," she said. "That's the best I can do. I just hope it's enough to keep you going until I can get help."

She eyed the telephone, then went over to give it another

try. Still no dial tone, not that she had really expected the line to get repaired so soon. She probably should have taken her sister's advice and purchased a cell phone as a backup for her stay here. At least the resort's electricity had a backup generator, so she wouldn't have to worry about being withou. power.

But she hadn't been expecting a situation like this to occur. How could anyone? When she had talked her cousin into letting her stay at Half Moon Bay, finding a frozen stranger on her doorstep hadn't been among the possibilities they had discussed. The resort was closed for the winter. The only problems she was likely to face in her role as caretaker were leaky pipes or too much snow on the roof.

"Mrrrow?"

At the indignant sound, Dana turned toward the kitchen.

Morty padded through the doorway, evidently fresh from his nap in the laundry basket. He yawned, extending his front legs in a bowing stretch, then arched forward and delicately shook out his back paws. His ears swiveled as he regarded the heap of blankets on the floor.

"No, you can't use them," Dana said.

Ignoring her warning, Morty picked his way past the puddles of melting snow and went to investigate. He sniffed lightly at the stranger's face, jumping backward to avoid a droplet of ice water that was dislodged by the man's shivering.

"Good point," Dana said. She retrieved a towel from the bathroom and squatted down to pat the man's face dry. The snow and ice that had clung to his hair had all melted now. His hair wasn't black as she had first thought but a deep, rich brown. It was long enough for the ends to brush his shoulders and curl against the sides of his neck. His mustache was thick and extended past the edges of his mouth, giving him the appearance of an old-fashioned desperado.

Dana paused. Desperado? Where had that thought come

from? Sure, he was big and well muscled, and his hair was a touch too long, and his mustache looked like something out of an old Western, but he was unconscious and helpless on her floor. He was as far from dangerous as anyone could get.

On the other hand, she was three miles from her nearest neighbor, cut off from the outside world by a blizzard, completely alone with a very large, strange man. Maybe she should have thought about that before she dragged him inside the cabin…

No, that was ridiculous, she told herself, dabbing at his wet hair. What did she think, that ax murderers made a habit of wandering around in snowstorms and this one just happened to choose her doorstep to collapse on? He was probably some poor soul who had gone off the road in the snow. Appearances weren't always a reliable gauge of character.

Take Morty. When she had found him huddled in that alley behind her apartment building, he'd looked like a ragged toy that someone had knocked the stuffing out of. All he had needed was a bath, food and some affection and he'd turned out to be a wonderful companion.

Of course, she wasn't comparing this situation to taking in a stray cat. And she wasn't looking for a companion. Besides, this man was probably in need of a lot more than just a bath, food and affection.

Dana wished she knew more about first aid. So far all she had done for him, getting him out of the cold and warming him up, was simply common sense. What if she was missing something important, something vital? It could be hours before she could get him medical help. What if his unconsciousness was due to more than the cold?

She pushed aside his hair to lay her fingertips over the thin skin at the side of his neck. In spite of his continued shivering, she found the throb of his pulse. To her relief, it was strong and steady. She ran her hands carefully over his head, sliding her fingers into his thick hair to check his scalp for lumps or gashes, but found none. She hadn't noticed any injuries when she had removed his clothes, but she lifted the blanket and looked, just to be sure.

There didn't appear to be anything wrong with his body. In fact, he was about as close to perfect looking as a man could get.

She quickly replaced the blankets and sat back on her heels. All right, now what? she asked herself for the second time.

Morty, evidently finished with his investigation of the stranger and satisfied that all was in order, leaped onto the blanket that covered the man's chest and curled up in a contented half circle.

Dana stared, her mouth going slack. Like most cats, Morty usually showed a regal disdain for strangers. Even if they coaxed him with food, he seldom approached. "Morty," she said. "Get off there."

He regarded her through half-closed eyes and didn't budge.

"Morty, he probably has enough trouble breathing without you sitting on his chest," she said, giving the cat a gentle shove. "Go back to the laundry basket."

Morty dug his claws into the blanket.

"Oh, for heaven's sake," Dana muttered, making a grab for the cat. She picked him up, detached his claws from the blanket and set him back on the floor.

His tail raised in offended feline dignity, Morty stalked over to plunk down at the man's feet.

Dana shook her head, bemused. "Okay, you can stay there," she said. "The extra heat will probably do him good."

A violent spasm shook the man's frame. His teeth began to chatter.

Not knowing what else to do, Dana reached beneath the blanket and caught one of his hands. It dwarfed hers as she pressed it between her palms. For the first time, she noticed the lumpy outline of calluses at the base of his fingers.

Evidently he worked with his hands. That detail made sense, considering his muscled arms. But if he did manual labor for a living, why was he wearing kid gloves and an expensive coat that would have been more suited to an accountant?

And why would anyone head up the road to the resort in a blizzard in the first place?

Speculation was pointless, Dana thought, pushing the questions to the back of her mind. He was alive; that was the most important thing. "Hang on," she said, squeezing his fingers. "You're safe now. Everything's going to be fine."

You're safe now. Everything's going to be fine.

Remy heard the voice from a long way off. It pounded at the ice that encased his brain, chipping away at the weakness that held his body.

You're safe now.

Was it true? No, not yet. He couldn't afford to rest. He had to keep moving. He couldn't let them find him.

But where was he? Why was he so cold? What was that clattering noise?

He forced his senses back to awareness. Pain shot up his arms from his fingertips, as if someone held a blowtorch to his frozen flesh.

Frozen. Cold. Images kaleidoscoped through his head. The storm, the snow. The fading light.

The resort. The cabin. Had he reached it?

He caught the aroma of woodsmoke. It mixed with the tang of wet wool and old wood and…lilies.

Lilies?

Someone was holding his hand. That's where the heat was coming from. Not a blowtorch. Fingers. Small fingers. But they hurt like hell. He tried to move away.

The fingers squeezed. "Mister?"

The voice was soft and female, like the hands that held his. But he could barely hear it over the clattering noise that filled his head. He clenched his teeth and the clattering stopped.

"Hello? Mister, can you hear me?"

Remy heard the woman's voice draw closer, and the scent of flowers grew stronger.

Something bumped his feet. Agony stabbed into his frozen toes. He tried to shift away, but his limbs felt bound, held down. Panic tripped his pulse. They must have found him after all. The safety was an illusion. He couldn't trust it. He couldn't trust anyone.

The woman released his hand. Fingertips feathered over his forehead before her palm settled warmly against the side of his face. "Hello?" She patted his cheek. "Hello?"

Remy struggled to open his eyes but his eyelashes seemed stuck together. He held his breath and tried again. He managed to crack his eyelids apart just enough to glimpse a face.

She was leaning over him, her hair falling in a blond curtain across her cheekbones. Her bottom lip was caught between her teeth and her pale eyebrows angled together in concern. She looked worried. She looked innocent.

And she wasn't wearing a uniform.

His pulse steadied. Gradually his surroundings started to solidify. He realized he was lying on his back, on the floor. There was a quiet crackling nearby, like a fire. Blankets weighed down his legs, not shackles. There was a flash of orange fur by his feet, and a marmalade cat raised its head to stare at him.

Remy closed his eyes and feigned unconsciousness, buying time to assess his situation.

It was okay. This couldn't be a hospital. It couldn't be a police station. They didn't have cats there.

So Sibley hadn't found him. There was still hope. All he needed was a chance to rest, to regain his strength. Then he'd figure out what to do.

Chantal.

The name echoed through his mind like the clang of a

locking door. Had he heard it? Spoken it? The last time he
had seen her he hadn't been able to speak at all. His throat
had been swelled shut with the sob he had been determined
not to let her hear.

Was she warm? Was she safe? Was she happy?

Did she believe what they said about him?

His pulse tripped with helpless, frustrated anger. It was
a familiar feeling. For seven months he had lived and
breathed it.

He couldn't waste time resting. He had to keep moving.
He had to find the key that would end the nightmare.

Would he ever see her again? Would he feel the sunshine
of her laughter and hear the lilting music in her voice when
she called him Daddy?

She would turn five next month. Five. And she was being
raised by people who called him a murderer.

No, he thought. *No!* He wouldn't give up. He couldn't.
Not until Chantal knew the truth.

Chapter 2

"John? Mr. Becker? Can you hear me?"

Remy floated back to awareness with a confused jerk. When had he drifted off again? How long had he been out? And who the hell was Becker?

"I'm just going outside to get some more firewood, Mr. Becker. The storm isn't letting up, and it's going to be a long night."

Gentle fingers brushed across his forehead, accompanied by the scent of lilies. There was the rustle of clothing and the rasp of a zipper. Remy squinted one eye just enough to see the blond woman pull the hood of a red parka over her head and move away. A door creaked, a blast of frigid air whistled inside for an instant, then the latch clicked shut. Remy waited another few seconds, listening to be sure he was alone before he opened his eyes fully.

Whitewashed beams crossed the ceiling above him, mottled with flickering shadows. A plaid couch with wooden arms loomed above him on his right, and to his left a fire burned low behind a mesh screen.

Right. The resort, the storm. It didn't take as long for his brain to click into gear this time. Good. That must mean his strength was returning. Remy stretched his arms, then his legs, one at a time. Aches and stiffness but no real damage, from what he could tell. He tried to flex his fingers. Pain, swift and white-hot, knifed through his joints from the thawing flesh. He took shallow, panting breaths until the pain eased, then cautiously lifted his head.

The room was large, taking up the entire front half of the cabin. Along with the couch, there were two overstuffed easy chairs, footstools, bookshelves and a table with a tilted top and a stool. It was a drafting table, Remy realized. Did it belong to the woman who smelled like flowers? Who was she? And what was she doing out here by herself?

Didn't matter, he told himself immediately. Whoever she was, she was one person too many. He never would have come here if he'd known the place was occupied. She was a complication he hadn't anticipated. He had to leave, he thought, pushing himself up on his elbows.

The room went gray and tilted. Remy waited until it righted itself again, then straightened his arms and levered himself into a sitting position.

A shudder shook his frame as the air hit his bare skin. He glanced down, puzzled, and noticed that he wasn't wearing a shirt. Using the heels of his hands, he clasped the edge of the blanket that had fallen to his lap and pulled it to his shoulders. That was when he realized he wasn't wearing any pants.

"What the—" Wincing at the rawness of his throat, he swallowed carefully. He spotted his shirt draped over a wooden rack near the fireplace, along with his jeans. Another shudder rattled through him, and he had to clamp his jaw shut to keep his teeth from clacking.

Damn, he was cold, so cold. But he had to get dressed. He had to leave. He hung on to that thought as he bent his knees and tried to stand up.

The floor was hardwood, he learned. It rushed upward and slammed into the side of his face.

A marmalade cat padded daintily into his field of vision. ''Mrrowww?''

Remy glared at the cat as he regathered his strength, then rolled to his back and gingerly assessed the additional damage. Everything throbbed now, and he tasted blood. He mouthed a string of silent curses as he wiped the blood from his lip. Taking care to move more slowly, he sat up again.

The cat sat back on its haunches and curled its tail around its feet. Its ears pricked forward as it studied him.

Remy ignored the animal's scrutiny and focused on the clothes on the wooden rack. They were wet. That must be why the woman had stripped them off him. He shuddered again as he realized how completely vulnerable he had been while he had been unconscious. He hadn't even been aware that a strange woman had taken off his clothes and wrapped him in blankets.

He should be grateful. Whoever she was, she had undoubtedly saved his life.

But she could just as easily have ended it.

He had to leave. He couldn't count on the charity of a stranger. He knew better than to trust anyone. During the past year, people he had believed to be his friends had turned their backs on him.

He hooked his elbow over the arm of the couch and tried once more to get to his feet. This time, he was able to lurch as far as the fireplace before his legs gave out. The blanket he'd draped around his shoulders tangled around his ankles and he crashed into the rack with his clothes. The thin wooden slats snapped, collapsing under his weight into a tangle of splinters and soggy denim.

Remy took a precious minute to catch his breath, then got to his hands and knees. Lifting his head, he looked at the snow that still swirled outside the window.

He couldn't make it across the room; there was no way

in hell he could make it across another ten miles of coun-
tryside in wet clothes. That would be suicide.

But he was risking far worse if he remained here. That
blond woman who smelled like lilies had helped him, but
the help would end when she discovered who he was. She
would call the authorities. He couldn't let her do that.

Frantically he surveyed the room once more. There on a
low table under the window was a telephone. It was an old,
black rotary dial set. He had to disable it.

He shook his feet clear of the blanket. Bracing his back
against the wall, hanging on to the stones at the edge of
the fireplace, he managed to get himself upright.

There was the stamp of feet outside the cabin. Seconds
later the door swung open on a blast of cold air.

Remy pushed off from the wall and staggered toward the
phone.

"What… Oh, my God! Mr. Becker!"

At the woman's voice, Remy tried to move faster. If he
could grab the wire and rip it from the connection—

"John, wait," she cried. She dropped an armload of firewood onto the floor. Tossing aside her mittens as she ran,
she reached his side before he made it to the phone.
"Here," she said, slipping her arms around his waist. "Let
me help you."

Only two more steps and he would be there, Remy
thought. But before he could lift his foot again, his knees
gave out.

"Oomph," the woman grunted. She swayed, propping
her shoulder under his arm to hold him upright. Stumbling,
she steered him toward the couch.

Remy didn't have the strength to fight her. He bit back
a moan as he fell backward onto the plaid cushions.

The woman landed on top of him, her face pressed into
his chest. She pushed off quickly and got back to her feet,
then retrieved the blankets he had scattered and covered
him up once more. "Don't move, John," she said. "Please.
I don't want you to hurt yourself."

"Who…" He swallowed hard and tried again. "Who?"

"My name is Dana," she said, tucking a quilt around his legs. She took off her coat and paused to look at him. "Dana Whittington."

She had misunderstood his question, Remy thought. He had been trying to ask who John Becker was.

"You're in my cabin," she continued. "At Half Moon Bay. I found you outside." She brushed his forehead with her fingertips. "How are you feeling?"

The last time she had touched him, her fingers had burned. They didn't anymore. They were gentle, and they felt good. Her cheeks were flushed, her forehead furrowed. No suspicion clouded her blue eyes, only innocent concern.

Remy scowled. No matter how innocent she looked, or how good her touch felt, this woman, Dana, was a threat. "'M 'kay," he said. He tried to swallow and started to cough.

"Let me get you something to drink," she said immediately. She hurried through a doorway that led to a kitchen. "Stay there," she called over her shoulder.

Remy shivered and eyed the distance to the phone. Before he could think about trying for it again, Dana returned. She propped a pillow under his back to help him sit up and brought a steaming mug to his lips.

He hated feeling helpless. He hated being fussed over, but Remy knew that for the moment he had no choice—he couldn't even hold the mug himself. He took a mouthful of what she offered, endeavoring not to gag as some kind of grassy-tasting liquid slid down his throat.

She smiled encouragingly. "Better?"

He made a noncommittal grunt. "Thanks."

She stroked his forehead again, then rested her hand on his shoulder. She left it there as his body shook with another round of chills. "You're still cold."

"Not…as…bad," he said through chattering teeth.

"Hang on. I'll put more wood on the fire." She set the mug on the table beside him and went over to where she had dropped the firewood. "I was going out for wood when I found you," she said as she stoked the blaze on the hearth. "You looked half-frozen."

"My...car went...off the road," he improvised. He coughed again to give himself time to think. "I got lost. Walking for hours. Lucky...I ended up here."

"Ah. I knew it had to be something like that." She came back to his side and pulled up a footstool to sit down. "I tried calling for an ambulance, but the lines are down. The storm's getting worse, so it's probably going to be a while longer before I can get you a doctor."

"I don't need—" Her words suddenly registered. "The lines?" he asked.

"The storm knocked out the phone service. I'm sure they'll fix it as soon as the snow lets up." She glanced toward the telephone, then back at his face. "I'm sorry. It happens up here from time to time."

If his lip wasn't stinging and his teeth weren't starting to chatter again, he could have smiled. As it was, all he could do was let out a relieved breath. The phone was dead. She wouldn't be calling anyone. All right. He could stay here a few more hours, maybe even another day. That would buy him some time for his body to recover.

"I guess you were trying to call someone when I came in," she continued. She held the mug up to his lips for another drink. "I know you must have people who are worried about you, John. I'm sorry I don't have a cell phone or anything."

Better and better, he thought. He took a second swallow of the hot liquid. It tasted like hay, but it was helping to warm him up. "You called me John."

"I hope you don't mind. When I was hanging up your coat, I found your day planner in the pocket," she said. "Your name was inside the front cover."

His coat? Remy felt a stab of confusion before he remembered. Of course. She meant the coat he'd stolen from the truck stop. It had been two sizes too small, and he had barely been able to squeeze his hands into the gloves that had been in the side pockets, but he hadn't been in the position to be choosy. The coat had kept him alive, and the gloves had probably kept him from losing his fingers to frostbite. When this was all over, he'd have to mail everything back to this John Becker, wherever he was.

When this was all over? Remy curled onto his side as a renewed wave of weakness surged through him. No, it was far from being over. He had too much to do before he was finished and a long, long way yet to go.

Dana put the cup of camomile tea on the side table and smoothed the blankets over John's shoulder. His knees were drawn up as if to hold in the heat of his body. His eyes had closed ten minutes ago. Thankfully, this time it seemed more like sleep than unconsciousness. His breathing was deep and even, and his shivering wasn't as violent. She hoped that meant he was recovering.

Considering his condition when she found him, he must have a formidable reserve of strength. Just look at the way he had tried to walk when he had barely been capable of standing. The poor man. Judging by the power that was evident in those muscles that ridged his arms and shoulders, he likely wasn't accustomed to being helpless. She had felt the quivering tension in his body when he had collapsed, and she had seen the frustration in his gaze. It must be horrible to be incapacitated like that and at the mercy of a stranger.

A gust of wind shook the cabin, and Dana glanced at the window. Until the storm eased, they were trapped here. Alone. Together.

John wasn't the only one at the mercy of a stranger.

She felt a tickle of uneasiness as she watched the snow. Now that it seemed safe to assume John wasn't about to succumb to hypothermia, she should be pleased. The evidence of his strength should come as a relief, not as a cause for misgivings.

She returned her gaze to her guest, noting how he filled the couch. She'd known he was a large man when she'd wrestled him out of his clothes, but she hadn't felt the full impact of his height until she had seen him upright…and practically naked. Although he'd been staggering on his feet, he'd nevertheless been an awesome sight, all taut skin and firm muscle. He had to be two, maybe three inches over six feet. That made him a full head taller than her. Still, his height shouldn't make her nervous, either. He was the same size as her cousin Derek, and Derek Johansen was as gentle as a lamb.

Tucking her hair behind her ears impatiently, Dana got to her feet and went over to untangle John's wet clothes from the broken drying rack. All right, under other circumstances she would be right to worry about being trapped alone with a very large, strange man, but it was too late to change her mind about taking him in now, not that she'd ever really had a choice. She'd always been a sucker for strays, no matter what size or species they happened to be.

Besides, as long as he remained in his present condition, there was no reason for her to be nervous. It was absurd to think, even for a moment, that John could be some kind of, well, ax murderer.

According to the well-worn agenda book he kept in his overcoat, John Becker was the head salesman for an industrial fasteners company. His home address was in Toronto—he had undoubtedly been trying to make it home before the storm closed the roads. That would explain what he had been doing on the highway. He probably had a wife and children waiting anxiously for his arrival.

Yes, of course. He must have a family. His not wearing a wedding band didn't mean anything. Neither did his mustachioed-desperado appearance. Why else would someone be anxious enough to risk traveling in this weather, if not for the sake of one's family?

In that respect, John was luckier than she was. Dana had no one to go home to. She had no child who would press her nose to the windowpane and peer through the snow in hopes of seeing a familiar car pull into the driveway. Apart from Morty, Dana was responsible for no one.

But there had been a time when she had dreamed of having more....

Yes, well, life moved on. She might not have a child, but she had her work. And because of her work, she touched the lives of thousands of children.

She added another few logs to the fire and finished tidying the main room, then gathered her papers from the drawing table and carried them into her bedroom. She was about to close her door when a flash of movement from the couch caught her eye. Despite her efforts to reason away her misgivings, she couldn't help the nervous little jump of her pulse as she gripped the door frame and looked over her shoulder.

John hadn't moved from where she'd left him. The blanket that stretched over his shoulders rippled as he shivered. He curled up more tightly. A lock of dark hair flopped over his forehead, softening the harsh planes of his face. It made him look vulnerable, almost...boyish.

There was another blur of motion near his feet. Morty, looking very smug, picked his way across the blanket and nestled into the crook of John's knees.

Dana turned back to her room. If John Becker had Morty's seal of approval, her qualms about his character had to be misplaced.

It was hard to tell when the night ended and day began. Beyond the white drift that piled against the window, the snow swirled as if from an endless gray tunnel. Between gusts, Remy glimpsed the shadows of other cabins and the hulking outline of the resort's main lodge, but he didn't see any lights. There was no sign of anyone else. The place was deserted.

Well, almost deserted.

He should have realized there would be a caretaker. Too

bad about the woman. If not for Dana Whittington, this place would have been perfect. Half Moon Bay Resort was isolated enough to provide concealment, yet close enough to the small town of Hainesborough to allow him access to what he needed. That's why he'd decided to head up here when he'd gotten out. He could have holed up comfortably in one of the outlying cabins. It had been fifteen years since he'd been at the resort, but he remembered every detail of the layout.

After all, he'd helped to build it.

He'd been eighteen and full of hope and ambition when he'd arrived here the last time. He'd seen the construction job as his ticket to the future, the first step toward his dream of making something of himself. He was fresh from the juvenile detention center, and he'd wanted to prove that the people of Hainesborough were wrong, that he was nothing like his old man, that he wasn't the boy they thought he was.

Ironic, wasn't it? He had come full circle. He was once more at Half Moon Bay, once more hoping to prove everyone wrong.

Only now the stakes were a hell of a lot higher.

Drawing in a steadying breath, Remy looked away from the window and turned his attention back to buttoning his shirt. His fingers still felt like slabs of wood, aching and unmanageable. He tried to make a fist. Pain screamed through his joints, but it wasn't as bad as it had been the night before. Ignoring the discomfort, reining in his impatience for his weakness, he curled his fingers into his palms until he had worked out the stiffness. Not 100 percent, but it would do. Clumsily he pushed most of his buttons through the holes, fastened the stud on his jeans, then braced his hands on his knees and stood.

So far this morning he hadn't fallen down, but he still wasn't steady on his feet. If he could hole up here until tomorrow, he would stand a better chance of finding some other base to operate from. In the meantime he had to make sure Dana kept on believing he was just some hapless traveler who had arrived here by chance.

He staggered to the wall where the overcoat he had stolen hung from a peg. The day planner Dana had mentioned finding was in the left pocket. Remy forced his aching fingers into motion once more and flipped through the pages, scanning for any clues to the identity he was temporarily assuming. There wasn't much personal information. Too bad Becker hadn't kept his wallet in his overcoat—

Remy drew in his breath. He still wasn't thinking straight. If there had been a wallet, there would have been identification. Photo identification. If Dana had seen it, his game would have been up before he'd regained consciousness.

He shoved the notebook back into the pocket where he'd found it, then looked at the closed bedroom door. He paused to listen for any hint of movement from within, but there was none. With one hand on the wall for support, he moved around the cabin, taking stock of anything else that might present a risk.

There was no television that he could see, but there was a CD player with a radio in the living room and a battery-powered radio in the kitchen. He didn't want to waste time searching for tools, so he took a butcher knife from the cutlery drawer, pried open the back of the kitchen radio and disabled it.

A check of the phone revealed there was still no dial tone. He couldn't gamble on the lines remaining down for much longer. He improved his odds by severing the input wire from the receiver, a sloppy but effective way to ensure it would remain out of order. He hesitated over the CD player, not wanting to do more damage to Dana's property than he needed to. In the end he merely cut the connection to the antenna—he knew without that, the set wouldn't be able to pick up a signal this far north.

A door creaked open behind him. ''Oh! I didn't expect to see you awake already.''

Remy straightened up from the CD player and turned around, using his motion to conceal the knife behind his back.

Dana stood in the doorway of her bedroom, her arms filled with a stack of loose papers and what appeared to be a large sketchbook. A bulky sweater came to the top of her thighs, obscuring much of her figure, but the black leggings she wore revealed long, slender legs. And despite himself, Remy felt his pulse move into a slow, steady throb.

He must have been in worse shape last night than he had thought. When he had looked at Dana then, he had only seen a threat. Now he was aware of much, much more.

Her hair wasn't merely blond. It was warm gold, somewhere between the color of wheat in August and aspen leaves in October. It tumbled around her face to brush her shoulders in sensuous waves. Her eyes weren't merely blue. They were pure cerulean and stunning enough to steal his breath.

And somehow, she looked familiar. He had the feeling he had seen her face before…

No, that wasn't possible. If he'd met her, he would have remembered. Any man would.

What had happened to Dana Whittington? Why would a beautiful woman with such a gentle touch choose to live by herself up here in the middle of nowhere?

Not that it should matter to him, he reminded himself. How she looked, who she was, made no difference. One more day, that's all he wanted. By then he should be able to move on. "Good morning," he said finally.

"How are you feeling, John?" she asked.

"Better, thanks."

"I can see that," she said, placing the papers and sketchbook on the drafting table. "I'm so glad."

She wasn't lying, he realized. She really was pleased that he was recovering.

No, she was pleased that John Becker with the fancy coat and the fat appointment book was recovering. Remy tightened his grip on the butcher knife. "I didn't get the chance to thank you last night," he said, taking a step backward. He had to find someplace to ditch this knife before she saw it—things would be far easier if he could avoid a confrontation.

"No thanks are necessary, John. Up here, everyone looks out for their neighbors."

God, he hoped not. That's all he needed, some nosy neighbor showing up to check on her. "I appreciate everything you've done for me, Dana. I'll be gone as soon as—" His words ended on a sharp curse. Instead of the hardwood floor, his foot came down on something soft. There was a sudden, high-pitched screech.

Damn! He'd forgotten about that cat. It had been following him around since he'd gotten up.

"Morty!" Dana cried, racing forward in a futile attempt to reach her pet.

Remy shifted quickly to avoid bringing his full weight down on the cat. Morty streaked away unharmed in a blur of orange while Remy staggered sideways, off balance and unable to catch himself without revealing the knife.

"Oh, no!" Dana exclaimed. She was by his side in an instant, sliding her arm around his waist and propping her shoulder under his arm. It was a position that was becoming much too familiar…and more comfortable than he would have liked.

She still smelled like lilies, he thought, feeling her hair brush his cheek. And she had a surprising amount of strength in her slender frame. He deliberately swayed against her as she helped him over to the couch. Allowing her to believe he was worse off than he actually was might help to lower her guard, and that could prove to be an advantage. He collapsed onto the cushions more heavily than necessary.

Her cheeks pinkened with her efforts as she disentangled herself from him and straightened up. A memory from the night before flashed into his mind. She had flushed like that when they had tumbled onto the couch together and she had ended up sprawled over his bare chest.

Was she blushing because of him? How long had it been since he'd known any woman who was innocent enough to blush? "Sorry," he murmured. "I'm not usually this clumsy."

"You need to take it easy. You probably shouldn't be up yet."

"No, I'm okay."

"I wish I could talk to a doctor. I'll try phoning—"

"The line's still out. I checked."

She hesitated, then went over to lift the receiver herself.

So she didn't quite trust him yet, Remy thought. Part of him was pleased that she wasn't completely naive, despite those innocent blushes. Living up here on her own like this, she was right to be cautious about strangers. After all, the stranger could turn out to be…someone like him.

Hell, what was he thinking? He should be concerned about Chantal's welfare—and his own—not this woman's. "I figured the snow would have stopped by now."

She glanced at the window, grimacing as she saw the height of the snowdrift. "I've never seen it this bad before. I'm not sure I'd be able to get my car through that snow, or even get it out of the garage."

"If you point me in the direction of the highway, I could try to hitch a ride," he said.

She shook her head quickly. "No, John. It's two miles away and you're in no shape to be on your feet."

"But—"

"I know you must be anxious to get home, but it would be crazy to go anywhere on foot in this weather, even if you were fully recovered."

He moved his lips into what he hoped would appear to be a grateful smile. "Thanks, Dana."

The flush on her cheeks deepened as she looked at his mouth. "I'll check the weather forecast," she said.

''Maybe we can get some idea how much longer the storm will last.''

Remy tried to ignore the whisper of guilt he felt as he watched her futile attempts to get a signal on each of the radios in turn. Instead, he took advantage of the moment her back was turned and slid the knife out of sight under the couch.

Chapter 3

It was the weather, Dana told herself, feeling yet another shiver tiptoe down her spine. The eerie grayness of the swirling snow outside the window and the moaning of the wind around the eaves as the afternoon wore on were like elements out of some horror film. Come to think of it, wasn't there a Stephen King movie about a man at a closed resort in the winter flipping out and using an ax? That character's name was John, too, wasn't it? But that man had been the caretaker, not an unexpected guest, right? Maybe this weather was going to make *her* flip out.

The kettle whistled beside her. Dana jumped, then shook her hair back from her face and forced herself to laugh. She was letting her imagination get the better of her, that's all. So what if both the telephone and the radio were out? Being cut off from civilization had never bothered her before. That's why she had come here, wasn't it?

Of course, she hadn't planned on having company. Especially someone who looked like John Becker.

On the other hand he didn't really look like a John

Becker. He looked more like a Tex or a Rocko or maybe even a dark-haired, brown-eyed Sundance Kid....

"Idiot," she muttered to herself. She measured out the tea and poured the boiling water into the pot. So far today John had been a quiet and unobtrusive guest. He hadn't made one move that could be interpreted as remotely threatening. She should stop obsessing over his appearance. He hadn't been able to shave, so he couldn't help it that the black beard stubble only made him look harder, almost...dangerous. He was frustrated over being stuck here by the storm, so it was only natural that there would be a troubled—at times desperate—gleam in his gaze.

And there was nothing suspicious about the way he was spending so much time dozing on the couch. He had been through a terrible ordeal—it was a miracle he hadn't lost any fingers or toes to frostbite. He needed rest to allow his body to recover. It was unkind of her to suspect that he was faking the extent of his weakness to avoid conversation. Just because he looked powerful didn't mean that he was. Not at the moment, anyway.

She was simply too accustomed to being alone. Maybe that's why she was feeling this constant awareness of his presence.

Or maybe the awareness was due to the fact that she had seen him without his clothes.

Dana pressed the heels of her hands to her eyes and stifled a groan. There was no denying he was a good-looking man. All that luscious dark hair, that bad-boy mustache, those chiseled features and that magnificent, powerful body....

Talk about a distraction. She hadn't gotten more than twenty minutes work done all day.

How could she be leery of him one minute and fascinated by him the next? This wasn't like her. It must be due to the isolation or the low barometric pressure in the weather system or maybe the phase of the moon. Right. She simply had to get ahold of herself. This would all be over in a few hours, or another day at the most.

Then everything would get back to normal. She would send the latest stray she had acquired on his way and she would be alone again, just the way she wanted.

He was awake when she returned to the main room. Firelight danced over the harsh planes of his face as he stared at the flames on the hearth. As usual, Morty was ensconced on his lap, purring like a train as John's long fingers moved lightly over the cat's fur.

"He seems to have adopted you," she said, carrying her mug of tea to her drafting table. "Do you have a cat?"

John turned his head to look at her. "No."

She noticed that the troubled gleam was back in his eyes. Well, why shouldn't he be troubled? Anyone in his situation would be. "You must like animals, though. Morty doesn't normally take to strangers."

John stroked behind Morty's ears. The cat closed his eyes and drew his head back into his neck in bliss. "Yeah, I like animals," John murmured.

"Then you probably have some kind of pet at home, right?"

His fingers stilled. A closed look came over his face. "The place I've been staying doesn't allow pets."

"That's a shame. I'm lucky my landlord doesn't mind Morty. He's such terrific company."

"With all the wildlife in the area, I wouldn't have thought the resort owner would kick up a fuss over one cat."

"Oh, I didn't mean here at Half Moon. I meant my apartment in the city."

"I see."

"You live in Toronto, too, right? In the Beaches?"

"Yes," he answered.

"Your address was written under your name in your day planner," she explained, even though he hadn't asked.

"Uh-huh."

As conversations went, it wasn't exactly sparkling, but it was better than silence for keeping her imagination under control. She plunged ahead. "The Beaches is a lovely neighborhood. Have you been there long?"

"No." He frowned. "If you have an apartment in Toronto, what are you doing up here? The place looks closed for the winter."

"It is. I needed somewhere quiet to work, so I convinced Derek to let me stay here at the resort as the caretaker. With no TV or newspaper delivery or Internet hookup to distract me, this cabin is perfect."

"Derek?"

"My cousin, Derek Johansen. He took over Half Moon Bay when my uncle passed away two years ago, and he hasn't had any time off until now. Considering the weather, he sure picked the right month to visit his mother in Florida."

"This storm might extend his vacation. Pearson Airport would be closed."

She hesitated. Should she tell John that Derek had left only a week ago? Would it be wise to let this stranger know that she wasn't expecting her cousin to return until next month?

Oh, come on, she thought. John was simply trying to make conversation, something she should be pleased about. "Derek wouldn't let a little detail like a raging blizzard interfere with his plans. He loves this place."

He nodded, and the stubborn lock of hair that she had noticed before flopped endearingly over his forehead.

"I do, too," she continued, as if to make up for her evasive reply. "In exchange for free rent, all I have to do is make sure the pipes don't freeze in the main lodge and keep the snow from collapsing the roof, which isn't much trouble since the roof was designed to be steep enough for the snow to slide off."

"Yeah, I know—" there was a split-second pause "—I

noticed that.'' His gaze moved over the room, then settled on her desk. ''What kind of work do you do, Dana?''

''I'm an author.''

His eyebrows rose.

She picked up the page she had been working on—or trying to work on—and held it for him to see. ''I write children's books. I illustrate them, too. This is for my current project.''

His gaze sharpened as he focused on her unfinished drawing. He leaned forward, his expression lighting up with interest. It was the first sign of animation he had shown all day. ''That looks like…''

''Morty,'' she finished for him. ''He earns his keep by serving as my model. I'm trying to deduct the cost of his cat food from my income tax, but so far I haven't had any luck.''

He transferred the cat from his lap to the couch beside him and rose to his feet. Moving carefully, his steps still wobbly, he crossed the floor to take the drawing from her hand. ''Morty. Is that short for Mortimer?''

''Yes, as a matter of fact, it is. How did you guess?''

He was silent for a moment. When he spoke again, his voice was laced with humor. ''It wasn't a guess. That cat has to be Mortimer Q. Morganbrood.''

She started in surprise. ''You recognize him?''

He grinned. ''Hell, yes, I recognize him. My daughter's crazy about that cat.''

Had she thought his rebellious hair was endearing? That was before she had seen his grin. It was as sudden and unexpected as a burst of sunlight from a storm cloud. And it zinged right through her caution to twang something in Dana's heart. ''You have a daughter?''

He hesitated. His grin wavered, then softened to a smile as he sighed. ''Chantal,'' he said finally. ''She's almost five, and she has every one of the Mortimer books.''

Dana forced herself to look away from his way-too-appealing mouth so she could concentrate on what he was saying. He looked like a different man when he smiled. She had the feeling he didn't do it often. "Really?"

"Really," he confirmed. "Starting with *Mortimer Ropes the Moon.*" He tilted his head. "Dana. You're D. J. Whittington?"

"Yes. Janelle's my middle name."

"Funny. I had thought you looked familiar, and now I see why. But the photo on your books doesn't do you justice."

She had heard that before. She knew the photo wasn't flattering, but her sister had taken it, and she hadn't wanted to hurt her feelings by asking for another. "My, uh, hair was shorter then."

"Even if I hadn't seen your photo, I should have recognized your name."

"It's not all that well-known."

"In our house it is." He studied the drawing again. "You said this is your current project. Is it for a new book?"

"Yes. *Mortimer and the Pirate Mice.* It's scheduled to be published this summer."

"That will make Chantal happy."

"I hope so." She made a wry face. "Assuming, of course, I get the thing done."

"Are you having problems?"

"No, just the usual. I procrastinate until I'm so close to my deadline that I have no choice but to work."

"Now I understand why you wanted to hole up here where there aren't any distractions. You're trying to finish your book."

"Exactly. It's my own private isolation chamber."

"This is unbelievable," he said. "I read a lot of stories to my daughter, but yours are her favorites."

"Thank you."

"They're my favorites, too. They haven't put me to sleep yet."

She laughed. "Good. I try to keep in mind the adults who will be doing the reading."

"It shows."

Usually, she could take praise in stride as matter-of-factly as she took criticism, yet John's compliments were igniting a warm glow in her cheeks. Or was it his nearness that was responsible? "You said that Chantal is almost five?" she asked, steering the subject away from herself. "What's she like?"

"Sweet when she wants to be, impulsive sometimes and smart as a whip." His voice rang with the unmistakable pride of a doting father. "Her laugh can make a stone smile."

Dana didn't doubt that. The mere mention of his daughter had caused a remarkable transformation in John. "She sounds adorable."

"Do you have any kids?"

She wouldn't think about the pain that stabbed through her at his question. She should be used to it by now. "No, I don't have any of my own, but I love all my young fans. I'm a real pushover when it comes to children."

"That shows in your stories, too."

"Well, thank you again."

"D. J. Whittington and Mortimer," he mused. "I can just imagine the look on Chantal's face when I tell her that I met both of you..." His words trailed off. Gradually his smile faded. "Damn," he muttered, putting the drawing back on the table.

The switch in his mood was as definite as a light going out. He was once more the intense, brooding stranger.

Yet the uneasiness Dana had been feeling on and off all day was gone. Morty had been a better judge of character than she had thought. Any man who was familiar with the Mortimer books, and who was so obviously devoted to his daughter, *couldn't* be bad. Impulsively Dana reached out to touch his hand. "You're worried about her, aren't you?"

"Yes."

"You'll be back home soon."

He glanced at her fingers where she touched him. "I intend to be."

"Maybe they've fixed the phone line by now. You could try again."

"It's still dead. I just checked."

"I'm sure she's fine. Your wife would be taking good care of her."

"My wife—" He stepped back, breaking her contact with his hand. "Chantal's mother…passed away."

This time the twang in her heart was deeper. Pieces of his behavior that had bothered her fell into place. He was a widower, a single father. Was it any wonder he was so anxious about being stuck here by the storm? Or that he preferred silence to conversation? What if his reserve was simply his method of handling pain? He might very well still be mourning his wife. "Oh, I'm sorry, John. That must have been so difficult for both of you."

"Yes." Remy moved to the window, bracing one hand against the frame as he stared into the snow. "It was."

Difficult? he thought. That didn't come close to describing it. His wife's death had been a nightmare.

He closed his eyes, trying to block out the image, but it was no use. It had played over in his head so many times, it had worn a path in his brain.

The scene flashed full-blown into his head. Sylvia was sprawled on the bedroom carpet. At first he'd thought she had been drinking and had passed out again. He'd smelled the brandy. But then he'd seen that her eyes were open. And he'd detected another smell, a bitter, coppery tang that rose from her red blouse…

He had shouted her name and dropped to his knees. She had still been warm. He'd called 911. He'd done CPR. He hadn't even noticed the blood that slicked his hands and spattered his shirt.

Thank God Chantal hadn't been there. The number of times Sylvia had left their daughter with her parents while she indulged herself had been another source of arguments between them, but on that day he had been grateful for her selfishness.

His hand curled into a fist against the window frame. Sylvia had had her faults—he'd known that when he'd married her—but she had been the mother of his child. He had loved her once. When had it gone wrong? What could he have done differently?

There was a featherlight touch on his shoulder. "John, you shouldn't be on your feet."

He opened his eyes and looked at Dana. The grisly image of his wife's death faded. Instead, he saw a blond angel and caught the scent of flowers. "I'm okay."

"I'm sorry for upsetting you. If there's anything I can do…"

For the first time he saw that the caution was gone from Dana's gaze. In its place was compassion.

Did she trust him now? He hadn't meant to tell her about Chantal. He'd done his best not to get personal. The less involved he got with Dana, the fewer complications when he left.

But the drawing she'd shown him had taken him off guard. When he'd seen the cat with the distinctive, impish face, he hadn't been able to stop the leap of pleasure he'd felt. Although it had been a rough sketch, the fluid lines that characterized D. J. Whittington's work were unmistakable. Her illustrations were as full of life and laughter as her stories. After the bleak existence he'd been living, the sight of that drawing had transported him back to a better time, a happier time, and he'd spoken before he'd thought.

Chantal would be thrilled if she knew that he was face-to-face with her favorite author. She would be tickled pink to discover he had held the real live Mortimer Q. Morganbrood on his lap.

But how could he tell her? Would he ever get the chance?

And now that he knew who his beautiful rescuer really was, how could he continue to lie?

Damn it, Dana didn't deserve this. No one did. What kind of man was he turning into? He should end this now, turn himself in before he hurt anyone else.

But then he thought of Chantal with Sylvia's parents. Would they be reading her favorite books to her at bedtime, or would they be filling her head with stories about her evil daddy? Would the children in the town point at her and call her names? Would she grow up the way he had, always trying to prove everyone wrong to atone for a father's sins?

He felt a chill that had nothing to do with the drafty window. He couldn't afford the luxury of a conscience. He'd use whatever—and whoever—he could in order to see this through. Another day to recover his strength, a head start on his pursuers, that's what he needed from Dana. And if playing on her sympathy would serve his purpose, then that's what he would do.

"Thanks, Dana. You're right, I shouldn't be on my feet."

She smiled without hesitation. Fitting herself against his side, she drew his arm over her shoulder and turned him around. "Come on, then. I'll help you back to the couch."

After the perpetual dusk of the previous day's storm, the sunrise seemed overly bright. It glared from the fresh snow that covered the frozen lake, it ignited the tops of the pines. It jabbed through the frost on the windows like a search-light. It also silhouetted John's broad shoulders and found gleaming chestnut highlights in his hair.

With another day's worth of beard, he appeared rougher than ever, yet when Dana looked at him now, she saw the echo of his smile as he'd talked about his daughter. His features no longer seemed harsh to her, and his strength no longer seemed threatening.

Was she nuts? Was her self-imposed isolation sending

her round the bend? Why else was she sorry to see the sunshine?

John wasn't some stray she could take in and coddle. He had a life to get back to. So did she. The sooner they got this over with, the better, right?

He raked his hair off his forehead and turned away from the window. "I have to get going."

"Are you sure you're up to it?"

"I'm fine."

And he was, she knew. His movements were smoother today, and he was much steadier on his feet. "The road is about two miles south," she said. "Just keep the lake on your left and follow the lane."

John leaned down to run his palm along Morty's back as the cat threaded himself around his ankles. "Now that the weather has cleared, I shouldn't get lost again."

"You don't have to walk. The snowplow should swing through in a few hours," she said, watching his large hand move along Morty's fur. How could he have once made her nervous? For a physically powerful man, he was incredibly gentle. "Once the lane's plowed, I could drive you to your car. Or you could wait until the phones are back up and call for a tow truck."

He gave Morty one last caress and straightened. "Thanks, but I can't stay any longer. Once I get to the highway, I'll hitch a ride to the nearest gas station and get a tow from there."

"I understand." She smiled. "If I had a child like Chantal, I'd be anxious to get home to her, too."

"She's the reason for everything I'm doing," he said.

The vehemence in his voice startled her. It shouldn't have, though. Throughout yesterday evening, he hadn't wanted to talk about his job or his home, but his daughter was one topic he didn't mind sharing. Dana had no doubt whatsoever that he loved his child fiercely.

Was that why she found him so attractive?

There, she'd admitted it. Yes, she found him more than

attractive. His outlaw good looks alone would have caught the notice of any red-blooded woman, but it was the sensitive—and vulnerable—man inside that really appealed to her.

Here was a man who knew what love and commitment were, she thought. He wouldn't disappear when the going got rough, the way Hank had. John would be willing to go to any lengths for those he loved....

She jerked her thoughts back from that useless direction. Her imagination was getting the better of her again. How could she think she could know a man after only a day in his company? She had spent four years with Hank, and she'd been wrong about him, hadn't she? Why would her judgment be any better now?

John picked up his shoes from in front of the hearth and carried them to the door.

"Wait," she said. "You can't go like that."

He paused. "What?"

"The snow's too deep for sneakers." She hurried over to take her coat from its peg. "I can get a pair of my cousin's boots from the lodge. He's about your size—"

"Dana..."

"It wouldn't be any trouble. I have to go over there later, anyway, to check the heat since I skipped yesterday."

"Dana, no," he said. "You've done more than enough."

"But those running shoes aren't meant for conditions like these."

He shoved his feet into the sneakers. "They got me here, they'll get me back to the road."

"At least let me give you a hat." She hung her coat up and stretched to take a knitted cap and a pair of padded snowmobile mitts from the shelf above the pegs. "Here, you can use these, too."

John shrugged into his overcoat. "I can't take those, Dana. I don't know when I can return them."

She held them out. "It doesn't matter. I trust you, John."

Something flickered in his expression. Beneath the bristling black beard stubble, his jaw flexed. He fastened his coat, then took the hat from her and put it on. He tucked the mittens under his arm. "Thank you. For everything."

"I only did what anyone would."

"No, Dana," he said quietly. "There aren't many people who would be so kind to a stranger."

"You've been good company. Besides, I always welcome an excuse to put off working for a little while longer," she said. "No self-discipline, you see. I don't know how I ever get a book done."

"We all have to do things we don't want to sometimes."

"Hah. I see you know about editors."

Her weak attempt to lighten the mood didn't work. He regarded her in silence for a moment, then extended his hand. "Goodbye, Dana."

She slipped her hand into his…and her breath hitched.

She had touched his bare skin before—heck, she had seen practically every square inch of skin he had—but this was different. She was aware of the firm warmth of his palm, the subtle swell of his calluses, the strength that pulsed beneath the surface of the polite gesture. And she was very, very aware of how close they were standing.

Oh, for heaven's sake, she told herself. It was only a handshake. "Goodbye, John."

"Take care of yourself."

"You, too." She swallowed, trying to keep her voice normal. "And say hello to Chantal from me."

A muscle twitched in his cheek. "I will."

Without thinking, she lifted her free hand to his face, pressing her fingertips to the tense knot in his jaw.

His gaze met hers, his dark eyes swirling with expressions she couldn't name. "Dana."

The way he said her name warmed her right through to her toes. This was too fast, she thought. Circumstances had thrust them together. They were like strangers on a train, two ships that passed in the night, all the old tired clichés. They would probably never meet again.

So she couldn't really be considering kissing him good-bye, could she?

He tilted his head, leaning into the gentle caress of her palm.

Yes, she could. That's exactly what she was considering. What did it matter how they had met or how long they had known each other? Maybe she had made the same kind of instinctive judgment as Morty. She tipped up her chin and focused on the lips beneath John's desperado mustache.

A log popped in the fireplace. In the silence that had fallen between them, it sounded like a gunshot. John jerked back. "Dana, I'm sorry."

"Mmm?"

"I've got to go." He dropped her hand and turned away to open the door.

"John…"

Cold air surged over the threshold. He pushed his way through the snow that had drifted over the yard, carving a knee-deep path in the blanket of white. He stopped when he reached the beginning of the lane and turned to look over his shoulder.

Dana waved, then stepped back inside and swung the door shut. Biting her lip, she let her forehead thud against the wooden panels.

Oh, God. What had she been thinking? She had almost made a complete fool of herself.

Must be lack of sleep or barometric pressure or phases of the moon or…

Or maybe she had been living on her own too long. It had been two years since Hank had left. Maybe that's why she was ready to throw herself at the first man who happened by.

But it wasn't just any man. It was John Becker, with his haunted eyes and his endearing, rebellious hair and his tender smile and his love for his child…

"You're pathetic," she muttered to herself. "Right

round the bend. First you're worried because you're trapped here with him, then you're upset because he leaves.''

Morty meowed and sat on her foot.

''It was my imagination, that's all,'' she said to the cat. ''All this creative energy floating around, ready to make up stories. I should put it to work, that's what I should do. That's what I'm being paid for, right?''

But instead of heading for her drawing table, she went to the window and watched until John was out of sight.

The rest of the day was a total loss. Dana did everything she could think of to get her mind back on her work. She put on her most comfortable sweater. She made endless pots of camomile tea. She organized her papers and sharpened all her pencils, but the drawing that took shape wasn't a marmalade cat and pirate mice. It was a man's face.

''Argh!'' Dana tossed her pencil on the floor and tunneled her fingers into her hair. It was more of a doodle than a drawing, only a few vague lines, but the long hair, the mustache, those dark, haunted eyes were unmistakable.

''This is pointless,'' she muttered. She needed some fresh air, she decided, going over to put on her coat. It was high time to switch into her role of caretaker, anyway.

She had almost cleared a path to the main lodge when she heard the clinking rumble of the snowplow. She leaned on her shovel and waved a greeting.

The driver turned around in the parking lot and lowered his window. ''Everything okay here, Miss Whittington?'' he called.

''Just fine, thanks, Mr. Duff,'' she shouted over the noise of the engine. ''That was some storm.''

''Forty centimeters. We been doing double shifts for three days and still aren't finished.''

''Did you see a car in the ditch?'' she asked.

''More like a few dozen. The roads are a mess with all the wrecks.''

''Any cars in the ditch near here?''

"Nope. Lucky, eh?" The engine revved loudly as the driver put it back in gear.

Dana smiled. John must have managed to get his car out and get home after all. "Thanks for swinging by," she called.

The driver touched his hand to his hat in salute. "No problem. Take 'er easy."

Dana waved and turned back to her shoveling. By the time she had cleared the front entrance to the lodge, she was out of breath and in need of a shower. She took the keys from her pocket and opened the front door.

A puff of warm air greeted her, along with the ringing of a phone. It had been so long since she'd heard the sound, it startled her. She stamped the snow off her boots and crossed the floor to the registration desk. "Hello, Half Moon Bay Resort," she answered.

"Dana! Are you all right?"

It was her sister, and she sounded on the verge of panic. "Hello, Adelle," Dana said. "I'm fine, how are you? Is everything okay?"

Adelle ignored the question and rushed on. "Why haven't you been answering the phone? I've been worried sick."

"The lines were down because of the storm."

"That's what the phone company said, but they claimed the problem was fixed last night."

It couldn't have been, Dana thought. She had checked an hour ago and there hadn't been any dial tone.

"I've been trying the number at the cabin all day," Adelle continued. "When you didn't answer, I started leaving messages on the lodge number."

Dana glanced at the answering machine behind the desk. Sure enough, the red light indicating recorded messages was blinking furiously. Why would the phone in the cabin still be out if the one here was working? They both branched from the same line, didn't they? "Adelle, relax," she said. "It was probably just some glitch at the switching

station or something like that. You know how things are
up north.''

''Yes, I do. Which is why I wish you'd come back to
the city.''

''I will come back. As soon as I finish my book.''

''What if the power had gone off? What if you had run
out of food?''

''There's a back-up generator for the power, and there's
enough food in the lodge freezers to keep me going through
ten books.''

Adelle paused, as if searching for something else to focus
her worry on. ''You sound out of breath. What's wrong?''

''I've been shoveling snow.'' Dana sighed and transferred the phone to her other ear as she slipped her arms
out of her coat. She grasped the front of her sweater and
flapped it away from her body to let in some cooling air.
''It's wonderful exercise.''

''That's what health clubs are for.'' Adelle huffed. ''And
doesn't that skinflint Derek have a snowblower?''

''Yes, he does, but it broke down last week. I really don't
mind, Adelle. It helps take my mind off…things.''

''Are you sure you're all right?''

''Positive. I'm sorry you were so alarmed. Is everything
okay with you?''

''Sure, everything's fine.''

''Did you get much snow down there?''

''I'll say! We got so much the mayor declared a state of
emergency and called in the army.''

''You're kidding!''

''Haven't you seen the news?''

''I don't have a TV in the cabin, remember? And the
radios there decided to break down yesterday.''

''Then you'll have to catch a newscast, now that you're
at the lodge. The blizzard shattered all the snowfall records
from here to Montreal.''

Dana toed off her boots and hitched herself up to sit on

the desk. "Wow. If it was that bad in the city, no wonder you were so worried about me."

"You're not the only one in the family with an imagination. Remember those stories grandpa used to tell us about trappers in the old days?"

"Vividly."

"When you didn't answer your phone today, I was picturing you lost out in the snow somewhere and slowly freezing into a lump of ice."

"Mmm."

"Don't say I'm overreacting. It could happen."

"Oh, I know. It almost did."

"Dana! You said—"

"Not to me, Adelle. Two nights ago I found a man on my doorstep. He was practically frozen."

"What!"

Briefly Dana told her sister about John Becker.

"Oh...my...God," Adelle said.

"He's okay now. He left first thing this morning."

"Oh...my...*God!* I can't believe you took a complete stranger into your home. Haven't you heard the news?"

"No. I told you, the radios—"

"Two days ago there was a prison break at the Kingston Penitentiary," Adelle said, her voice rising again. "Three of the convicts are still at large."

"Kingston's a long way from here. And those guys would head for the city or the border. They'd be crazy to head for the bush, especially in the winter."

"So? They might *be* crazy. What if this John Becker was one of those escaped prisoners?"

It was hard for Dana to believe that her thoughts had once gone along those same lines. Was it only yesterday that her visitor had made her nervous, with his height and his desperado aura?

But that was before she had seen the naked love in his eyes as he'd talked about his child. "That's impossible," she said. "John's no criminal. Morty adored him."

"As if a cat can judge someone's character."

"Morty hated Hank," she pointed out.

"Hank was an idiot. But, Dana, this isn't funny. That man could have been anyone."

"Well, he wasn't. He's a salesman whose car went off the road in the storm when he was trying to get home to his daughter. And he's one of the sweetest, gentlest men I've ever met," she said firmly.

Dana wasn't sure whether she had placated her sister by the time Adelle got off the phone. One thing was for certain. If she'd shoveled her way to the lodge in order to her mind off John, it hadn't worked.

She went to the floor-to-ceiling window that dominated the south wall of the lounge. From this vantage point, she could see the entire resort complex, from the caretaker's cabin to the boathouse that was nestled by the shore. It all looked so peaceful now. The frozen lake glittered like powdered diamonds in an unbroken expanse of white. Melting snow winked golden from the tips of the pine boughs. It was hard to believe a vicious storm had raged through here less than twenty-four hours ago.

As a matter of fact, it was hard to believe anything that had happened. Fresh drifts had obliterated any tracks John may have made on his way to the cabin, and the snowplow had cleared away the tracks he had made when he had left. Had she really saved a man from freezing to death? Had he been as drop-dead gorgeous as she remembered, or had the whole incident been twisted by her lonely imagination?

"Get a grip," she muttered to herself. Of course it had happened. Even *her* imagination couldn't have conjured up someone like John Becker. Instead of wondering about him, why didn't she just give him a call and check to make sure he had reached home safely? That would be the decent thing to do, wouldn't it? And it would prove her sister's ridiculous suspicions were wrong. Maybe then she would be able to get her mind back on her work.

She returned to the front desk and retrieved the Toronto

telephone directory from one of the shelves. There were half a dozen John Beckers, but she couldn't remember the exact address she had read in John's day planner. She chose a street that seemed familiar, then, before she could give herself time to reconsider, she picked up the receiver and dialed.

The voice that answered was that of a stranger. Assuming she must have been mistaken about John's address, Dana tried the next John Becker. She went through all six, then started on the listings for J. Becker, but still no success. Maybe her John had an unlisted number.

Her John? She closed the phone book and sighed. No, he wasn't hers. This was pathetic. Why was she doing this? If he had wanted to extend their relationship, he could have called her, couldn't he?

But he didn't know her number at the cabin, did he? Unless he had already tried to contact her through the lodge...

Quickly Dana pressed the button on the answering machine to play the messages. One was from Derek, giving her his schedule for the week, one was from the local marina to say that the new snowmobile Derek had ordered was in, and the rest were from Adelle. Nothing from John.

Could he have been delayed getting home? If the storm had been as bad as Adelle had said, the highways north of Toronto would be terrible. They might even be closed. She glanced at the clock on the wall and saw that it was four sharp. The headline news channel would be starting its report.

Dana returned to the lounge and clicked on the television there. The storm and its aftermath was the number-one story. She gasped at the footage of the ravaged city—entire streets were still blocked as the public works department tried to cope with the mountains of snow. Emergency services were overloaded, and a plea was going out to the public to check on their neighbors.

Slumping down on the couch, Dana muted the sound.

Perhaps it was lucky that John had ended up at her cabin. If he hadn't gone off the road when he had, he might not have made it back to the city, anyway. At least here he'd been safe.

A face flashed on the screen, and Dana's heart thumped. The picture was stark black-and-white, but she recognized it instantly. Long dark hair, outlaw mustache, harsh features… It was John! Oh, God. Had he been in an accident? Fumbling for the remote, she turned the sound back on.

"…still at large."

She frowned, certain she must have heard wrong.

"The other two prisoners were apprehended without incident this morning in Montreal," the announcer continued. "Police are asking for the public's help in locating Remy Leverette. He is thirty-three years old, stands six feet three inches, weighs two hundred pounds and has dark-brown hair and a mustache. If you have any knowledge of his whereabouts, please contact the authorities immediately."

It was a mistake, Dana thought, staring at John's face. Somehow the TV station had gotten the pictures mixed up. Or maybe it was a bad photograph. The photo on her book covers didn't look anything like her. Maybe the camera had made this Leverette person look like John.

But even as she scrambled for explanations, she knew it was no use. The truth was there in the numbers that were held in front of his chest. It was a mug shot, and there was no denying that it was John. The camera had even captured the desperate edge to his haunting gaze.

"…exercise extreme caution," the newscaster droned on. "Leverette has served four months of a life sentence…"

A life sentence? But how could that be possible? The gentle, quiet man who had shared her cabin couldn't have hurt anyone, could he? And if he had, it must have been an accident, or self-defense, or…

The excuses she had been grasping scattered like snow-flakes on the wind with the announcer's next words.

"In the trial that shocked the quiet town of Hainesbor-ough last year, Remy Leverette was convicted for the brutal stabbing death of his wife."

Chapter 4

Dana crossed her arms tightly and rubbed her palms over her sleeves. Once the sun had gone down, the temperature had plummeted. She had heaped more wood on the fire and had plugged in the electric heater, but it hadn't helped. The cold she felt went through to her bones.

It didn't have much to do with the temperature, though. This cold was harder to shake off because it came from within.

How could she have been so wrong? she thought, for what had to be the hundredth time. How could he have deceived her so thoroughly? And how could she have wanted to kiss him...

Damn it all, after two years of keeping to herself, of avoiding the possibility of any kind of relationship with a man, why did she have to choose now to lower her defenses? And why choose *him?*

He could have killed her while she'd slept. He could have done anything he'd wanted to her, and she wouldn't have been able to stop him. No, she would have *let* him. Welcomed him.

He must have pegged her for a soft touch the minute he'd seen her. He knew about her books and decided to play on her ego. That wouldn't have been hard to do—all writers were eager for even a crumb of praise. It had all been an act, a lie.

There had been so many inconsistencies, but she hadn't wanted to see them. The expensive coat he had worn didn't match his plain chambray shirt and jeans. The salesman's agenda book in his pocket didn't go with the workman's calluses on his palms. The look in his eyes wasn't haunted, it was *hunted*.

She swallowed hard to get rid of the lump that rose in her throat. What a fool she had been. About everything. And God help her, the worst of it was that even now she didn't want to believe she could have been that wrong about John.

No, not John. Remy Leverette. Escaped prisoner. Convicted wife killer.

The sudden knock on the cabin door made her jump.

"Miss Whittington? It's Constable Savard."

Dana recognized the gravelly voice of the provincial police officer who had arrived twenty minutes ago. She hurried over to unbolt the door. "Did you find anything?"

"No, ma'am." He knocked the snow off his boots on the doorstep and stepped inside. With his gray eyebrows and round, ruddy cheeks, he looked more like a kindly farmer than a policeman. "I've been all around the lodge buildings," he said, pulling off his gloves and stuffing them in the side pockets of his jacket. "If anyone had been there, I would have seen his tracks. The snow hadn't been disturbed."

"I told you, he wasn't at the lodge, he was here at the cabin."

"I didn't see any tracks here, either."

"That's because I shoveled the snow after he left. The plow went through, too."

"Ah. Did anyone else see this person?"

"Well, no. And he said his name was John Becker."

"Yes, I made a note of that. Did you call anyone, ask for help?"

"The phone lines were down. And the phone in this cabin wasn't working. I think—" She paused, but then decided she might as well tell him her suspicions. "I think he did something to it. I replaced it with one from the lodge and that one's working fine."

"I see. Do you live here year round, Miss Whittington?"

"No, I'm acting as caretaker while my cousin's in Florida. I needed someplace quiet to complete my book."

"You're a writer?"

"Yes. I write and illustrate children's books."

He pulled a small notebook from inside his jacket and scribbled a few words. "So you make up stories for a living."

She frowned at his tone. "You sound as if you don't believe me."

A flat voice crackled from the radio that was clipped to Constable Savard's belt. He retrieved it and said a few words, his cheeks flexing with a suppressed yawn. "I'm sorry, ma'am, I didn't mean any offense, but between the traffic accidents from this storm and the sightings of the fugitive it's been a long day."

"Sightings? You mean he's been seen somewhere else, too?"

Savard nodded. "Since the picture hit the news two days ago, I've heard he's been spotted everywhere from Kapuskasing to Kenora."

"Wait, I can prove he was here. I have a picture of him."

"Why would you take his picture?"

"It's not a photograph," she said, going to her desk to retrieve the doodle she had made. "It's a sketch."

He studied the paper briefly, then handed it back to her.

"It looks kind of like the picture on the news, all right."
He jotted something else in his notebook and slipped it
back inside his coat, then withdrew a card and handed it to
her. "Thank you for your cooperation, Miss Whittington.
We'll be in touch. If you remember anything more, please
call this number. That's for Detective Charles Sibley. He
dealt with Leverette before."

"That's it? You're not going to post someone here in
case he comes back?"

"Did this person threaten you?"

Dana shook her head. The only thing that had been in
danger from John had been her heart. "No, he didn't make
any threats."

"We'll investigate this report as thoroughly as possible,
ma'am," Savard said, his voice rough with weariness as he
pulled his gloves back on. "But rest assured that if the
person you claim to have seen really was Leverette, he'd
probably be halfway to Calgary by now."

The diner next to the gas station had been doing a brisk
business right up until dusk. Located just before the turnoff
to Hainesborough, it was on the main route between Toronto and the Trans-Canada Highway. It was a good place
for snowplow drivers to stop and fill their thermoses with
coffee and grab a few doughnuts, or for travelers who'd
had to postpone their trips because of the storm to rest long
enough to wolf down hamburgers or sandwiches before
they got back on the road, trying to make up for lost time.

But now the crowd was thinning out. With nightfall,
most people had already reached their destinations. The bell
over the door remained silent, and the buzz of conversation
had been replaced by the drone of a small television behind
the counter.

Remy knew he could allow himself another five minutes
tops before he would have to move on. Although his stomach was growling audibly, the coins he'd found on the floor
of the phone booth wouldn't stretch to buy him dinner. He

would have preferred to stay here long enough for his feet to warm up past the numb stage, but the waitress had been by twice already, eyeing the coffee he'd been nursing, and he didn't want to risk becoming conspicuous.

His immediate problem was where to go once he left the diner. Because of Dana, he couldn't use Half Moon Bay as a base to work from, so his first priority was to find somewhere else to stay. But where? No one could survive in the bush at this time of year, and he sure didn't have the means to pay for a motel. He had no friends he could count on— the events of the past year had proven that much. If he was lucky he might stumble over a cottage in the area that was empty for the winter…as long as his feet didn't freeze solid while he was wandering around the bush looking.

It appeared as if he had to risk going into Hainesborough earlier than he would have wanted. Hopefully, the news of the breakout would have died down by now. He could find shelter in his office or in the construction trailer in the yard. It had been two days, and the Kingston pen was hundreds of miles from here. Besides, no one would expect to see him—escaped felons generally knew better than to return to the scene of the crime, right?

Wherever he ended up, he couldn't count on luck being with him this time. He'd probably used up a lifetime's quota of luck getting this far. Being in the exercise yard just as the leading edge of the storm had disrupted the power to the electric fence had been a fluke. A one-in-a-million opportunity. Two men had gone over the wall before Remy had fully understood what was happening.

The decision to follow them had been instinctive. After being a law-abiding citizen for his entire adult life, he had escaped custody without a qualm or a backward glance. Odd, how easily the old skills had come back to him. He wasn't as agile as he'd been as a juvenile, but he'd known how to avoid detection by sticking to the alleys and back roads. He'd ditched the prison issue jacket and stolen that poor sap Becker's overcoat. He'd hitched a ride with an out-of-province trucker. Then he'd lied to the innocent woman who had saved his life.

Damn, he'd already been through this in his mind, he thought, scowling into his cold coffee. He'd do whatever it took. He wasn't going to leave a legacy of shame for his daughter. Somehow he was going to find a way to prove his innocence.

He lifted the mug to his lips and drained the last of his coffee, then counted out enough coins to cover it. He slid to the edge of the bench and glanced around the diner, preparing to leave when his gaze was caught by the face on the TV screen.

It was his mug shot.

The shock of seeing himself like that kept him motionless for a vital second before his pulse tripped into overdrive. Hunching his shoulders, Remy ducked his head, as if concentrating on fastening the buttons on his coat while he watched the screen out of the corner of his eye.

''...six feet three inches, weighs two hundred pounds...'' Snatches of the newscaster's voice drifted across the diner, listing details of his appearance.

So much for hoping the news of the breakout would have died down. Remy felt a prickling sensation on the back of his neck, but he resisted the urge to look around. He turned up his collar and nodded to the waitress, forcing himself not to hurry as he walked toward the door.

A man who was sitting on a stool at the counter was talking to the waitress. ''Too bad they don't have the death penalty anymore, eh, Maggie? After what Leverette did to his wife, he deserves to fry.''

''My cousin was on the jury. She said she had nightmares about the way he used that knife.'' The waitress took the carafe from the coffeemaker and topped off the man's cup. ''I hope they catch him. I hate to think of him getting away with it.''

''They'll get him.''

''Where do you think he went?''

"Probably Quebec, like those other two that escaped with him."

"Or down to the States." She lifted her head. "Excuse me, sir?"

One foot in front of the other, Remy told himself. All he needed to do was make it outside and he could disappear.

"Sir?"

Remy coughed into his hand as an excuse to cover the lower half of his face. "Yes?" he asked, half turning.

"You forgot your hat."

It took an extra ten seconds to retrieve the hat Dana had given him, but by the time Remy made it outside, his heart was beating as if he had run a marathon. He gulped in a breath, and the cold air hit him like a punch to the solar plexus. The people in Hainesborough wouldn't care if he froze—they were ready to see him fry.

He slipped around to the side of the coffee shop, staying close to the wall while he surveyed the area. He thought about hot-wiring one of the cars in the parking lot, then dismissed the idea. It would be better to hike the remaining miles into town than to draw the attention of the police by stealing a car.

Keeping to the shadows, he walked toward the highway, his shoes squeaking on the packed snow. His toes throbbed as the cold knifed through the rubber-soled sneakers, but at least his fingers wouldn't freeze, thanks to Dana's mitts. Too bad he couldn't have continued his charade and stayed on in her cabin. She was from Toronto, and the news media there hadn't given as much coverage to the trial as the local paper had. Add to that the fact that she had cut herself off from the world in order to write, and he might have been safer there than he had thought at first.

She was a bright, compassionate woman, and under other circumstances he would have enjoyed his time with her. She wasn't anything like Sylvia. If things were different, maybe he would have taken her up on the invitation he'd seen in her eyes.

Oh, hell. He'd spent most of the day trying to forget about that moment at the door. He'd known from the first time he'd seen her that he'd have to leave, but that hadn't stopped him from enjoying the feel of her body next to his. And when she'd laid her fingertips on his cheek so tenderly...

It must have been adrenaline. Something to do with the tension of the situation, because he couldn't remember wanting to kiss a woman more.

He hadn't wanted to leave her.

And that was precisely why he had. He had to keep his goal in mind. He couldn't afford to—

A siren wailed from the highway behind him. Acting instinctively, Remy leaped over the snowbank the plow had left and dove into the ditch.

Snow slithered up the legs of his jeans as he sank past his knees. He tried to move forward. If he could make the cover of the trees, there was a chance they might not spot him, but each step in the drifted powder was like pushing against a ten-ton weight.

Red lights flashed on the tops of the pines that flanked the highway. The siren grew louder. The people in the diner must have recognized him after all, Remy thought. The cruiser couldn't have been more than a few miles away for them to get here so fast.

He pushed himself harder, the muscles in his thighs burning, his breath steaming. The pines didn't seem any closer. In desperation, Remy half ran, half jumped toward the shadows beneath the trees. His sneakers slipped and he went down face first in the snow.

Headlights brightened the pine boughs overhead. The siren shrilled higher. There was the roar of an engine from the other side of the snowbank and then...

And then the noise swept past.

Remy lifted his head and looked around just in time to see an ambulance disappear down the Hainesborough turn-off.

He wiped the snow off his face and rolled to his back to catch his breath. The siren hadn't been for him. This time.

His plan wasn't going to work, he realized. Walking along the road like this left him too exposed. And the news of his escape hadn't died down at all. His face was on every TV screen in town. People in the area remembered the trial. Could he risk continuing to Hainesborough, when there was no guarantee he would find anyplace safe to stay?

Half Moon Bay would have been perfect, if it weren't for Dana. She posed a threat not only to his freedom but to his peace of mind, so the place was out of the question.

Or was it?

Shivering, Remy crawled back to the snowbank and hauled himself up. There might be a way to use the place after all. Dana was staying in the caretaker's cabin, not the lodge itself. It was a big complex, and he probably knew its layout better than she did. If he was careful to avoid her, and if he was lucky, he could lay low for another few days, maybe a week, before he risked going into town again.

She wouldn't even have to know he was there.

It was a wild idea, but was it any worse than walking into town when his picture was on the news? Or staying here to freeze to death in a snowbank?

"Don't look at me like that," Dana muttered to the cat as she hauled the vacuum cleaner out of the closet. "I'm working, I really am. I'm just taking a break, that's all."

Morty blinked at her from his perch on the back of the couch.

"You don't have to hold the pose anymore," she said. "You can take a break, too."

The tip of his tail twitched lazily. He continued to regard her flurry of activity with the tolerant detachment most felines exhibit for the antics of their humans.

Dana threw a sidelong, guilty glance at her work table as she ran the vacuum along the hardwood floor. The drawing was coming along fine, it really was. Mortimer was manning the wheel—or was it catting the wheel?—of his little sailboat in hot pursuit of the sloop full of piratical mice.

She was quite pleased with the mice. It had been a challenge to strike the right balance. They were mischievous enough to be interesting, but not menacing enough to frighten her readers. She had given one a twig for a sword and had put a clover-leaf eye patch on another. Everything had been progressing well this morning. Yes indeed.

Until the leader of the pirate mice had unexpectedly developed a desperado mustache.

Dana pushed aside the footstool and aimed the vacuum nozzle at a cluster of dust bunnies. She wasn't normally particular about housekeeping, but somehow when she was working on a book, these otherwise boring tasks took on a glow of attractiveness. It was a good thing she had cut down on as many potential distractions as possible, because even in an isolated cabin that was stripped down to the bare essentials, she still managed to find plenty of things to do. And plenty of other things to think about.

Where was John now? Had he really gone out West? Had he fled the country?

Was he safe? Was he warm?

"Stop it, just stop it," she told herself, dragging the chair out of her way. It had been five days since he'd left. Almost a week. Even though she had deliberately restrained herself from checking any more newscasts, she couldn't put him out of her mind. She didn't know which would be worse, knowing he had been recaptured...or knowing he hadn't.

More than once she'd found herself looking over her shoulder when she was up at the lodge, or catching a glimpse of movement through the windows of her cabin at night. At odd times she seemed to feel his presence, as if he were somewhere nearby.

But that was ridiculous. She would never see him again.

She didn't *want* to see him again. So why couldn't she forget about him?

Why? Because she wanted to believe she had made a mistake.

Wasn't that why she hadn't told her sister about what had happened? Adelle had called yesterday, just to check on her, but Dana hadn't said a word about Leverette or the police. Part of it was because she didn't want Adelle to know how big a fool she had been—her sister wasn't above a few I-told-you-so's. Yet the main reason she had remained silent was because of her own doubts.

What if the tall, compelling stranger really was just a luckless traveler named John Becker? What if there were reasonable explanations for the things that didn't add up about him?

The police didn't believe that the man she had met could have been the escaped criminal they were seeking. Oh, sure, Constable Savard had gone through the motions, but Dana could tell by his lack of interest that he considered finding Leverette around here was about as likely as spotting Elvis.

She couldn't blame him for questioning her credibility. After all, it was a bit eccentric to want to live like a recluse and sketch mice.

Was she wrong?

"Excuse me," she told Morty. He yawned, then jumped to the floor as she pushed the couch aside. She rammed the vacuum into the dust that had been underneath, but paused when she heard a clink.

Dana shut off the vacuum and bent down to take look at what she had unearthed.

There was a glint of metal from the floor at the edge of the couch. She reached out to grab it and felt something sharp prick her thumb. Reflexively, she drew back her hand and stuck her thumb in her mouth, then got down on her knees for a better look.

"What on earth...?"

There was a knife on the floor. Using her other hand, she cautiously picked it up and shook off the dust.

It looked like the butcher knife that belonged in the kitchen drawer, but how had it ended up here? She knew she was an indifferent housekeeper, but even she wouldn't have any reason to carry a butcher knife into the living room....

"Oh, God," she whispered, rocking back on her heels. Her gaze flicked from the long, sturdy knife blade to the couch. This was where John had spent most of his time. He had sat right here in this corner. This knife would have been within his reach the entire time.

Remy Leverette was convicted for the brutal stabbing death of his wife....

Dana's stomach knotted. No. John wouldn't have wanted to hurt her. He'd had plenty of opportunity, and he hadn't done anything to harm her. He couldn't have hidden the knife here. And if he had, there must be some other, innocent explanation.

...brutal stabbing...

She dropped the knife on the floor and put her face in her hands. She was doing it again. Making excuses for him, trying to talk her way out of the facts. What would it take to convince her?

"You *are* a fool," she muttered. "A complete and utter idiot."

Remy shut off the water and toweled himself dry, then carefully wiped the water drops from the glass walls and tile floor of the shower stall. He'd learned that the exhaust fan in the ceiling would eliminate the remaining moisture in the bathroom within fifteen minutes. The scent of soap would linger a while longer, but that didn't concern him. It was Derek Johansen's bathroom, so it would be expected to smell like Derek's soap.

Along with the glass shower, the bathroom also had a sunken whirlpool tub. A long mirror stretched over the granite counter and twin sinks. The fixtures weren't the original ones Remy had helped install. Dana's cousin must have renovated when he had taken over the management of the resort. The floors in the rest of the suite had been redone in pegged oak, and an open stone fireplace had been added to the main room.

Apart from a few surface changes, though, the place was essentially the same as it had been fifteen years ago. This suite had been built for the owner's use. Shaped like a sprawling pentagon, it perched atop the main lodge building where it had a commanding view of the outbuildings and private cabins. Through the telescope that sat in front of the south window in the main room, Remy could observe anyone who came within half a mile of the resort. He could also see the moment Dana stepped out of the caretaker's cabin.

For the past five days her schedule had been as regular as clockwork. She made her rounds of the outbuildings and the lodge in midafternoon, her red parka as eye-catching as a flag against the neat paths she had cleared. Each evening just before dusk she went to the woodshed and carried back an armload of firewood. After dark, she usually worked at her desk until midnight or so before she went to bed.

He had learned that her nightgown was ankle-length fleece. It was a practical choice for a cabin in winter. It covered her from her neck to her feet, yet when she moved it gave fascinating outlines of her curves. Sometimes she read when she couldn't sleep right away. Once she had fallen asleep with a book in her hands and her light had burned until morning.

Remy's lips twitched. If he stayed here much longer, he would have to add Peeping Tom to his growing list of crimes.

Nevertheless, he had good reason to keep track of Dana's movements, he told himself. He couldn't let her discover he was here, and he had to stay alert to any change in her routine that might mean her cousin was returning. So far he'd been lucky, but he couldn't afford to relax. The longer he remained, the more chance he'd be discovered. He had to risk going into Hainesborough soon. He'd start with his office—there must be something among all the scraps of paper that would back up his alibi.

Leaning forward, Remy cleared the mist from the mirror, then braced his hands on the edge of the sink and scrutinized his image.

This morning's newscast hadn't broadcast his picture. Did he dare to hope that meant it would be safe for him to show his face?

Perhaps. Another two or three days would improve his odds. In the meantime he might as well prepare himself.

Twisting his mouth to one side, he picked up the pair of scissors he'd found earlier and began to clip away at his mustache. He used a razor to finish the job, then retrieved the scissors and started on his hair. By the time he was done, the face that stared back at him from the mirror jarred him. His lip looked naked, and his hair looked like the handiwork of a drunken barber.

He grimaced and took another stab at evening up the haircut, but the shorter he cut it, the more his hair curled. It didn't matter, he decided, as long as he looked different from his mug shot. He swept the hair off the counter and flushed it down the toilet. Next, he replaced the shaving gear and scissors exactly where he had found them. Finally he rolled up the used towel and padded toward the bedroom.

Dana had once offered to lend Remy a pair of her cousin's boots. What would she think if she knew he had been helping himself to her cousin's entire wardrobe? Along with Remy's list of crimes, his list of IOUs was continuing to grow, too. Once this was over, he would have to—

He paused in midstride, certain he had heard something creak. A glance at the clock showed it wasn't yet noon—

he should have several hours yet before Dana made her rounds. Nevertheless, he listened intently.

A sound barely on the threshold of hearing drifted through the silence of the lodge. It was the slam of a door.

Remy mouthed a curse and spun around. He returned to the bathroom to shut off the exhaust fan, then glanced at the suite's door. Could he risk making a run for it? There was only one staircase to this top floor suite. If whoever was in the lodge came directly upstairs, there was no way he could avoid them.

He quickly surveyed the suite. The open concept design of the living area wouldn't provide any concealment. The balcony off the bedroom might, but in the buff as he was, he wouldn't last more than a few minutes outside.

There was the scuff of footsteps outside the door.

Remy sprinted for the bedroom. He scooped the clothes he had picked out earlier off the bed and slipped into the closet. He was just drawing the closet door closed behind him when he saw a flash of red go past the bedroom doorway.

It was Dana. She was early. Was she alone? Remy aligned one eye with the closet opening and strained to listen, but all he could hear was the crash of his pulse in his ears.

He breathed shallowly through his nose, forcing himself to remain motionless. She was talking, but it didn't mean that she had anyone with her. Over the past few days, he'd noticed that she often talked to herself. He'd never been close enough before to hear what she was saying, though.

"...complete idiot," Dana mumbled. "Can't trust a cat." Her voice grew louder. "Should have gotten over it by now."

He held his breath as she walked right past the closet.

"Stupid, stupid, stupid," she said. "If Adelle ever found out she'd have me committed to a—" The rest of her sentence was lost in a blur of muttering. She strode back across the floor.

Remy only had a glimpse of her face, but he saw immediately that something was wrong. Her forehead was furrowed, and her usually generous mouth was drawn into a tight line. Who was Adelle? Her editor? No, Dana had mentioned a sister with that name. Were there family problems?

The front door of the suite slammed.

Remy didn't move from the closet until he had counted off two full minutes of silence. If Dana followed the pattern of her other visits, she would work her way through the guest rooms on the ground floor now and then do a check of the service areas.

But she had broken the pattern by coming here early. Did it mean that her cousin was returning? Remy hoped that the change in routine had more to do with whatever was troubling her.

Was it her work? She said that she had sought the isolation of the closed resort in order to finish her manuscript in peace, but he thought there was more to her desire for seclusion than that. Once again he wondered what had happened to Dana Whittington. She was such a warm and generous person, and she was so clearly fond of children, it was surprising that she hadn't wanted to settle down and start a family of her own.

Yet in the five days that Remy had been watching her, no man had come to visit. Did that mean she was unattached? If he had been the man in her life, he sure as hell wouldn't have left her alone up here for this long. She looked so lonely in that big bed of hers, with the quilts tucked up to her shoulders and her blond hair spread over the pillow. The night she had fallen asleep reading, he'd been tempted to go over there and take the book from her hands and slide beneath those quilts with her. It had been a long time since he'd had a woman in his arms.

Would she smell like flowers all over? Would she taste as sweet as she looked? Would she be as generous in bed as she was everywhere else?

The blood that had been pumping through his muscles

settled low in his groin. Remy exhaled hard and glanced down at the physical reaction his thoughts were producing.

They were useless thoughts, and an even more useless reaction, but he had plenty of things to feel guilty about without adding a perfectly normal erection to the list. He was a healthy male and it *had* been a long time. Even before he'd gone to prison, his sex life had been practically nonexistent. Sylvia had lost interest in sex shortly after Chantal had been born. Sure, she had humored him for a while, feigning interest in order to placate him. During the last year, though, she had stopped pretending. She hadn't cared about their marriage, their child, their future…

He smiled crookedly as his arousal subsided—thoughts of his late wife were as effective as a cold shower. Considering the circumstances, it was for the best. He had other much more urgent matters to worry about.

Remy dressed swiftly and carried the boots he was using to the door. He could hear Dana clunking around on the first floor—she would be going through the kitchen by now. It was a good thing that he had made it a habit to clean up any traces of his presence each time he used a room. Unless she took an inventory, she would never know the supplies in the freezer were going down.

There was the stamp of booted feet. He guessed the sound was coming from the main entrance. His guess was confirmed seconds later by the solid slam of the front door, followed by a low, rumbling echo.

Remy frowned. Something definitely was bothering her. Normally she was even tempered, as sweet as the flowers she smelled like. The pressure of her book deadline must be getting to her.

The rumbling noise increased in volume, then ended in a loud thump. It seemed to have come from the roof. His frown deepening, Remy went to the side of the window and looked out, waiting to see Dana's red parka. When she didn't appear, he edged closer and peered downward, but all he could see was a tumbled pile of white.

That's what the noise must have been, he thought. The snow that had built up during the storm had finally slid off. The steep pitch of the roof had been designed for that purpose. Considering the record amount of snow that had fallen, it was no small weight that had crashed to the ground.

Concerned now, Remy moved right up to the glass. He would be in full view of anyone looking upward, but Dana wasn't there. He had been certain she had gone outside, so why couldn't he see her?

He replayed the sequence of sounds in his head. No more than a few seconds had elapsed between the slam of the door and the resulting snowslide. Anyone caught beneath it…

Remy jammed his feet into his boots, grabbed his coat and raced through the empty lodge to the front door. For all he knew, Dana could be standing beneath the porch overhang and be perfectly safe. He didn't know how he would explain his presence to her if she saw him, but if the sick feeling in his gut was anything to go by, he didn't think he *would* see her.

The door was stuck. Remy put his shoulder against it and shoved hard, but it wouldn't budge. Not wanting to waste more time, he headed out the service entrance and ran around to the front of the lodge.

He saw immediately why the door hadn't opened. It was blocked by a ten-foot-high pile of snow.

"Dana?" Remy shouted.

There was no movement. No sound. Just a sparkle of snowflakes that trickled from the roof.

"Dana!"

Still nothing.

A truly ruthless man would have saved his own skin rather than risk revealing himself. No one knew he was here. No one else had witnessed this accident. If he left her, that would be one less complication, one less threat to his freedom. There would be no questions he couldn't answer, no lies to tell. Dana believed she was alone, anyway. If he did nothing, her fate would be the same as if he hadn't been here.

All he had to do was walk away.

But not for a second did Remy consider any alternative. He thrust his bare hands into the snow and started to dig.

Chapter 5

The face above hers was hazy. The light behind it was too bright. Everything looked white. She winced, squinting her eyes.

"Dana?"

She knew that voice. She wanted to tell him so, but she was having trouble drawing air into her lungs. She wheezed.

There was the brush of fingers against her cheek. "It's okay, Dana. You're all right. You're out now."

Out? What was he talking about? She lifted her hand to shield her eyes and saw more white on her arm. White? It was snow. Her arm...no, her coat was covered with snow.

She blinked in an effort to adjust her eyes to the brightness. Sunlight reflected from the front windows of the lodge and bounced from an unending mountain of jumbled white.

What she was seeing suddenly clicked into place. Full consciousness flooded over her and her chest heaved. "Oh, my God!" she croaked.

"Shh, it's okay, Dana," he repeated, wiping the last of

the snow from her face. His touch was achingly tender. "You're all right now."

"It fell on top of me," she said. "I couldn't get out of the way. I couldn't move. I…couldn't breathe."

"You had passed out when I got to you, but you were still breathing." His hand settled on her shoulder. "You weren't out for long."

They were still in the snow, she realized. And she was lying across his lap, cradled in his arms. She tipped back her head to bring his face into focus.

Was she imagining this? Was she still stuck under that snowpile somewhere and having a hallucination? His image had been in her thoughts so often, for a moment she wondered whether he was really here.

But the arms that held her were warm and strong, and the chest she leaned against was broad and solid. She could see his pulse beat at the side of his neck, and she could feel the warmth of his breath on her face. He was real.

"John," she whispered.

His lips curved into one of his rare smiles. Yet something was different. Wrong. Where was his lush, sexy mustache? What had happened to his long hair? It had been lopped off into short layers that curled haphazardly over his head. He no longer looked like his photo—

The air that she'd managed to draw into her lungs rushed out as if she'd been struck.

No, he wasn't John. He was Remy Leverette.

Oh, God. He wasn't out West or up North or out of the country; he was here. Right here.

"I'd better get you back to your cabin," he said, shifting his grip. He tightened his arms around her and rose to his feet.

Dana squirmed, bringing her hands to his chest to push herself away.

John staggered but didn't release her. "Dana, relax. You're safe now."

Safe? She was being carried by an escaped felon. A murderer. A man who had stabbed his wife, and who had hidden a knife under her couch....

But this murderer had just dug her out of the snow. If he hadn't been there, she would have suffocated. It happened to children when snow tunnels collapsed. It happened to skiers in avalanches, and it could have happened to her...if it hadn't been for John.

No, not John. Remy was his name. She would do best to think of him that way.

She went still. "You saved my life."

He resettled her more comfortably in his arms and started down the path to the cabin. "Then I guess we're even."

Dana didn't know what to think. If he was Remy Leverette, convicted wife killer and desperate prison escapee, why had he helped her? Why not simply let her die? He had to know she would turn him in....

Or did he? She had automatically called him John. He had smiled when he'd heard her use that name. Could he believe she didn't know who he really was?

And was that why he felt he could risk exposing himself to save her?

She grabbed the front of his coat to keep steady as he strode forward. He walked easily, despite the slippery footing and the weight he was carrying. The strength that she had suspected while she'd watched him recover from the cold was evident in every move he made.

Oh, God. What was she going to do? She was no match for him physically. It would be futile to struggle. And even if she managed to get out of his grasp, she would never be able to outrun him. It probably would be wiser not to confront him. As long as he didn't know that she knew he was Remy Leverette, then he would have no reason to harm her, right?

They reached her cabin before she could form a plan. He carried her inside and kicked the door shut behind him.

She glanced at the telephone. She didn't dare use it now. She would have to wait until she was alone.

Remy walked as far as the couch, then leaned over and laid her on the cushions. He tugged off her boots and tossed them aside. "How are you feeling? Do you hurt anywhere?"

If she was hurting, it wasn't anywhere physical. Her emotions were another matter. "I'm all right."

"You must be cold." He brushed some snow off her jeans, the warmth of his hand going right through the denim. He unzipped her coat. "Let me help you out of those wet clothes."

The situation was familiar, only this time the roles were reversed. A memory of the way *she* had undressed *him* flashed into her mind. The sculpted arms, the broad chest with the feathery black hair, the slim hips, the long legs. He'd been so large, so muscled, so…male.

Her pulse thudded as he eased the sides of her coat apart. What was the matter with her? Did she need to remind herself of what a fool she had been? She had trusted him, liked him…and had been completely duped by him.

Wriggling away from his touch, she sat up and drew her arms out of her sleeves herself. "Only my coat's wet. I can get it off myself," she snapped, dropping the garment on the floor.

At her sharp tone, he shot her an assessing look.

She forced herself to move more slowly as she leaned back against the arm of the couch. Letting him think she was worse off than she was might prove to be an advantage. "I guess I'm still shaken up a bit."

"Anyone would be." He took the wool throw from the back of the couch and tucked it carefully around her legs. "Take it easy. I'll fix you something hot to drink."

Evidently Morty had heard the familiar voice. He padded in from the kitchen and started twining himself around Remy's ankles.

Remy stooped to run his palm over the cat's arched back, his touch as gentle as ever.

Damn him, Dana thought. He was making fools of them

both. Why did he have to come back? Why hadn't he just kept on going all the way to Alaska? "What are you doing here, John?" she burst out.

He straightened up. A look of wariness flickered in his eyes as he regarded her in silence.

She pasted on a smile. If she didn't curb her temper, he might realize that she knew the truth. Her only chance was to bluff him until she could get help.

Think, she ordered herself. How would she have behaved if she hadn't known John was Remy?

How? She probably would have been twining herself around him as pathetically as Morty.

What are you doing here, John?

Remy knew he had to come up with something. Fast.

At least she had called him "John." He hadn't expected that. It had been five days since he'd left her—could she really have kept away from the news all this time? Did she truly not know who he was?

Perhaps it was possible. He knew she hadn't turned on a television while she'd made her rounds of the lodge, and she didn't have one in this cabin. She hadn't taken a trip into town or had any visitors, so she couldn't have seen a newspaper. Even if she had heard a radio newscast of the prison break, she wouldn't have any way of knowing they were talking about him. He still had a chance to keep one step ahead of the law, as long as he could spin a feasible story.

Yet somehow his brain couldn't produce an available lie. He'd spent so many days watching her from a distance that her proximity was muddling his reason.

"I came to your cabin first," he said, stalling for time to think. "When you weren't here, I looked around a while. Thank God I saw what happened."

"It was lucky that you were at the lodge to dig me out of that avalanche," she said.

He remembered how pale and still Dana had looked when he'd reached her, and how hollow he had felt until

he had verified that she was still breathing. He had only
met her a week ago, had spent barely a day with her, yet
her welfare had come to mean so much to him. He reached
out to brush some remaining snow from her hair, then
stroked her hair back from her cheek. "Yes," he said, relieved to feel that her skin was warming up. "It was
lucky."

She accepted his caress for a moment before she glanced
down at the cat. Setting her chin, she tilted her head away
from his touch. "I didn't mean why were you at the lodge,
I meant why did you come back to the resort at all?" she
asked. "John," she added.

What could he possibly say? The truth was out of the
question. No one else believed him, so why should Dana?
Sure, she was a compassionate woman, but he couldn't rely
on her compassion stretching that far.

Still, he had to say something. Desperately he searched
his thoughts but all he could think of was how good it was
to see her again, no matter what the circumstances…

That was it! he decided quickly. The best lie was always
one that had a core of truth.

He pulled a footstool beside the couch and sat down. "I
have a confession to make, Dana."

Her eyes widened. "You do?"

"I could say that I was on my way to Hainesborough
and decided to drop in, but that's not the whole truth." He
reached out and took her hand. "The truth is, I came back
because I couldn't stay away from you."

"I'm not sure I understand."

"I had to see you again."

The color that was returning to her cheeks suddenly
deepened. "What?"

"Since I left here, I haven't been able to get you out of
my mind."

"*What?*"

"I'm sorry. I hadn't meant to spring it on you like this,"
he murmured. "I'm not expressing myself very well."

She looked down at their joined hands. "Uh…"

"I thought I'd take this slow, but when I held you in my arms after I pulled you out of the snow, I realized time is too precious to waste. We don't know what will happen tomorrow."

"But…"

"I understand that you're busy, and that you came up here to be alone. I'm not expecting you to neglect your work, yet I was hoping that we could get to know each other better."

She lifted her gaze back to his. "You want me to know you better?"

God, no, he thought. That was the last thing he wanted. "I realize this is sudden, Dana. We only had a day together, but somehow it doesn't seem to matter to the way I feel."

"I don't…know what to say."

Remy could tell that she was having difficulty believing him. Of course she would. She may be generous and compassionate, but she wasn't stupid. He needed to work harder at convincing her. Holding her gaze, he lifted her hand and pressed a soft kiss on her knuckles.

The sensation of her skin beneath his lips set off a jolt of awareness. He didn't need to fake the way his pulse accelerated and his body tensed. Damn it, this was supposed to be a lie.

Her hand trembled.

He wanted to kiss more than her hand. He wanted to stretch out beside her and hold her close and feel her entire body tremble. Instead he turned her hand over and brushed a kiss across her palm. "There's something special between us, Dana. You sense it, too, don't you?"

"John…"

"Something must have brought me to your doorstep in the storm. And it brought me back again when you needed me. I'd like to believe it was fate."

She parted her lips, but she didn't speak.

Remy watched her carefully. He couldn't tell what she

was thinking. Still, there was a spark of awareness in her eyes. It wasn't as clear an invitation as it had been six days ago, when they had been saying goodbye, yet it was a step in the right direction. Was she buying the act?

He'd been safe with her before. As long as he continued to keep her away from the news reports, there might be a way to salvage this situation yet. And what better way to ensure that than to play the attentive admirer? "I'm not expecting anything except a chance to find out where this leads. No pressure, Dana, and no strings," he said. "All I want is a few more days—"

"Days?" she repeated. "Are you saying you plan to stay here? With me?"

"It worked out well before. We'll have the same arrangement."

"Arrangement?"

"I'll sleep on the couch." He curled her fingers into her palm and held her hand to his chest. "But the rest of the time, Dana, I don't want to let you out of my sight."

Suds geysered upward as Dana thrust another plate into the sink. Remy had insisted on helping cook dinner, but it was probably due more to his desire to keep an eye on her than to share her company. And while she had gone through the motions, playing along with this farce, the whole time they'd been smiling across the table at each other, all she could think of was how to slip away and call the police. She would probably have permanent indigestion from the tension that had accompanied this meal.

The smart thing to do would have been to reject his transparently phony advances right at the beginning, ask him to leave and bolt the door. But he had taken her by surprise. And hadn't she already decided it would be best not to have a confrontation? What would he have done if she had called his bluff?

He was lying, of course. All that nonsense about not being able to get her out of his mind and wanting to see her again and hoping they could discover where things led, it had to be lies.

Well, one thing was undoubtedly true. Whatever else Remy was, he was an excellent liar. Although she caught occasional glimpses of the brooding stranger he had been when she had first met him, he was doing his best to behave like a love-struck suitor. He was trying to charm her the same way he was charming Morty. He could be waiting for a chance to catch her off guard and then—

And then what? Kill her, the way he had killed his wife? If he was a murderer, if he intended to harm her, then why hadn't he left her in the snow to suffocate?

As it had at least a hundred times over the past few hours, her mind returned to the moment she had opened her eyes and seen his face. He had saved her life. She simply didn't want to believe the worst about him.

But that was nothing new, was it? She had been struggling to make excuses for him from the start.

She was a complete idiot. A first-class fool. Because deep in her heart she wished she could believe his phony advances and ridiculous lies.

If only they really had been fated to be together. It would have been so romantic, like a story of love at first sight, just the two of them in a cozy cabin in the woods. Wouldn't it have been nice if Remy really had been as affected by her as she had been by him? Wouldn't it have been wonderful if the thrill she had felt when his lips had met her skin had been the real thing?

But nothing was real here, she told herself. Not his feelings, not even the name she was calling him. The sooner she phoned the police and ended this game, the better.

The problem was, Remy was keeping his word. He wasn't letting her out of his sight.

"Where does the colander go?" he asked.

"Second cupboard to the left."

He flipped the dish towel over his shoulder and bent down to open the cupboard.

Dana tried very hard not to notice how his movement made his jeans pull taut to mold a set of firmly rounded buttocks. Averting her gaze, she plunged a pot lid into the soapy water that filled the sink.

Did all ruthless wife killers volunteer to help with the dishes? And did they all have to possess such a tantalizing set of buns?

At the touch on her shoulder, she jumped back with a cry and spun to face him.

"I'm sorry, Dana," Remy said. "I didn't mean to startle you."

She took a deep breath to settle her pulse. "It's okay."

Remy dabbed the towel he held to a spot at the base of her throat. "You have some suds here."

"Oh."

He brushed the towel lower. "Here, too."

It was no use trying to settle her heartbeat, Dana thought. Not with his hand so close to her breasts. He would be able to see the way her pulse raced and her breath was growing short.

But why should she try to hide her reaction? This would be how he would expect her to react if she believed he was John, right? She would respond to his touch because of that "something special" he sensed between them, right?

Playing along had seemed like a good idea at the time. Now all she had to do was keep reminding herself that it was an act.

"Is there anything else I could help you with, Dana?" he asked, leaning closer.

"No, I—" She thought quickly. "As a matter of fact there is, John. We'll be needing more wood for the fireplace."

"Would you like me to get it for you?"

"Yes, please. It's in the woodshed."

"I'd be happy to," he said, hanging up his towel.

She turned back to the sink, pretending to be absorbed in scrubbing the pot lid while she strained to hear the sounds from the next room. She detected the rustle of fabric as Remy put on his coat, the stamp of his boots, the click of the latch on the front door...

Yes! she thought, wiping her hands on her sweater. This was her chance. She pivoted and raced to the living room. The woodshed stored firewood for the entire resort, and it was closer to the lodge than to the caretaker's cabin, nearly fifty yards from here. As long as Remy didn't hurry, that would give her plenty of time to reach the phone and—

"How much do you need?"

She skidded to a halt in the doorway. Remy was still inside the cabin, his hand on the front door latch. "Lots," she answered immediately. "You'll probably have to make two or three trips."

"No problem."

"Thanks." Bypassing the telephone, she walked over to the fireplace. The blaze was burning well, but she crossed her arms and drew in her shoulders as if she were cold. *Go,* she thought. *What are you waiting for?*

"Dana?"

"Mmm?"

"Are you really all right?"

"What do you mean?"

"No lingering aftereffects of your accident this morning?"

"No, none at all. I'm perfectly fine."

"Great." He smiled and held out his hand. "Then could you show me where the woodshed is?"

Did he know? she wondered as she put on her coat and led him outside. Did he realize that she knew who he was, and that she was waiting for the opportunity to turn him in? Was he merely being cautious, playing it safe?

Or was he toying with her the way Morty toyed with the mice that were foolhardy enough to bumble within his reach?

She shivered as she started down the path she had shoveled. Moments later she felt the warmth of Remy's arm around her shoulders. He drew her close to his side and shortened his steps, as if he really did care about her comfort.

Damn him, how could he do this to her? Why did he have to come back?

Dana looked around. The moonlight reflected starkly from the snow, illuminating the area. She suddenly realized what she wasn't seeing. "John, where's your car?"

"My car?"

"I don't see a car."

His breath puffed whitely in the moonlight. "I did more damage than I had realized when I hit the ditch in the storm. My car is still in a garage in Hainesborough. The mechanic has to wait for parts."

"Then how did you get home last week?"

"The tow truck driver dropped me off at the bus station and I caught the first southbound to Toronto."

"Why didn't you rent a car?"

"My wallet must have fallen out of my pocket while I was wandering around in the snow that first night, so I didn't have my driver's license or any ID."

"How...inconvenient. But how did you get here?"

"I got a ride with a friend who was on his way north. He dropped me at the end of the lane."

If she hadn't been listening for it, she might have missed the slight pause before each of his answers. She had to hand it to him. He had an excuse—a lie—for everything. And she thought *she* was the one with the imagination?

All right, if he wanted to toy with her, two could play that game. "I thought you were anxious to get home to your daughter," she said, wondering how he'd lie his way out of this one. "I'm surprised you'd want to leave her alone so soon."

"My daughter—" The pause was longer this time. "Chantal will be fine."

"I guess you have a good baby-sitter?"

"She's staying with her grandparents." He cleared his

throat. "As a matter of fact, when I told her about you, she wanted to come here herself."

Dana frowned. He had lied about everything else. Had he lied about having a daughter, too?

Somehow she didn't think so. Obviously, she had huge gaps in her judgment when it came to men, but she was sure Remy couldn't have fabricated Chantal. He might have lied about her name, and about her fondness for the Mortimer books, but the love on his face when he'd spoken of his child had been too pure to be faked. So had the note of sadness in his voice when he'd spoken of her now. Dana had spent too much of her life longing for just that kind of bond with a child of her own. She was certain she was able to recognize it in someone else.

If he did love his child as much as it seemed, then it must have been hell to be locked up where he couldn't see her. No wonder he had liked to talk about her so much. He was probably eaten up with grief over missing her....

She grimaced. She was doing it again, making excuses, trying to see some good in him. Before she started sympathizing with Remy Leverette, it might be good to remind herself that he couldn't be with his daughter because he had killed his daughter's mother.

"Please feel free to call Chantal whenever you want," she said. "I have a good long-distance plan."

"Thanks. That must mean the phone is working again."

"Yes." She watched him out of the corner of her eye. "It was the weirdest thing. At first I thought the line was down, but then I discovered it was my phone that was the problem."

"Oh?"

"I replaced it with one from the lodge and the line worked fine."

"Whatever the cause, I'm glad it's fixed. I hated to think of you completely isolated out here." He squeezed her shoulders. "That's another reason I had to come back."

He was piling it on thicker, she thought. But there was

some truth in what he said. He had probably wanted to return to the resort because of the complete isolation. After all, it had worked out well as a place for him to elude the authorities before.

She swung open the door to the woodshed and flipped on the light. The glow from the solitary bulb that hung from the rafters was swallowed by the rows of stacked firewood, but it was enough to illuminate the chopping block in the middle of the floor...and the shiny new ax that was embedded in it.

"Want me to split some kindling for you?" Remy asked, reaching for the ax.

An image flashed into her mind from that Stephen King horror movie about the caretaker at the closed resort. She saw Jack Nicholson grinning maniacally and wielding an ax.... "No!"

Remy cocked his head and looked at her, one eyebrow lifting. "Relax, I've done this before. I wouldn't chop off my foot."

"No, of course not," she said. "It's just not necessary. Derek provided plenty of kindling before he left."

He shrugged and went over to the nearest stack of firewood. One by one he piled the short logs on his forearm. "Let me know if you change your mind."

She swallowed hard, her gaze on the ax. What was she doing? This wasn't a game. Instead of matching wits with Remy, she should be worried out of her mind.

So why wasn't she?

Chapter 6

Remy angled the screwdriver against the valve and pressed down on the pin in the center. Air hissed out in a steady stream as the last tire slowly deflated.

Satisfied, Remy rose from his crouch beside Dana's car and replaced the tool on the workbench, shining the flashlight around the garage. Like the woodshed, this building was closer to the lodge than to any of the scattered cabins, including the caretaker's. It sheltered several all-terrain vehicles, about a dozen mountain bikes and a pickup truck that he assumed belonged to Derek. The ATVs and the bikes would be useless until the spring thaw, and he'd removed the battery from the pickup. Now that the remaining car was unusable, Dana wouldn't be going anywhere in a hurry without his knowledge.

All right. That was one more loose end tied up...and at least a hundred more to go. He'd been lucky so far that Dana hadn't asked him about his lack of luggage, considering his claim that he had wanted to stay with her. He had covered that problem as soon as he'd gotten up this morning by returning to the lodge and filling a gym bag with Dana's cousin's clothes. He was gambling that she didn't see Derek often enough to recognize his clothes, but if she did, he could say it was merely a coincidence. The deceptions kept adding up, didn't they?

As had happened all too frequently, a whisper of guilt stirred, but he tamped it down. Whatever it took, he reminded himself. For Chantal, he would do whatever was necessary.

Keeping the light low, he moved to the side door and looked outside. There was the hint of a glow on the southeast horizon—it would be dawn soon. He hoped Dana would still be asleep. Not even twenty-four hours had gone past and already he was sick of the lies.

He knew this charade couldn't go on indefinitely, but so far, things had worked out better than he could have imagined. He could go into town in a few more days anyway, just as he'd planned, but he could claim he wanted to pick up his car. Dana might even give him a ride, once he installed the battery in the truck. As long as she didn't learn the truth, she could be useful. She seemed to be as interested in him as he pretended to be in her.

Pretended? Scowling, he grabbed the bag of borrowed clothes and started back to the cabin. That was his problem in a nutshell. The smitten-suitor role was coming far too easily to him. He had barely slept last night. His mind was too full of images of Dana in her bed. The image had been tempting when he had been separated from her by hundreds of yards and the lens of a telescope. Separated by nothing but a wooden door that was thin enough to hear the creak of the bedsprings through had been a test of his willpower.

She had been restless last night. Although the sliver of light beneath her door had gone out shortly after midnight, he had heard the bed creak as she tossed and turned. Had she been thinking about him as he had been thinking of her? How would she have reacted if he'd gone to her?

That was the question that wasn't letting him rest. They

were two adults. They were attracted to each other. They were alone in an isolated cabin. What would be the harm in finding out? If they let nature take its course…

He swore under his breath and reached for the cabin door latch. A quick one-nighter wasn't his style, and he doubted it was Dana's, either. She was an innocent, as sweet and trusting as the characters she wrote about. Despite his growing list of lies, he still had some scruples left. He needed to remind himself of that, he thought, opening the door.

The interior of the cabin was lit only by the fire on the hearth, but Remy immediately saw a figure in front of the window. Dana stood beside the low table there, her hair tousled with sleep, her nightgown covering her to her ankles. For a crazy moment he thought she might have come into the living room looking for him. Maybe she hadn't been the only one wishing there hadn't been a door between them. Could she have arisen early to join him on the couch or invite him back to her bedroom?

But the crazy moment passed. A log shifted in the fireplace, and in the sudden flare of light, Remy saw the gleam of the telephone receiver in Dana's hand.

Not taking his gaze from her, he kicked the door shut behind him and dropped his bag on the floor. "Good morning, Dana. I hadn't expected to see you up so early."

"Me, neither," she said. "I thought you'd still be asleep."

"I'm an early riser."

"I had forgotten. Where were you?"

"I went out to look for my bag."

"Your bag?"

He gestured at the gym bag by his feet. "I had packed some spare clothes before I came up north. I had dropped it when I went to dig you out of the snow."

"Oh. Lucky you found it."

"Yes. Who are you talking to?"

"What?"

He nodded to the telephone.

"No one."

Another log popped. In the silence that followed, Remy heard the buzz of a dial tone.

"It was a wrong number," she continued, replacing the receiver. She pushed her hair behind her ear. "It woke me up. I rushed out here to answer it so it wouldn't wake you up, too, but then I noticed you weren't asleep anyway so it hadn't mattered."

Across the width of the room in the firelight, he couldn't see the expression in her eyes. He didn't know whether or not she was lying. He supposed it was possible that she was telling the truth.

Just like it was possible that she didn't know who he was?

Oh, hell. What if somehow she had known all along? What if she had been about to call the police right now? Or worse, what if she had already reached them?

No, he'd heard a dial tone. If she had gotten through, there would have been a voice. If she had completed her call, she would have hung up the phone.

Dana flicked her hair behind her ear again, although it didn't need it, and moved forward. "How did you sleep, John?"

"Fine. What about you?"

"Not too well. I was thinking about you."

"Really," he said.

"Uh-huh." She halted in front of him and reached up to unbutton his coat. "You were right. There is something special between us. I felt it, too, but I hadn't believed it could happen so fast."

Was she humoring him, trying to allay his suspicions so she could try her call again?

Or was she telling the truth? What if it really had been a wrong number that had brought her to the phone?

He felt the gentle touch of her hands as she continued to open his coat. He drew in his breath and tasted the scent of lilies and sleep-warmed female. How was he supposed to think straight when she stood this close?

He could see her pulse beating fast in the vein on the side of her neck. Was that because she was telling the truth about her feelings? Or was it because she was nervous about lying?

He peeled off his gloves and put his knuckles under her chin, lifting her face so that he could meet her gaze.

"I enjoyed the evening yesterday," she said. "It was nice getting to know each other better."

Despite his doubts, his body was reacting to her as if nothing was wrong. If she honestly wanted to know him better, all she had to do was take another step closer. His hands tingled with the urge to pull her against him, to run his palms over her nightgown and feel the warm curves the sensible fleece fabric hid.

If this was an act, if she was only humoring him, how far would she be willing to go?

She smiled shyly. "Do you mind if I ask you something personal, John?"

"Go ahead."

"Why did you get your hair cut?"

"It was getting into my collar."

She raised up on her toes to run her fingers through his hair, smoothing it back from his forehead. "It's nice."

"Thanks, but I think the barber was in a rush." He tipped his head into her touch. "Maybe you could even it up for me later."

"Mmm. Sure." She tapped the side of his mouth with a fingertip. "Why did you shave off your mustache?"

"It was itchy. Don't you like the change?"

"You look nice either way."

He moved his hand, placing his palm over her pulse. Her neck was so delicate, his thumb stretched across her throat. "There was another reason I got rid of it."

"Oh?"

"I didn't want anything to get in the way when I kissed you."

He felt her throat work against his thumb as she swallowed. "Oh."

"Feel like trying it out?"

Her gaze dropped to his mouth.

He leaned closer. *How far would she be willing to go?*

She ran her fingertips across his upper lip. "Nice," she said. "But I think you need another shave."

He sighed against her fingers. "Dana…"

"Over easy?"

"Mmm?"

"Your eggs." She stepped back. "Since we're both up, I might as well fix breakfast."

Dana jabbed at the logs with the poker, rearranging them so that the unburned sides lay across the embers. She watched as flames licked upward, first blackening the wood, then turning it orange. The blaze strengthened until the warmth that bathed her face became uncomfortably hot. Just before the heat on her skin reached the point of pain, she pulled back. She closed the mesh curtain spark-guard and sat down on the braided rug in front of the hearth, wrapping her arms around her knees.

Well, that's what you got when you played with fire, she thought. You got burned.

She had to be insane to think she could outbluff a liar who was as skillful as Remy Leverette. Where did she think this flirtation dance she had entered into would lead? How long before she was trapped in her lies, outsmarted by her own scheme, or as Mortimer and his pirate friends would put it, hoisted by her own petard?

But there had been no choice, she told herself yet again. When Remy had caught her with the phone in her hand this morning, she'd had to come up with something. Fast. He hadn't seemed to buy her story about the predawn wrong number. So she had tried to distract him with the same methods he had used so effectively on her.

It hadn't been difficult. That was the trouble. Pretending to welcome Remy's supposed advances came all too naturally to her.

The floor creaked behind her, but she wasn't startled. She had already sensed Remy's approach. It had been that way all day. Ever since she had followed up on her offer and had trimmed his jagged haircut for him, she had become intensely attuned to his presence.

He had such beautiful hair, thick and surprisingly soft. It had been impossible not to notice how it had slid so sensuously over her fingers. She could understand why he had worn it long before—it was almost a crime to take scissors to it. Whatever barber had left it in such a mess belonged in jail. No, wait. If Remy had trimmed his hair himself in an effort to disguise his appearance, then he already belonged in jail. Oh, God, this was so confusing.

"I fixed you some hot chocolate," he said, lowering himself to the rug beside her. He handed her a steaming mug.

She took the mug from his hand and blew on it. The aroma of chocolate curled temptingly over the rim as half-melted marshmallows bobbed on the surface. It was a drink that evoked memories of skating parties at her grandparents' house and the Christmas Eves of her childhood. It was what she would expect John Becker, solid citizen and family man, to offer. It wasn't what she would associate with a desperate killer.

She pursed her lips and blew harder, then gulped a mouthful of chocolate. "Thanks."

He stretched out his legs in front of him. "Are you finished working for the day?"

Working? Right, sure. She'd sat at her desk for an hour and pretended to work, hoping he would get bored or inattentive and wander off somewhere. She should have known better. She'd finally given up the pretense when the layer of eraser crumbs had begun to obscure the paper. "For now, anyway," she replied.

"How's the book coming along?"

"Fine," she lied.

"What's the story about?"

"Mortimer has to save an island village from raiding pirate mice. He gets captured, but he manages to escape and round them up."

Remy shifted closer until his hip nudged hers. "How does he escape?"

"He distracts them." She sipped her cocoa and tried not to be distracted by the heat that was spreading from the place their bodies touched. "With, uh, cheese."

"That sounds like something Mortimer would do." He covered her hand with his and guided the mug to his own mouth. Placing his lips over the same spot on the rim she had used, he took a drink.

There wasn't anything sensual about hot chocolate with marshmallows, Dana told herself. It was ordinary and wholesome. Her pulse shouldn't be speeding up at the way Remy had shared it. No, indeed.

He released her hand and draped his arm over her back. "I wish I had thought of bringing some wine."

Wine? If his proximity was making cocoa so potent, she sure didn't need anything stronger... No, wait, she thought. This opportunity was too good to waste. "I have an idea, John."

"So do I, Dana. You show me yours and I'll show you mine."

She sputtered. "What?"

"I meant ideas." He smiled, playing his fingers over her ribs. "What's yours?"

"Everything pretty well shuts down after supper in Hainesborough, but if we leave right now, we might have enough time to drive into town and pick up some wine before the stores close."

"Okay. Sounds good."

Startled, she turned her head to look at him. She hadn't expected him to agree to go into town.

"I'd like to buy some groceries, too, if we get there in time," he continued. "I know you weren't counting on having a visitor." His thumb rubbed her sweater a hairbreadth from the side of her breast. "Not a visitor with my appetite, anyway."

Wasn't he afraid of being recognized? Wasn't he worried that she might go straight to the first cop they saw and turn him in?

On the other hand, he *did* look different from the photo that had been on the news, she thought. Without the long hair and the mustache, he looked less like an outlaw, but if he thought he would pass unnoticed, then he was seriously underestimating the eyesight of the female population.

Silence lengthened as she studied him. There was another explanation for his willingness to go into town. What if he was telling the truth? What if he really was a innocent traveler named John who was infatuated with her and—

No. No, no, no. She wasn't going to go there. It just wasn't possible.

But it had been a week since she had seen that newscast. And she had only seen the photo for less than a minute, and the policeman who had come here hadn't believed John could be Leverette, and there had been reasonable explanations for everything...

Just stop it, she told herself. Was she so desperate to believe the romantic fantasy he was weaving that she was willing to disregard her logic? That was downright pathetic. She put the mug of hot chocolate on the floor. "All right. I'll get my coat."

"Just a minute," he said. "Don't you want to hear my idea?"

"What? Oh, sure. What was it?"

For such a large man, he moved remarkably quickly.

Without knowing exactly how he did it, Dana found herself lying on her back on the rug, staring up at Remy's face.

He placed his hands on either side of her shoulders, straddling her legs as he balanced himself on his knees and his outstretched arms. His dark eyes sparkled with what appeared to be mischief. "Comfortable?" he asked.

"Uh…"

"It's not bearskin, but it should do."

"What are you talking about?"

"If we're going to get some wine, we need to have a bearskin rug, right? Can't very well make love in front of a blazing fire without one."

"John, that's not… I mean, when I agreed to get wine, I hadn't meant…"

He grinned and ducked his head to kiss the side of her neck. "You wanted to know my idea," he murmured against her skin. "That was it."

Oh, why did he have to kiss her? she thought. If he was trying to distract her, he had chosen an effective tactic. The kiss hadn't even been on her mouth, yet it sent awareness tingling through her body. Except for the whisper of his breath on her neck, he wasn't touching her. Nevertheless she could feel him everywhere.

She could probably move away if she wanted to. The way he straddled her left him completely vulnerable to a well-placed knee if she chose to fight him. Yes, a sharp blow to his groin and a follow-up smash to the nose with the heel of her hand could slow him down enough to allow her to get away. The poker was still within her reach, too. She could knock him out with a quick blow to the head and make a run for it—

Bile rose in Dana's throat. Just the thought of hurting this man made her feel ill. He hadn't threatened her, he hadn't harmed her, he had saved her life. As if to make up for her vicious thoughts, she placed her hands hesitantly on his shoulders.

"Maybe we can skip the wine," he said. He touched his tongue to her earlobe. "What do you think?"

His shirt crumpled beneath her fingers. "I think you're trying to seduce me."

"You might be right." He pressed his nose to her temple. "You smell like lilies, did you know that?"

"What?"

"It's one of the first things I noticed about you. I hadn't been able to open my eyes, but I caught your scent."

"It must be my shampoo."

He gradually lowered himself until his chest was just touching her breasts. "I was in about this spot, I think. I remember the warmth of the fire."

"I had to leave you on the floor because I hadn't been able to get you onto the couch." Beneath her sweater, her skin tingled from the whisper of contact. She should push him off, or wriggle out from under him. Anything instead of lying here waiting…

Waiting? Was that what she was doing?

Yes, she thought, moving her hands to his back. He pressed more firmly against her and she closed her eyes at the mindless surge of pleasure. Despite who he was and what she knew about him, her body was reacting as if this wasn't a lie.

He shifted his weight, leaning on his elbow to free the opposite hand. He trailed his fingers down her side, following the curve of her hip, then slipped his hand beneath the lower edge of her sweater.

Her breath caught. "John?"

He made a deep noise in his throat as his fingertips touched her bare skin. Inch by tantalizing inch, he moved his hand upward.

She should stop him now, Dana thought. Right now. This instant. It had gone far enough. There was no way to justify what they were doing—

In one bold move, he closed his hand over her breast.

Oh, damn. Damn. Even as more pleasure shot through

her body, Dana's eyes filled. Why did this have to be a lie? Why did it have to feel so good? She arched her back, filling his palm for a greedy, guilty moment before she grasped his wrist.

He moved his lips over her cheek, kissing his way to the corner of her mouth.

A heartbeat before he would have reached her lips, she turned her head aside. "John, no. We can't do this."

He went still. Underneath her fingertips she could feel his pulse throb. "Why not?"

"It's too fast," she said, blinking hard.

"Dana…"

"You said you wouldn't pressure me, remember?"

He exhaled hard, his breath hot on her cheek. He gave her breast one last, lingering caress then slowly withdrew his hand. "I'm sorry, Dana," he said, his voice hoarse. He rolled to his side. "I didn't mean for this to happen."

She stayed where she was and focused on the ceiling. "That makes two of us."

"When I touch you I seem to forget…" He paused and cleared his throat. "I forget my good intentions."

"I tend to forget things, too."

He placed his index finger under her chin and gently turned her face toward him. "You're a very attractive woman, Dana. A man would have to be made of stone not to notice." He smiled crookedly. "I know. When I was half-frozen I noticed."

The fire crackled quietly. The clock on the mantel ticked. Bit by bit, Dana felt herself relax. She looked at the way Remy's smile softened his sharp features and deepened the lines beside his mouth. Even her amateur haircut couldn't diminish his appeal.

There were so many lies between them, at least she could be honest about this one thing, couldn't she? "You're a very attractive man."

"I've been a lonely man, Dana. It's been a long time since…" His smile dimmed. "I'll spare you the details."

"How long… I mean, when did your wife die?"

"Last year."

"You must have loved her very much."

"We made a wonderful child together."

She realized he hadn't really confirmed her statement.

He rested his hand on her shoulder, his fingers toying with the ends of her hair. "What about you, Dana? Have you ever been married?"

She hesitated, but what harm would there be in telling him the truth about this, too? "Yes."

"What happened?"

"It didn't work out. I couldn't give him what he wanted. We divorced two years ago."

"I'm sorry."

"It's okay. I have my career, and my family. I have a great life."

"Your life is so great, you like to cut yourself off from the world in a closed resort in the winter."

"I'm staying here to work."

"Is that the only reason?"

"Of course," she answered a little too quickly.

He curled a lock of her hair around his index finger and brought it to his lips. "Don't you ever get lonely, Dana?"

She didn't like where the conversation was leading. How much honesty did she want to allow herself? Yes, she got lonely. Damn right, she got lonely. Why else would she be stretched out on the floor beside a convicted killer and wishing she could believe this whole crazy charade they were playing?

"Dana?"

"Sometimes," she murmured.

"I think the nights are the worst," he said. "When everything's quiet, and there's nothing left to keep your mind busy, and all the small things from the day start to swirl around your head. Don't you wish you had someone beside you then, to talk to?" He stroked her cheek with the ends of her hair. "Or just to hold in the dark?"

She moistened her lips. "Sometimes."

Firelight reflected in his eyes, making the brown depths glisten. He watched her without speaking for a while. "When we find someone," he said finally, "it's not always logical or convenient, is it?"

He's got that right, she thought. There was nothing logical or convenient about the way she was feeling right now. She had just finished pushing his hand away from her breast, but now she wanted him to touch her again.

He leaned closer.

Oh, God. Was he going to kiss her? What would she do if he did? How could she stand it if he didn't? Was she crazy?

"Do you believe in fate, Dana?"

Before she could think of an answer—to any of the questions—the hush of the cabin was split by the shrill of the telephone.

Dana started. Her gaze flicked to the phone, then back to Remy's face.

His hand tightened in her hair, his touch no longer a caress. "Let it ring," he said.

She tried to move her head but stopped when her hair tugged uncomfortably against her scalp. "It might be important."

"If it is, they'll call back."

The phone rang again. Dana's stomach lurched. She had been prevented from calling for help this morning. Remy had effectively kept her under surveillance since then. Regardless of who was on the other end of the phone now, this might be the chance she had been waiting for. "John, I have to get that."

"It could be another wrong number."

Was she imagining the note of steel in his voice? Was there a tinge of suspicion? "No, I have to—"

"You have to stay here with me," he said, throwing one leg over hers. "Please, Dana."

For a mad instant as she looked into his troubled gaze,

she almost did what he asked. *What if she was wrong?* she wondered yet again. What if he really was a lonely widower who was falling in love....

Or what if he decided to drop the act and force her to do what he said? He could. She felt the strength in his thigh where it rested over hers, and she could see the tendons in his neck stiffen as he held himself motionless. He was no longer vulnerable—she had been fooling herself to think that he ever had been.

Yet somehow Dana still couldn't believe that he would knowingly harm her.

Another ring.

Was she going to lie here forever? Dana decided to go with her instincts. She braced her elbows on the rug and carefully began to lever herself upward, wincing at the pull on her scalp. "Let go of my hair, John," she said.

"Dana..."

"You're hurting me."

Remy saw the flicker of pain in Dana's eyes and felt as if he'd been struck. Instantly he released her hair and rolled away from her.

She jackknifed to her feet and lunged for the phone. "Hello?"

Remy sat up and rubbed his face. What the hell was he doing? He had been wondering how far she would be willing to go to perpetuate the charade. He should have been wondering how far *he* would go.

He hadn't wanted her to answer the phone. Not because she might learn about him or might give him away. No, he hadn't wanted to let her escape from his arms. He raked his hair off his forehead and rose to his feet. At his movement Dana watched him warily.

He did his best to arrange his face into a harmless John Becker expression as he approached her.

She pressed the receiver to her ear. Her brow furrowed briefly before the corners of her mouth firmed with what appeared to be disappointment. "Yes? Yes, I am."

Remy weighed the consequences of dropping the pretense and ripping out the phone cord. If Dana knew who
he was, she could give him away to whoever was on the
other end of the line in the next second. But if she didn't
know who he was, by overreacting now he would give
himself away. The best course of action would be to play
this out and see what happened. He moved to her side and
slid his arm possessively around her waist.

He could hear the tinny drone of a man's voice from the
receiver. He gave Dana a squeeze, pulling her securely
against him so that he could hear better.

She smiled tightly at him and shifted the phone to her
other ear.

Remy moved behind her back and folded his arms over
hers, enclosing her in a lover-like embrace. He dropped his
chin to her shoulder to bring his ear next to the receiver.

"...then you might be interested in our pay-as-you-go
plan. For a two-hundred-dollar deposit..."

Remy frowned. What was going on?

"I'd like to see some more information," Dana said.
"Could you send someone out to talk to me? I'll give you
directions."

"I'm sorry, ma'am, but with the demand for these con-
dominiums we wouldn't be able to do that. I'd be happy
to mail the brochures..."

It was a telemarketer, Remy realized. Not the police, not
a concerned friend or a relative, just an anonymous stranger
trying to sell something.

Under other circumstances he might have laughed. As it
was, he merely pressed his lips to the side of Dana's neck
and sighed.

Was he imagining the delicate shudder that traveled
through her body? He didn't think so. That should have
made the role he had to play easier, yet somehow it didn't.

The conversation ended. Remy loosened his embrace, allowing Dana to pull out of his arms and hang up the phone.

She stared at it blankly for a moment, then turned around and looked out the window.

He followed her gaze. Darkness had fallen completely. Against the black shadows of the trees and the deep-blue swaths of snow, the reflection of the softly lit cabin seemed to float just outside the glass. This is what he had hoped would happen when he had initiated that embrace on the rug. The flat tires on her car and the missing battery from the truck would have delayed their departure anyway, but there was no reason for her to find out about the disabled vehicles unless she had to. "The stores would be closed by now, wouldn't they?" he asked.

She crossed her arms. "Yes."

"Sorry. I guess we got sidetracked. We'll have to take that trip into town another day."

"Right."

"Who was on the phone?"

"Just somebody selling time-share condos in Florida."

"You sounded interested."

"Sure. I'm always on the lookout for a quiet place to work."

"There could be a lot of distractions in Florida."

"There seem to be a lot of distractions here," she muttered. She turned back to face him. The soft, almost confused expression she had worn while she'd been lying beneath him was gone. In its place was frustration and something that looked suspiciously like...challenge. "You mentioned that you were lonely," she said.

"Yes. I do get lonely."

"What about Chantal? I'm surprised you haven't wanted to call her yet."

At the sound of his daughter's name, his muscles knotted. "I...uh."

"Go ahead." She watched him steadily. "I wouldn't mind."

"I don't want to impose—"

"As I said, I have a great long-distance plan." She

picked up the receiver once more and held it out to him. "She's probably eager to hear from you."

Did she know? he wondered. Was she trying to test him, to call his bluff?

Or did she actually care?

The moment dragged on. He had two choices. Either he played along, or he ended this now.

"Well?"

Remy took the receiver from Dana's hand. He thought for a moment, then dialed the number of the airport weather service. There was a short beep, followed by a long tone. When the recorded forecast began, he forced a smile. "Hi, Mom. It's John."

Dana started. Was it surprise? he wondered.

"Fine, fine. How's everything with you?"

The temperature would dip to minus twenty-one Celsius overnight and rise to minus twelve tomorrow.

"Yes, I'm still at the resort. How did things go at school today? Did Chantal take her new rabbit for show-and-tell?"

Winds were calm, barometric pressure at one hundred and one kilopascals and steady.

"Yes, that would be great." He paused. "Hello, pun'kin. It's Daddy."

As Remy listened to the details of the low pressure system over the American Midwest, in his head he imagined the sound of his daughter's voice. It had been months since he'd heard it. His late wife's parents had found one excuse after another to keep her away from the phone each time he was allowed to make a call. They had never brought her to the Kingston Pen to see him, either. He wasn't sure he would have wanted her to see him there, caged up like an animal. That wasn't how he wanted her to think of her father.

But how was she thinking of him now? Did she remember how he used to hold her over his head and spin around to make her giggle? Did she slip her hand into someone else's as she walked to the playground? Did she still need him to check under her bed for trolls?

Remy pinched the bridge of his nose and swallowed hard. Of all the acts he'd had to put on, this one was the worst. If only it could be real. What he wouldn't give to be able to hear his daughter's voice, to be finished with the lies.

"Did Grandma take you tobogganing at the park?" he asked. He paused, as he always did to allow Chantal time to chatter. "You kept your hat on for the whole time? Hey, good for you."

The chance of precipitation was zero for tonight, ten percent for tomorrow.

"We'll build a snow fort when I come home, okay? And I'll make a slide in the backyard, just like last year."

Ceiling unlimited.

"You be a good girl for Grandma and Grandpa."

Sunrise at 7:56 tomorrow.

"I promise I'll be home soon."

Sunset at 4:20.

"I love you, too." Heat rose behind his eyes. The recorded voice crackled to a stop. There was a long beep. The line clicked and went dead. "Goodbye, Chantal."

He leaned over to hang up the phone, exhaling slowly to regain control. When he straightened up, Dana was staring at him. Was it a trick of the lighting, or were her own eyes moist?

"Thanks," he said, his voice rough.

She rubbed her eyes and turned away. "Don't mention it."

Chapter 7

Mortimer should have escaped from the pirate mice's island by now. He wasn't stupid. He had stockpiled the cheese and was about to make a dash for his ship, but instead he was watching the pirates play tag with their children. Cute little baby mice were romping and laughing with the desperate outlaws. How could these evil pirates be such caring parents?

Dana groaned and dropped her head to the table. It should have been a simple story, a tale of right and wrong, but the plot that had seemed so straightforward was splintering out of control.

Next time she signed a contract for a book, she would have her publisher provide a sensory deprivation tank. Yes, one of those fluid-filled boxes from a research lab where she could be locked in with absolutely no distractions. That would be perfect.

"Dana? Is something wrong?"

Whoa, not only was he a good liar, he was perceptive as hell. Something wrong? What had been his first clue?

Could it be the dark circles under her eyes this morning? How about the overflowing wastebasket beside her work table? Or maybe it was the way she didn't know how to meet his gaze.

She wasn't normally a cruel person. Yesterday she had been frustrated by this cat-and-mouse game they had been playing. That was why she had dared him to make that phone call.

He had faked the whole thing. Sure, he had been clever enough to dial a number with the Toronto area code, but he hadn't counted on how quiet the room had been. He had pressed the receiver tightly enough to his ear to keep her from hearing the voice on the other end of the phone, but he hadn't been able to muffle the beeps and clicks that signaled a recorded message.

The problem was, the call hadn't been entirely faked. The things he had said, the way his voice had softened, she would bet her next royalty check those had been real.

At least one thing had been settled. She no longer held out even a smidgen of hope that she might have been wrong. He *was* Remy Leverette.

Yet instead of the fear she should logically be feeling, she felt anger. She was angry over his continuing deception. She was downright livid at the way he was using her cabin as a hideout, toying with her emotions and playing her for a fool.

Most of all, though, she was furious at the guilt she felt over forcing him to pretend to talk with Chantal.

It had hurt him. He loved his daughter. He missed her, and it had caused him pain to pretend. What had started out as a dare, as a petty bit of revenge for the game he was playing, had backfired on her when she had seen that faraway sheen in his eyes. Physically he was such a ruggedly powerful man that it made the depth of his emotions all the more compelling.

She couldn't be developing sympathy for the person who was essentially holding her captive, could she? Wasn't

there a psychological term for that? Some kind of syn-
drome? How humiliating. Was that why she had welcomed
his touch?

A broad hand settled on her shoulder. "You look as if
you could use a break. Let's go for a walk."

She straightened up, brushing off the eraser crumbs that
clung to her forehead. "No, you go ahead, John. I have to
get this finished."

He squeezed lightly, then rubbed his hand over her back.
"I'll wait."

Of course he wouldn't go without her. It hadn't even
been worth a try. She mouthed a curse and stood up. "On
second thought, I might as well do my check of the lodge."
She watched him carefully. "We could take a shopping trip
into town afterward."

Remy probably had no more intention of going into town
today than he had yesterday, Dana thought. But if he
thought another seduction attempt was going to work this
time...

"Sure," he said, going toward the kitchen. "Let me put
some food in Morty's dish before we go."

As soon as he saw where Remy was heading, Morty
leaped down from his perch on the back of the couch. Ears
forward, tail held high, the cat pranced adoringly in his
idol's wake.

Pathetic, Dana thought. Yet more proof that her judgment was no better than a cat's. Gritting her teeth, she went
to get her coat. She was almost across the living room when
a glint outside the front window caught her eye.

Sunshine reflected from the windshield of a car as it
drove out of the shadows at the bend in the lane. Her gaze
went to the light bar on the roof. It wasn't just any car. It
was a police cruiser.

For a paralyzing moment, all she could do was stare.
Could it be this easy? After the head games of the past two
days, all her attempts to outwit Remy, could it really be
over?

The whirr of the can opener came from the kitchen. Morty meowed loudly, doing his starving cat imitation. Dana heard the low rumble of Remy's chuckle—he was accustomed to Morty's dramatics by now.

The cruiser slowed to a stop near the garage, where the snowplow did its turnaround. A heavy-set officer emerged from the vehicle, pausing to pull a handkerchief from his pocket to wipe his nose.

Dana felt her heart thump hard against her ribs. It was the policeman who had been here before, Constable Savard. He had said he would follow up on her reported sighting of the fugitive. She hadn't thought he had taken her seriously enough to do it, but obviously he had.

Oh, God. It really *was* going to be this easy. All she had to do was run outside and cry for help. Savard had a radio. And a gun. He wouldn't have any trouble overpowering Remy and taking him back to prison.

Yet instead of racing for the door, she hesitated for a crucial instant. She had seen Remy's mug shot, but she couldn't picture him locked up. She couldn't picture him hurting anyone, either. His touch was so gentle, so considerate—

The policeman slammed the car door and started toward the cabin.

Remy's voice came from behind her. "Dana? It sounded like we have company."

She looked around. He stood in the kitchen doorway. Or filled it would have been more accurate. Why did she keep forgetting about his size? "Uh, yes."

His gaze went to the window, then snapped back to her. His jaw hardened. His nostrils flared.

She edged away from him, suddenly breathless.

"It's a cop," he said.

"Yes."

"Why would a cop come up here, Dana?"

She mentally measured the distance to the door. This was

no time for doubts, and it was too late for finesse. She spun around and ran.

Had she thought he had moved quickly yesterday when he had tumbled her to the floor? That was nothing compared to the speed with which he moved now. Before she could take more than two steps, he grabbed her by the arms and hauled her back against his chest.

Where was the man who had just chuckled over her cat? Where was the tender lover who had kissed the side of her neck and spoken of loneliness?

"What have you told them?" he demanded.

Should she play dumb? Should she try to continue the act? "John, what are you talking about?"

He turned her around and loomed over her, his gaze boring into hers. "No more lies, Dana. You know who I am, don't you," he stated.

"What do you mean?"

"You know damn well. You've known all along."

"No, I—"

"Why else did you run?"

She tried to hold his gaze, she really did. She had lied just fine for two days, but now his mask of harmlessness was gone. Even without the long hair and the outlaw mustache, there was no mistaking the dangerous look in his eyes. She glanced out the window at the approaching policeman. If she broke away, could she make it to the door? Would a scream carry all the way to the path?

Something of her thoughts must have shown on her face. Remy's breath hissed out on a curse. It didn't seem possible, but his features hardened even more. "I hadn't wanted to believe it," he muttered. "I'd hoped you were different, Dana."

How dare he? she thought. Out of the turmoil of her emotions, the anger she had been feeling minutes ago resurfaced. He was the criminal here. He'd been the one to initiate all the lies, so how could he be looking at her as if she had disappointed him? She threw her weight backward and kicked out, trying to break his hold.

He grunted when her toe connected with his shin, but he didn't release her. He changed his grip to enclose her wrists with one hand and put his other arm behind her back, lifting her from the floor. In two strides he pinned her to the wall with his body. "Please, don't fight," he said. "I'm not going to hurt you."

She continued to struggle, but his body was as solid as the wall at her back. "Let me go, Remy."

It was the first time she had spoken his real name aloud, and it was obvious by the way his eyebrows angled together that it jarred him. She parted her lips to scream.

Remy stretched her arms over her head and covered her mouth with his palm. "I'm sorry, Dana. I had hoped it wouldn't come to this, but I have no choice. I can't let you turn me in."

From the corner of her eye she could see that Savard was less than twenty feet from the cabin now. She shook her head.

"I need your cooperation."

She squirmed and made a noise in her throat.

He held her in place effortlessly while he glanced over his shoulder. A muscle twitched in his cheek. "For God's sake, Dana, there's no time for this. Keep still and listen."

His order only made her struggle harder.

Remy swore and brought his face so close to hers their noses touched. "That cop is going to be here any second. When I answer the door, you follow my lead."

"Mmph!" she grunted.

"We're crazy about each other, got it?" he said through his teeth. "You didn't have any trouble playing along up to now. You were so good, you almost convinced me. All you have to do is keep it up."

She narrowed her eyes and considered biting his hand. Keep it up? Play along? What kind of fool did he take her for? The truth was out in the open now. How could he possibly expect her to pretend—

"Tell the cop we're engaged. I'll explain everything to you later."

Her pulse was pounding in her ears, her breath coming in short, sharp pants. His grip and his body were like steel, hard and unyielding. His face was as cold as the black-and-white mug shot she had seen on the news.

If there ever had been a time to get frightened, this was it. He was twice her weight. He was a convicted killer. She knew it, and now he knew that she knew it.

Yet she still didn't fear him. Was it adrenaline? Was she nuts?

"Dana, please!"

The naked desperation in his gaze bypassed her brain to stir something deep inside her. For an instant she almost complied.

But then sanity reasserted itself. She wrenched her mouth free from his hand. "No!"

"Then I'll tell that cop you're my accomplice."

She jerked her head back. "No. You can't."

"You took me into your home. You've sheltered me for days," he said, his voice fast and harsh. "That's called aiding and abetting a fugitive. No one's going to believe you weren't willing. It'll be your word against mine."

There was the sound of boots on her doorstep. A series of sharp knocks rattled the cabin door.

Remy released her wrists and grasped her by the shoulders. "I know how it works. You'll be arrested. You'll go to court. All it takes is an accusation and people will believe you're guilty."

She hesitated, his threat finally sinking in. "You wouldn't."

He stepped back suddenly, and she staggered against the wall. "Believe me, Dana, I would do anything," he said. "Whatever it takes."

Another series of raps vibrated the door. A voice sounded faintly from outside. "Miss Whittington?"

Remy moved to the door. He paused with his hand on the latch and fixed her with a hard stare. "Don't even think about calling my bluff. I'm not bluffing. I have nothing left to lose, Dana, but you do."

She looked wildly around the cabin. No one would believe him if he named her his accomplice, would they? Surely justice wouldn't be that blind. An innocent person wouldn't be convicted. Her family would stand by her. So would her friends...

But she had cut herself off from them in order to write. They already thought she was eccentric. And what about her publisher and her fans? Who would buy her books for their child if she was accused of helping a murderer? Even if the charge was thrown out of court, the damage would be done, her reputation would be tarnished.

This could end her career. What would she do if she couldn't create stories, if she couldn't share with her readers the love she would have given her own child? That was all that had kept her going. That was all she had left.

Damn him! she thought, blinking back a sudden rush of tears. He was right. He had nothing left to lose, but she did. Oh, God, did she ever.

Remy heard the third knock and knew he couldn't delay any longer. Had the alterations he'd made to his appearance been enough to pass a cursory inspection? If they hadn't, he was about to find out. Slumping his shoulders in an attempt to take a few inches off his height, he yanked open the door.

The policeman was heavyset, on the far side of middle age and—thank God—a complete stranger. He had the relaxed posture of a neighbor paying a social call, but Remy didn't underestimate him for a second. It took all his self-control not to flinch at the sight of the uniform. "Good morning," he said. "What can I do for you?"

The man coughed, then whipped a handkerchief from his

pocket and blew his nose. "I'm looking for Dana Whittington," he said when he was done.

Remy forced himself to project a facade of calm. He'd found that people saw what they expected to see. When he'd appeared in court shackled by handcuffs and leg irons, no one had seen an innocent man. He hoped the reverse held true and that no one would be expecting a wanted fugitive to answer the door boldly in broad daylight. Nor would anyone expect a respectable citizen to vouch for him. He turned his head and called, "Honey?"

Dana was still standing by the wall where he had left her. Her cheeks were flushed, her hair was in a tangled cloud, and her sweater was twisted tightly across her breasts. Her chest rose and fell rapidly with her unsteady breathing.

Was she going to go through with it? Would she do what he'd said? Remy had hated coercing her, but what choice had there been? He only hoped that Dana believed he was enough of a bastard to make good his threat. He looked at her hard and held out his hand. "There's a policeman here to see you."

She took a moment to regain her breath before she came forward. "Yes. Hello, Constable Savard."

"Good morning, Miss Whittington. Is everything all right?"

Remy's stomach turned to stone. She knew this cop by name. They didn't appear to be friends, so she must have dealt with him on a professional level. And he had obviously noticed how disheveled she was.

Thinking fast, Remy took Dana's hand and twined his fingers with hers. "Sorry about taking so long to answer the door," he murmured, dropping his voice. "Dana and I were..." He paused, hoping the man would assume they had been busy doing what most couples would do together in a private cabin. Her flushed cheeks and disordered clothing could have been the results of passion rather than a physical struggle. "We were...talking."

Savard's face remained impassive. "I'd like to follow up the report you made last week, Miss Whittington," he said. "Do you mind if I come in?"

Remy felt Dana's hand tremble as they moved aside to let the policeman enter. Whether it was from fear or frustration or anger, he couldn't tell. It didn't matter, he reminded himself, as long as she played her part.

Now he knew for certain that Dana had been lying all along. Somehow she must have heard the news, put the facts together and reported him to the police the day he had left. She must have met this Savard before Remy had returned to the lodge. She had been playing him for a fool for days while she waited for the chance to alert the authorities.

Considering the way he had used her—and was continuing to use her—he had no right to feel betrayed.

Constable Savard's gaze went from Remy to Dana. "Perhaps you'd prefer it if we could speak privately, Miss Whittington?"

Remy gave her hand a warning squeeze.

She shook her head. "No, this is fine. My...fiancé and I don't have any secrets."

There was no time to even begin to feel relief. This was merely the first hurdle.

The cop pulled out a notebook from his coat and flipped it open. "And your name, sir?"

Remy was about to use John Becker's name again, but paused when he saw Dana glance up at him. She had made a report. That meant she had probably given the name he had been using. "Josh Lawrence," he said, picking a name out of the air.

Savard scribbled in his notebook, then used his handkerchief to smother a sneeze. "Excuse me. I picked up this cold three days ago. It's a real killer."

"I'm sorry to hear that," Dana said. "There's a lot going around."

"This weather doesn't help." He wiped his eyes. "How have things been up here?"

"Uh, quiet."

"No more trouble?"

"No."

He had been right not to underestimate the cop, Remy decided. Savard was being deliberately cagey with his questions, despite Dana's claim that she had no secrets from her fiancé. It was time to take a gamble, he decided.

"Have you caught him yet?" Remy asked.

Savard looked up quickly. "Who?"

"That murderer, Leverette." He wrinkled his forehead. "That's why you're here, isn't it?"

"Yes, it is."

"Dana told me all about the way he showed up here in the storm, pretending to be some stranded motorist." He rubbed the back of Dana's hand with his thumb. "It scared the hell out of me when I heard what had happened. I got here as soon as I could."

"You told me that you lived alone," Savard said, turning his attention back to Dana.

Beneath his light caress, Remy could tell she was as stiff as a block of ice. "Yes, most of the time," she said.

"Our wedding date's not until the spring," Remy improvised. "In the meantime, we have to be discreet because of Dana's fans. My fiancée told you she's a children's author, didn't she?"

"Yes, Miss Whittington did mention something about writing."

At the mention of her profession, Dana stiffened even more. "This whole thing has ruined my concentration," she said, her voice unsteady. "I keep thinking about how there was a murderer right here in my cabin."

Savard cleared his throat. "I did some checking, Miss Whittington, but I haven't yet been able to confirm your story."

"What do you mean?"

"Apparently there was a man named John Becker from Toronto who was in this area during the storm, but I've been unable to contact him. It's possible that your visitor was exactly who he said he was."

Remy was a long way from being able to smile, but he felt the lump in his stomach loosen. This was a stroke of luck he hadn't anticipated, yet it made sense. Becker was a salesman, according to the day planner that had been in his coat pocket. It wasn't unreasonable that he would be off on another business trip.

But what about when Becker returned? Once the cops had a chance to talk to him, it would be only a matter of time before they put together the truth. When they did, they would come back to the resort, and next time they would bring a lot more firepower than one, lone middle-aged cop with a bad cold.

How long did he have? Days? Hours?

All the more reason to establish a rock-solid identity as Dana's fiancé so he could make the most of the time he had left.

"But whether this turns out to have been a false alarm or not," Savard continued, "it would be a good idea to be careful about who you let in your door, Miss Whittington, considering how isolated you are out here."

"Yes, I'll have to remember that," she said.

"Have you made any progress tracking down that fugitive?" Remy asked. "We haven't seen anything on the news lately about him."

"No, Leverette is still at large," Savard said.

"Then that settles it, honey." Remy brought Dana's hand to his mouth. He kissed her knuckles, hoping Savard didn't notice how white they were. "I don't care what your publicist says about the gossip. With a maniac like Leverette on the loose, I'm not leaving you alone again."

"Gee, thanks *Josh*," Dana said, her tone as cold as her fingers.

The policeman's gaze narrowed.

Remy tensed. He couldn't tell whether Savard was buying the act yet. It could go either way, but he didn't know what else he could do without coming on too strong. He didn't want to overplay his hand. An innocent man wouldn't feel the need to prove he was telling the truth. He would assume the truth would speak for itself.

Then again, he'd learned the hard way that truth didn't always work.

Something bumped against his shins. There was a familiar meow before Morty sat on his toes and screeched.

Savard appeared startled. "What's wrong with that cat?"

Remy bent down to scoop Morty up and settled him in the crook of his arm. "I was just about to feed him when you arrived. He likes to pretend he's starving."

"Your cat was a lot quieter when I was here before."

"Morty's shy with strangers," Dana said.

Remy rubbed the spot behind Morty's ears that made the cat purr and close his eyes in pleasure. "Hang on there, old fella," he said. "I haven't forgotten you."

The policeman continued to scrutinize him. "My wife has two cats. Persians."

"Those are lovely animals," Dana said.

"Picky animals. They've been with us two years and they're just starting to tolerate me." He closed his notebook and stuffed it away with his handkerchief. "Well, thanks for your time, folks. I'll let you know if there are any developments."

Remy saw that Savard's suspicions were waning. Thank God for the pesky cat, he thought. Morty's fondness of him seemed to have tipped the balance in his favor. Too bad he couldn't get Dana to purr like that...

Or maybe he could. They were supposed to be engaged, weren't they? And he'd already implied they had been doing a lot more than holding hands when Savard's arrival had interrupted them. Remy put the cat back on the floor and shooed him toward the warmth of the kitchen. Slipping his arm around Dana's waist, he drew her firmly to his side as they ushered the policeman to the door. When Savard started up the path to where he had parked his car, Remy dipped his head and whispered in Dana's ear. "Smile."

"What?"

"The cop can still see us."

"I can't—"

"Don't forget, we're in this together now." He moved his hand lower and splayed his fingers over her hip. Framed in the doorway as they were, he knew the action would be clearly visible. "If I go down, so do you. Now smile and look as if you mean it."

Her lips curved woodenly.

"More," he whispered.

She flicked her gaze to the policeman and inched her smile up a notch so that her teeth showed.

From the corner of his eye, Remy could see that Savard had paused on the path to glance back at them.

Moving swiftly, Remy lowered his head and pressed his lips to Dana's.

Shock must have kept her immobile. He had a quick impression of moist warmth and a sweet yielding, but then she tensed. Before she could pull away, Remy reached out with his free hand and swung the cabin door shut.

Instantly Dana twisted out of his grasp. She drew the back of her hand across her mouth. Color flooded her cheeks. "Why did you do that?"

Why? It probably hadn't made that much difference to the cop—he had been leaving, anyway. Had it been the defiance in Dana's gaze?

Or had it been because he'd been wanting to do that for a week and had decided not to let the opportunity pass?

"It's all part of the act," he said, giving her the easiest answer.

Chapter 8

Dana had never hated another human being before. Even when she had returned from the hospital after the miscarriage to discover Hank had walked out on her, she hadn't hated him. Oh, she had felt hurt and disillusioned, but she had been too numb inside to spare the energy to hate anyone. Or maybe by that time she hadn't felt strongly enough about Hank to let him trigger such an ugly emotion.

That wasn't the case with Remy. He had inspired strong feelings in her from the start. She had been anxious, fascinated, fearful, sympathetic…but now she was very close to hating him.

She loosened the shoulder strap of the seat belt and leaned against the door of the pickup truck, putting as much distance between them as possible. She felt him look at her, but she didn't turn her head. Instead she watched the ridge of snow at the side of the lane blur past as he steered toward the highway.

They were using Derek's truck—now that Remy had reinstalled the battery—because her car had four flat tires.

Remy had readily admitted that he had been responsible for the sabotage. He hadn't wanted her to leave the resort. He hadn't wanted her to tip anyone off to his whereabouts.

But he no longer seemed worried about that. Not only was he going into town with her, he was going to extend the engaged-couple act they had played for Constable Savard to provide himself with a cover. And why not? He knew she would keep her mouth shut.

You took me into your home. You've sheltered me for days. No one's going to believe you weren't willing.

What Remy had said was true. All of it. No one would believe she couldn't have turned him in somehow. She wasn't sure she believed it herself. What about when he'd been asleep? Or in the bathroom? She had been worried that he would hear her, but couldn't she have slipped out her bedroom window and made use of the phone in the lodge without him knowing?

And what about the moment when she had seen Savard arrive? She could have ended it then, couldn't she?

Of course she could have. She was no match for Remy physically, but she wasn't a helpless ninny. Instead of playing along with him, she could have knocked him out with a skillet the first time his back had been turned and made a run for it. There had been countless opportunities to escape her predicament...if she'd honestly been looking for them.

She'd been an idiot, that's all. A softhearted, lonely fool, making excuses, taking in another stray.

Except this particular stray had turned around and bitten her. In return for her generosity, he'd gone straight for her most vulnerable spot. If he carried through with his threat to name her as his accomplice, he could ruin her reputation, end her career and take away the only joy she had.

Yes, she could easily hate him.

"Are you cold?" Remy asked, reaching for the controls of the heater.

"There's just the two of us here," she snapped. "You don't have to keep up the act."

"I can understand your anger, Dana. If there had been any other way—"

"And you don't have to pretend you're sorry. I'll co-operate with you because you gave me no choice. Just leave it at that instead of insulting my intelligence."

He adjusted the setting for maximum heat and turned up the blower. "I have great respect for your intelligence. The way you strung me along like you did was quite ingenious."

"And speaking of ingenious, you sabotaged my phone that first night, didn't you," she stated. "And my radios."

"I did it the next morning. I couldn't risk you hearing a news broadcast before I had left."

"Is that when you slashed my tires, too?"

"No, I did that yesterday. And I didn't slash them, I just deflated them."

"Wow, what a prince. I suppose you expect me to be grateful for that."

"Dana—"

"And when you showed up at the lodge two days ago, that wasn't a coincidence, was it?"

"No, it wasn't. I was using your cousin's suite at the top of the lodge. These are his clothes."

She didn't see her cousin frequently enough for her to recognize his clothes, but she should have wondered where Remy was getting his wardrobe. She "should have" done a lot of things if she'd been thinking with her brain instead of her too-soft heart. "You were at Derek's place?" she asked. "For how long?"

"All week. I made sure to keep out of your way when you made your rounds."

So she hadn't been imagining his presence. He really had been nearby the whole time. She had already known he had deceived her, but it was still a blow to discover the scope of his deception. "Why?"

"I left you because I hadn't wanted to involve you any further, but my face was all over the news. I came back because I needed to keep out of sight until the heat died down."

She shook her head. "No, I mean why here? Why aren't you in Alaska or Mexico or wherever it is that escaped murderers go?"

"I'm not a murderer."

She pressed more tightly against the door.

"I didn't kill my wife, Dana, and I intend to prove it. That's why I came back to Half Moon Bay instead of running farther. I needed somewhere to stay that was close to Hainesborough so I could search for evidence to clear my name."

"After all the lies, how can you expect me to believe that?"

He was silent as he geared down to take a bend in the lane. The back end of the truck slid sideways a fraction, then straightened out as he expertly corrected the skid. "I didn't like the lies any more than you did, but they were necessary," he said finally.

"And you'll do whatever it takes, right? That's what you said. You don't care who you use or who you hurt as long as you get what you want."

The silence lasted longer this time. "Yes, that pretty well sums it up," he said.

"At last, an honest answer," she muttered.

"No more lies, Dana," he said. "Not between us. From now on, I'm going to tell you the truth."

"Right, sure."

"Starting now." He slowed the truck to a stop at the bottom of the lane and set the brake. Draping his arm over the steering wheel, he turned to face her. "My name is Remy Leverette."

She snorted. "Gee, I kind of figured that out already."

"Until I went to prison for a murder I didn't commit, I

lived on River Road in Hainesborough in a house that I built myself. That's what I do. I'm a builder.''

"I realized you weren't a traveling salesman. Not with those calluses on your hands.''

He took off his gloves and regarded his palms. "I intend to return John Becker's belongings to him when this is over. And before you start wondering, I didn't kill him, either. I just stole his coat.''

Dana couldn't miss the ice in Remy's tone. She hadn't even considered the possibility that he might have killed the man whose identity he had assumed.

That was yet another of those "should have's.'' Constable Savard had said he hadn't been able to contact the real John Becker to confirm her story. Was Becker out of town on a business trip? Or had he never made it home after encountering Remy?

Why hadn't she thought of that earlier? How could she have allowed Remy Leverette into her home even for an instant? And how could she dare to sit here arguing with him?

"I know it looks bad, Dana," he said. "But think for a minute. If I really was a hardened killer, then why would I risk returning to a place where I could be recognized? Why would I have saved your life? It would have been a hell of a lot more convenient for me if I'd left you to suffocate in that snowpile, stolen this truck and headed for a place where no one knows me.''

She had come to this same conclusion herself, but had it been her logic that had led to it...or her heart? "You saved me because you wanted to use me.''

"Do you really believe that's all it was?''

She didn't reply. She didn't want to soften. She had made that mistake before, and look what it had gotten her.

He caught her chin and turned her face toward his. "Dana, answer me.''

She batted his hand away. "Don't touch me.''

His gaze bored into hers. "We've touched each other before."

"That was different."

"We're still the same people."

"No. It was all a lie."

"Was it a lie that first night in the storm, when you took off my clothes and wrapped me in your blankets?"

As if it had been just under the surface, waiting to emerge, the memory seeped through her brain. He'd been so vulnerable. And he'd needed her. Once more she felt the texture of his skin, the firm curves of his muscles, the silky hair on his chest... She shook her head. "I didn't know who you were."

"Do you remember what you said to me? I do. You told me I was safe, and all the while you stroked my forehead so gently I almost believed you."

"As I said, I didn't know who you were."

"What about afterward, when I came back? You knew who I was then, but you didn't push me away. Instead you let me hold you, laugh with you, put my hand on your breast."

"I was acting. Just like you were."

"All the time?"

"All the time."

"Now who's lying?"

Oh, yes. She definitely could hate him. He was forcing her to face facts she wanted to deny. Even now, after everything that had happened, her body tingled at the memory of his touch. The truck was a full-size pickup, and the cab was large enough to fit three passengers across the bench seat, yet it might as well have been a phone booth. "Back off, Remy."

"This is about that kiss, isn't it?"

She didn't know how she managed not to drop her gaze to his mouth. An echo of the intimate contact he had forced on her this morning whispered across her lips. "What kiss? A kiss is a gesture of affection or love. I don't consider what you did in front of Savard a kiss. It was a sham. A travesty.''

"It was necessary for our act.''

She pressed her mouth into a tight line.

"I said I wouldn't lie to you,'' Remy told her, "so I won't deny that I'm attracted to you. I have been from the start, and I'm not going to pretend otherwise just to make this situation easier.''

"If you think we're going to pick up where we left off, you're crazy.''

"Don't worry, I have other priorities. All I want from you right now is your cooperation.''

"Fine.''

"But make no mistake, if I decide it's necessary, I will kiss you again, Dana.''

"Go to hell.''

He laughed without humor. "I'm already there.''

The starkness in his gaze tugged at her. She dug her fingernails into her palms to keep from reaching out to him.

"Over the past year I've lost my home, my family, my livelihood and my freedom,'' he said. "In the eyes of the law and most people in Hainesborough, I got exactly what I deserved. I'll be the first to admit that I've made plenty of mistakes in my life, but I'm no murderer. I didn't kill my wife, Dana. I swear it to you.''

"Then why were you convicted?''

He was silent for a moment, as if gathering his thoughts. "My wife was Sylvia Haines. She was the only child of Marjory and Edgar Haines. Her father runs the local bank, her grandfather served three terms as mayor and the town of Hainesborough was named after one of her great-uncles.''

"If this is where you tell me what an upstanding citizen you are—''

"No, I'm going to tell you the truth,'' he said steadily. "My father was the local drunk until he got into one bar fight too many and ended up in prison. My mother ran a souvenir stand for the tourists each summer until she ran off with a bass fisherman from Michigan. By the time I was a juvenile, I had racked up a police record almost as long as my old man's. I cleaned up my act once I started doing construction, and I worked my butt off to found my own company, but some people never forgot where I came from.''

The twinge of sympathy she felt was unwelcome, a reflex response to strays and underdogs. She told herself to ignore it. ''Go on.''

He frowned down at his hands, rubbing one of his calluses with the tip of his thumb. ''Sylvia was killed last April. I had been ten miles north of town all day, checking over a new job site. I found her dead on the bedroom floor when I got home. I didn't do it, but everyone naturally assumed I did.''

''Why? Just because of your background?''

''The detective in charge of the case had been on the force when I was a juvenile, and he had a long memory. Sibley had me tried and convicted the minute he saw me.''

The name sounded familiar. Dana realized the number Savard had given her when he had come to the cabin the first time was for a Detective Charles Sibley. ''Are you saying this detective was biased against you?''

''I know for a fact he was, but even if he didn't know anything about me, it wouldn't have mattered. Sylvia's blood was all over my hands and my clothes because I had been trying to revive her before I had realized it was too late. My fingerprints were on the knife because I'd removed it when I'd turned her over to do CPR.''

Dana rubbed her palms over her arms. Her imagination readily filled in the details from Remy's terse description. She had seen countless detective shows on TV, and she often read mysteries, but hearing these details, knowing it had actually happened, was something else entirely.

''The circumstantial evidence alone was damning enough,'' he continued, ''but there was motive, too. It was no secret that Sylvia and I had been having problems with our marriage. Her family closed ranks against me, and the Haineses have a lot of clout. They're big supporters of the police. People practically lined up to testify to the arguments they had witnessed between Sylvia and me. On top of all that, I had been alone at the job site, so I had no alibi.'' He closed his hands into fists. ''Hell, if I had been on that jury, I would have found me guilty, too.''

The blower motor whirred as warm air puffed from the dashboard. On the highway beyond the lane, a transport truck whined past. Dana felt her anger fading, and she struggled to revive it. She needed the barrier it provided. ''Didn't you have a lawyer? Didn't he look for proof of your innocence?''

''It didn't work out that way. When Sylvia and I got married, I made her joint owner of my company. Our house, our bank accounts, everything was shared equally, because that's the way I believed a marriage should be. I hadn't known that she had named her father as her executor and beneficiary. At her death, he had all our joint assets frozen, so I had no money to hire a lawyer. Legal Aid provided one for me, but I probably would have been better off without him.''

''Why?''

''The lawyer I got had more experience dealing with small claims and welfare fraud than a criminal case. He was out of his depth from the start. Once he realized that I had no intention of pleading guilty and taking a deal, he did try to find evidence the police had overlooked, but it was too little and too late.''

''If he couldn't find any evidence then, what makes you believe you can find any now?''

He took a deep breath and released it slowly. ''I've had plenty of time during these past ten months to think about where to look. And I'm a lot more motivated than a Legal Aid lawyer.''

''But why not launch an appeal? There are groups that

help the wrongfully convicted. There are legal ways to gain your freedom.''

''The justice system failed me once. I'm not putting my faith in it again. By the time my appeal would be heard, if it ever is, it would be too late.''

''Too late? There's no death penalty in Canada.''

''Not too late for me, too late for Chantal.''

At least her instincts had been right about one thing, Dana thought. He hadn't lied about having a daughter, and her name really was Chantal.

''She's going to be five years old next month,'' he said. ''My in-laws are raising her. They'll give her everything their money can buy, just like they did with Sylvia, but they won't be able to shield Chantal from the shame.'' His voice hardened. ''I know what it's like to grow up in a small town with a father in prison, Dana. No child of mine is going to go through the same thing.''

''She's that important to you.''

He pulled on his gloves, released the parking brake and eased the truck onto the road. ''She's the reason for everything I'm doing.''

He had said that once before, the day after the blizzard ended, the first time he had left. She hadn't fully understood what he had meant then, yet she had been moved by his obvious love for his daughter. She still was.

It would be so much easier to hate him if he was doing all of this only for himself. If he claimed he wanted to prove his innocence for the sake of his personal honor or some kind of macho principle, or because he didn't like being cooped up in prison, that wouldn't excuse the dishonorable things he had done.

Yet how far would *she* be willing to go for the sake of a child? She had only carried hers for a few months, but she would never forget the bond that had already begun to grow. What would she be capable of doing for someone she loved that much?

Dana sighed and turned her gaze back to the blurring

snowpiles. Even crocodiles loved their young, but that didn't make them any less dangerous.

The traffic on Main Street was sparse. Hainesborough was always quiet during the winter, when the area lakes were frozen over and deserted except for the occasional intrepid ice fishermen or snowmobilers. The cottagers and tourists from the city who drove a large chunk of the region's economy didn't venture north until May. Nevertheless, Remy was excruciatingly careful as he steered the pickup through town, making sure to keep under the speed limit as he drove past the courthouse.

The last time he had seen this street had been the day after the guilty verdict. It had been a gray November dawn. Through the back window of the prison van, he'd watched the closed stores and empty park benches slip past like neighbors turning their backs. It was a feeling that hadn't been due entirely to his imagination.

The Haineses had never trusted him. They had tolerated him because he'd fathered their only grandchild, but they had disapproved of their daughter's marriage from the start. They'd had higher hopes for Sylvia. She was supposed to choose a man who belonged to the country club, not one who had been hired to build the club's new addition.

Remy glanced critically at his reflection in the rearview mirror, then took one hand off the wheel to turn up the collar of the down-filled ski jacket he had found at the back of Derek's closet. It was shiny silver, fancier than anything he usually wore—he thought it made him look like a well-off yuppie on vacation. The sunglasses he'd found in the glove compartment helped, too. So did having an innocent-looking blonde sitting on the seat beside him, but he didn't want to push his luck. He continued down the street until he reached the crossroads at the edge of town, then turned left at the municipal works yard.

Five minutes later he slowed as they neared the chain link fence that enclosed Leverette Construction. There wasn't much left, only the small trailer that he'd hauled to job sites and the square cement-block building that had served as his office. No one had bothered to lock the gate or plow the yard where his equipment had been stored, probably because there was no longer any equipment.

Exhaust puffed past them in a white cloud as Remy let the engine idle. He'd known his father-in-law had laid off the workers and disposed of the assets of his company shortly after the guilty verdict had been handed down. Acting as Sylvia's executor—and as the banker who had financed Remy's company—Edgar Haines hadn't wasted any time wreaking his own personal vengeance on the man he believed to be his daughter's killer. The business that Remy had spent a decade building had been wiped out by the stroke of a pen.

Remy couldn't really blame him. If anyone ever hurt Chantal, he would probably want to do a lot worse than merely destroy the man's company.

He switched the truck into four-wheel drive and eased the heavy vehicle through the snowdrift that spanned the gates. When they reached the office, he gunned the engine and yanked hard on the wheel, spinning the truck in a circle so that they faced out the way they had come.

Dana quickly flattened her palms against the dashboard to keep from leaning into him. "What are you doing?"

"Making sure we can leave in a hurry if we have to."

"What is this place?"

"It's what's left of Leverette Construction."

"How are you going to get in? You wouldn't have a key…" Her words trailed off and she frowned. "Silly me. You didn't have a key to the lodge or Derek's suite, either."

"One of the skills I learned in my misspent youth." He shut off the engine and got out.

"I'll wait here," Dana said.

He slammed his door and went around to open hers.

She pressed back into the seat. "I said I'll wait here," she repeated.

He held out his hand to help her down. "It'll get too cold to sit in the truck."

"Not if you leave the heater on." She held out her own hand, palm up. "Give me the keys."

"Sorry, I can't do that."

"You still don't trust me?"

"I don't think you'd turn me in, but the way you've been glaring at me for the past hour, I wouldn't be surprised if you decided to drive off and leave me stranded."

"I don't know how to drive a stick shift."

He couldn't afford to believe her. He grasped her hand and hauled her out.

She landed off balance against his chest. Remy reacted immediately, wrapping his arms around her and bracing his legs apart to steady himself. "Careful," he said, holding her close. "There's a layer of ice under the snow."

"I wouldn't have slipped if you had waited for me to get down on my own," she said into his coat. She pushed a fist into his stomach. "Let go of me, Remy."

"Josh," he corrected, dropping his arms and stepping back. "Or darling or sweetheart."

"What?"

"I don't want you calling me Remy in public."

Instead of using his name—any of them—or an endearment, she pulled up the hood of her parka and followed him to the office door.

He was seeing a different side of Dana from the generous innocent he had first thought she was. Her temper surprised him—there was obviously a well of passion beneath the gentleness she had displayed during their first days together. She was going along with him, but she was making it clear that she wasn't happy about it. No, that was an understatement. His sweet, gentle Dana looked as if she would happily back the truck over him.

Her anger was understandable, considering the way he

had coerced her. He wished that he could tell her he would never carry out his threat to implicate her as his accomplice, but what would be the point? He needed her cooperation, not her approval. It didn't matter what she thought of him, right?

Sure. Maybe if he told himself that enough times, he'd be able to convince himself.

Using the tools he'd brought with him from the garage, Remy had the door of the building open in less than a minute. Even though he had been expecting it, he still was jarred to see the condition of his office. The phones, the computer, the photocopier...everything of value had been stripped away. The drawers of the filing cabinets and his desk hung open, papers spilling haphazardly onto the floor.

Dana pushed back her hood as she moved beside him. "What happened here?" she asked. "Who could have done this?"

"Take your pick," he said. "Kids, Sylvia's friends or relatives, anyone."

"What a mess."

"Yeah." He left his boots by the door so that he wouldn't track snow over the papers and went to the storage room. Not much was left there, either, but he did find some garbage bags and two stray cardboard boxes. He returned to the filing cabinet and began removing what was left inside and stuffing it into one of the boxes. "We can't afford the time to sort through all this here," he said. "I'm going to grab what I can and take it back to the cabin."

"Exactly what kind of evidence do you think you'll find?"

"I'm hoping there might be some paper trail that could support my alibi. I don't believe my lawyer looked very hard." He found a file of telephone bills and emptied it into the box. "The day of Sylvia's murder, I was waiting to meet a potential client at a lakefront building lot. He had phoned me the day before to give me directions, claimed he wanted to talk about building a cottage, but he never showed up."

"Couldn't he have testified that he was supposed to meet you?"

"I took his call myself. No one else talked to him. The name and phone number I took down turned out to be dead ends, so either I had copied it down wrong and the guy changed his mind about the job—" he slammed the filing cabinet shut and went over to his desk "—or someone wanted to be sure I was out of town."

"Are you saying that man might have been the real murderer?"

Should he tell her his theory? Given Dana's present state of mind, what would be the point? There had been no evidence to support his suspicions of who had killed Sylvia any more than there had been evidence of his alibi. "Yes, it's a good possibility. I had no reason to suspect anything at the time, since a lot of my business involved building vacation homes for people from the city. It was only afterward that I started to think I'd been set up."

She hesitated. "It's also possible that you made up the whole story."

He shot her an impatient look. "That's what the prosecution claimed, but why would I risk my neck to come to this office to look for something that I knew didn't exist? Why would I need to pretend for you?"

"Maybe you want to be sure I'll cooperate."

"Now who's insulting whose intelligence?"

Dana didn't reply. She watched him in silence as he went through his desk. Finally she toed off her boots and grabbed one of the garbage bags. Squatting down, she started scooping papers from the floor.

Remy paused briefly to watch her. She was helping him. Did this mean she finally believed his claim of innocence? Or was she worried that she might get caught along with him if they stayed here too long?

He told himself it didn't matter, but he didn't believe

that now any more than he had before. It *did* matter. He didn't want to see that mixture of hurt and suspicion in her gaze when she looked at him. He wanted to see her smile again. And the next time he took her in his arms, he didn't want her to fight him....

The next time? He finished filling the first box and started on the next. Even if he convinced Dana that he hadn't killed his wife, it might not make any difference to her opinion of him. As far as she was concerned, he didn't have to be a murderer to be a first-class bastard.

Chapter 9

"The story's taking a few twists I hadn't expected, but I'll get it done, Gillian." Dana shifted the phone to her other ear. "When have I ever missed a deadline?"

"Did I say I was worried?"

"Well, no."

"Dana, I didn't call to nag."

Dana bit the inside of her cheek, regretting her defensiveness. Gillian Wychuk was a wonderfully supportive agent. She never nagged, and she never bullied. She trusted Dana to handle the creative side of producing books while she stuck to the business side. "Sorry. I guess I'm a little tired."

There was a pause. "Is everything all right?" Gillian asked.

Dana glanced at where Remy sat on the couch. He was still going through the papers they had brought from his office the previous day. He'd sorted the mess into various piles that he'd placed on the floor, but she didn't know how he'd be able to find anything worthwhile.

The whole idea was a long shot anyway, and he was smart enough to know it, yet he had been busy long after she had gone to bed last night and had already been working at it when she'd gotten up this morning. The bruised skin under his eyes and the stubble of his unshaved beard made her wonder whether he had slept at all.

"Dana? Are you still there?"

She turned her attention back to the phone. "Yes. Sorry. Everything's fine and dandy, Gillian. Peachy keen and tickety-boo as always."

Another pause. "Dana, if you want me to talk to your editor about getting more time—"

"No," she said immediately. "This is what I do. It's all I do. I enjoy it. I don't want to stop."

"Okay, okay." There was a light laugh. "I wouldn't want you to. I'm only calling to find out where you want me to send your check."

"Oh. Right."

"It's the advance for *Mortimer and the Pirate Mice.* I wasn't sure how much longer you were going to be up in the boonies, so I thought you might want me to send it directly to you there instead of to your home address."

She thought for a moment. With the free rent and food she was getting here in exchange for her caretaking duties, she wasn't in any immediate need of money.

Remy could use some, though. He was going to need a competent lawyer before this was all over. Dana had seen for herself how his father-in-law had stripped his business bare. If he'd had the money for a proper defense, he might not have been convicted in the first place.

Yet money might not have made that much of a difference. From the sound of it, the evidence had been overwhelmingly stacked against him. It was almost too incriminating to be believed…as if someone had planned it that way.

She dropped her head in her hand. No wonder the plot of her book was taking a few unexpected twists. It was merely reflecting the convoluted tangle of the rest of her life. "You might as well mail it up here, Gillian," she answered finally. "Care of Half Moon Bay Resort. I'll pick it up at the post office the next time I'm in Hainesborough."

Remy looked up and frowned when she finished the phone call. "You're not going into town on your own," he said.

She was about to snap at him, but instead she sighed. Being angry all the time was too draining. She had kept it up for more than a day now, and she simply didn't have the energy anymore. "You made sure I can't use my car, and I don't know how to drive Derek's truck. You pack up this phone when you're not around and you hide the keys to the lodge, so I can't call a cab. What's next?" She held out her hands. "Are you going to tie me up so I can't walk away?"

"Don't tempt me, Dana. I might take you up on that suggestion."

Shaking her head, she moved away from the phone. "I don't want to argue, Remy, but I'm getting sick and tired of you issuing orders."

"That's not what I'm doing."

"Yes, it is, and it isn't necessary. I've cooperated with you so far, haven't I?"

He nodded. "You have."

"Like you said, we're in this together now. I don't want to get my name and reputation dragged through the courts any more than you want to go back to prison. We've already established that, haven't we?"

He nodded again.

"So let's move on."

"And how would you suggest we do that?"

"For starters, you can stop bossing me around."

"All right." He leaned forward, propping his elbows on his knees. "Dana?"

"What?"

"When you want to go into Hainesborough, would you let me drive you, please?"

There was still an underlying tone of command in his voice, but at least he had phrased it as a request. He'd even said please. "I'll consider it," she said. "How's your evidence search coming?"

In reply, he held out the paper he had been studying.

She crossed the floor to take it from him. The small piece of lined paper looked as if it had been torn out of a notebook. It was creased and smudged, but she could still read several sets of numbers that had been penciled across the top. "What's this?"

"My mileage log."

She pulled up an ottoman and sat down to face him. "What does it mean?"

"See the numbers across the top of the page? That's the date."

"April seventeenth of last year," she read.

"It was the day of the murder."

"Oh."

He leaned closer to point out the next two sets of numbers. "I kept track of the distance from my office to the job site. This is the reading when I left, and this is when I returned. There's a difference of almost thirty-four kilometres. And see down here in the margin?" he asked, tapping against more scrawled numbers.

She tilted her head and squinted. "Not really."

"My handwriting isn't the greatest, but those are the times."

"Then this should back up your alibi," she said immediately.

"Not necessarily."

"Why?"

He lifted his shoulders in a shrug. "If you think like a Hainesborough cop, I could have made up those numbers, or I could have written them in right now. I could have fabricated the whole thing."

"No, you couldn't have. I would have seen you."

"It doesn't matter. A judge would never buy it. It's not definitive proof."

She smoothed the creases from the paper. It wasn't definitive enough for the courts, but it did support his story as far as she was concerned.

The doubts about Remy's innocence that she had clung to yesterday had been steadily fading along with her anger. Her heart had believed in him from the beginning. Her brain was rapidly following suit.

Yet she still wasn't completely ready to trust either one.

And why should she? His threats had guaranteed her cooperation, whether she believed he was guilty or not. It might be cowardly to continue avoiding the issue, but it sure was easier.

"You're right," she said. "It isn't proof."

"I was hoping to find a receipt or the credit card bill for the gas I bought that day. I've been through everything we brought from the office, but there's nothing like that here."

Could someone have already taken those receipts? Was that why his office had looked like ground zero of a tornado? "What are you going to do?"

He rubbed his face, his palms scraping over his stubbled cheeks. "I'm going to try one more thing. Some correspondence might have trickled in after my father-in-law shut down the business. With all the other evidence against me, the police wouldn't have any reason to seize the mail, so anything that came in should still be there. The box is paid up until next month."

"And where's that?"

"At the Hainesborough Post Office."

"Are you nuts?" she asked. "You can't break in there, it's a federal building. If you get caught—"

"What's the worst they could do to me, throw me in prison for life?" He put his hand on her knee. "Relax, Dana. I wasn't planning on breaking in. We're going to walk in together."

"And that makes it better?"

"All I need is a minute near the box. It's too late today. We'll get there tomorrow just before closing time. Most people will have already picked up their mail. No one's going to be suspicious of the famous author who happens to be the caretaker of the Half Moon Bay Resort and her fiancé."

"But a post office? Remy, your mug shot is going to be on the wall."

He moved his hand higher and spread his fingers over her thigh. "Then we'll have to put on a very convincing act."

She glanced down at his hand. Right. Their act. Could she be a convincing fiancée when she had spent the last day doing her best to hate him?

"So have you considered it yet?"

"Considered what?"

"Whether or not you will let me drive you into Hainesborough. I did ask, Dana, I didn't order."

"Fine. I think I might be heading that way tomorrow. Since you asked nicely, I'll let you come this time." She grasped his wrist and removed his hand from her leg. The ottoman rolled backward as she stood up. "And I know you were bluffing, Remy."

He lifted his eyebrows. "About what?"

"About tying me up to keep me from leaving on my own."

"What makes you so sure?"

She shook back the cuffs of her sweater and held out her arms. "Rope burns around my wrists would be hard to explain if you want to stick to your willing-accomplice story."

"Not necessarily." He gave her a long, slow look. "There are other reasons a man might tie a woman up."

"Remy," she said warningly.

"Besides, I wouldn't have to leave rope burns. While I was at the lodge, I noticed that Derek had a collection of silk ties. Real supple, high-quality stuff. If I used them and put lotion on your skin first, I'd make sure not to leave any marks.''

''That's not funny.''

''What makes you think I'm joking?''

Her stomach did a tingling little dance as she stared at him. No, he wasn't joking. The quirk of his lips and the hot gleam in his eyes weren't from humor.

''Your bed is a four-poster. If I knotted a silk tie to each of your wrists I could loop the ends around the posts.'' His voice dropped. ''I'd make sure you were very…willing.''

What would it be like to be tied to the bed by Remy? With strips of silk? And his large, gentle hands slicking her skin with lotion…

Oh, hell. Where was that anger when she needed it? ''Save it for town, Remy,'' she said, turning away. ''There's no audience now.''

Was this how Bonnie and Clyde got started? Dana wondered. First a minor bit of break and enter where there were no witnesses, then a daring daylight robbery? This pounding nervousness she was feeling was heightening her senses. Everything looked sharper. Sounds were amplified. If it wasn't for the underlying fear that someone might recognize Remy, she would find it almost…invigorating.

Only it wasn't really a daylight robbery—they weren't actually stealing, because it was Remy's mail, and soon it would no longer be daylight, as the sun was skimming toward dusk on the horizon. Still, she couldn't prevent the nervous skittering of her pulse as she walked into the post office with a wanted criminal at her side.

A weary-looking woman stood in front of the counter, a toddler propped on one hip and a small boy hanging on to the bottom of her coat. The lone postal worker was busy weighing a package and didn't look up as the door opened.

Dana's gaze darted to the bulletin board across from the counter. It was crowded with the usual community notices, some hand-lettered ads with fringes of tear-off phone numbers and what appeared to be a poster about a lost dog. Nothing about... Oh, God. Could that black-and-white sheet of paper in the top corner be a wanted poster? She squinted, trying to make out the photo, but she was too far away.

"Go to your right," Remy murmured, his breath warm on her ear. "To the boxes by the far wall. It's on the third row from the top."

Her pulse skittered again. This time it wasn't from nervousness, it was from Remy's proximity. Even through her parka she could feel the pressure of his palm at the small of her back. It wasn't just her surroundings that she was sensing so sharply. Her heightened awareness of Remy was more than invigorating, it was downright stimulating.

She suppressed a grimace. There was probably a psychological term for this, too, she thought, as she headed toward the rows of boxes.

Remy stayed at her side, keeping her between himself and the other people in the post office. When they reached the far wall, he took two long, thin pieces of metal from his pocket and inserted them into the keyhole of one of the boxes.

Dana swallowed a gasp and positioned herself between Remy and the door.

He didn't take his gaze off what he was doing. "Thanks for the screen. Too bad you're not a bit bigger."

She unzipped her parka and shoved her hands into its pockets, trying to make as wide a profile as possible. "Hurry," she whispered.

"You're shaping up to be a natural at this."

"I don't consider that a compliment."

"Just another second...ah," he said. The lock clicked. Remy swung the small door of the compartment open and reached inside.

Behind her back Dana heard someone else enter the post office and stamp their feet to get rid of the snow. She couldn't prevent herself from glancing guiltily over her shoulder.

The person who had entered paid no attention to them, instead hurrying over to another post office box. But before Dana could turn around, the woman with the children who had been at the counter glanced their way.

The woman's eyes widened.

Dana averted her face immediately. "Oh, please hurry," she whispered to Remy. "I think someone just noticed you."

"Stay calm." He closed the box and turned toward her, then smoothly slipped his hand inside her coat and yanked the hem of her sweater above her waist. "Act natural."

"Natural? Remy, I know you wanted to put on an act but this is no time for—"

His knuckles brushed her bare midriff for an instant before she felt the cool slide of paper against her skin. Seconds later he tucked a thin stack of envelopes down the waistband of her leggings and flipped her sweater back into place.

"Darling," he said, his gaze steady on hers. "Or sweetheart or Josh."

Everyone in the place had to be able to hear her heart beating, Dana thought. The noise from that alone would have drowned out her slip with his name. "Now what?"

"Now we leave," he said.

Had she thought this was invigorating? She was nuts. Cracking up from the prolonged strain. She crossed her arms, holding the envelopes securely in place, and turned around. Remy draped his arm casually around her shoulders and guided her toward the door.

The woman was still watching them. Her forehead furrowed briefly with uncertainty, but then she appeared to come to some kind of decision. She hitched the toddler more securely against her hip, grabbed the boy's hand and started forward, heading straight for Remy.

Dana felt him tense. "Oh, darling," she said, pretending

not to notice the woman drawing closer. "I just remembered we need to pick up some more cat food."

"No problem, honey," he said. He coughed, turning his head aside and lifting his hand to cover his mouth.

"And we'd better pick up some cough syrup, too," she went on quickly. "What was the kind that worked before? It was in a red box, wasn't it? I hope—"

"Excuse me."

Dana stopped walking, not because she wanted to, but because the woman had stepped directly into their path. She forced a smile and decided to do the talking. "Yes?"

"I thought you looked familiar, but I wasn't sure until you turned around and..." She paused. "I'm sorry. I'm making a fool of myself. You're D. J. Whittington, aren't you?"

It took a second for the question to sink in. The woman wasn't looking at Remy at all. She was looking at Dana. So was the child beside her knee.

Dana nodded.

"I wouldn't have believed it could be you but I heard from my brother-in-law's cousin that you were staying near Hainesborough for the winter. He plows your lane."

"Oh." She was still trying to take it in. "You mean Duffy?"

"Uh-huh. I wouldn't have recognized you from that picture on your book covers, but I saw you a few years ago when you did a reading at our branch library. We were still living in Toronto then. I had to leave early to feed the baby but I wanted so much to tell you how we all love the Mortimer books...."

While Dana normally enjoyed meeting her fans, she wasn't able to enjoy this encounter in the least. All she could think about was Remy. He mumbled a greeting when she introduced him as her fiancé, continuing to hide his face by alternately coughing or dabbing at his nose. The longer they stayed here, the greater the chances of someone recognizing him instead of her. She extricated herself as soon as she could with an autograph for the woman's son and a promise to talk to the Hainesborough librarian about arranging a reading. It wasn't until she and Remy were back in the truck that she allowed herself to breathe freely again.

"Oh, my God," she muttered. "That was horrible."

"I think it went very well," Remy said, pulling out onto the main street. Streetlights winked on in the gathering dusk. Traffic was busy as the stores were beginning to close for the day.

"Are you kidding?" Dana asked. "I should have realized I could draw attention to us."

"To you."

"What?"

"You're the one who drew the attention. It's exactly what I'd hoped. That woman was so busy fawning over you, she never gave me a second glance."

He was right. As incredible as it seemed that any woman could fail to notice a man like Remy, in this case he had been virtually ignored. "She was probably worried about catching your cold."

"Yeah."

"That was quick thinking, by the way."

He gave her a lopsided smile. "Thanks. You're pretty good in a crunch yourself."

It was the stress of the situation that made his smile so attractive, wasn't it? And made her pulse jump that way? Leftover exhilaration from their daring almost-daylight robbery?

Who was she fooling? Not herself, anyway. It didn't matter what he did, she found him attractive. His smile was so rare, it never failed to stir a response, whatever the situation.

Belatedly she remembered the envelopes Remy had stuffed in her waistband. She opened her coat and pulled up her sweater.

The truck swerved. Someone honked. Remy muttered

under his breath and corrected the skid. "Next time, could you warn me before you start undressing?"

She yanked out the envelopes and smoothed her sweater back into place. "Well, next time you could warn me before you stuck your mail down my pants."

"Inside your pants seemed like a good place at the time. It's so snug and private. And warm."

"So's your pocket."

He glanced at her sideways. "You thought there was another reason I was trying to get inside your pants, didn't you?"

"Of course not."

He lifted one eyebrow.

"All right, I wasn't sure," she said. "I thought you might have been getting overenthusiastic about trying to play the part of my fiancé."

"A fiancé who was so overcome by lust in a post office that he couldn't keep his hands off you?"

"Let's just forget it, okay?"

"I don't know if I can. Kind of hard for me to forget such a snug, private, warm—"

"Oh, shut up."

"Now who's issuing orders?"

She slapped the envelopes against her palm. "Can we stick to business here?"

His grip on the steering wheel tightened. His smile disappeared. "Right. What did we get?"

"Not much." She flipped through the mail, surprised that more hadn't accumulated. Judging from the return addresses, there was nothing here from a credit card company as Remy had hoped. "I can't tell whether any of this would be useful to you."

"I'll take a look at it when we're back at the cabin. I don't want to spend any more time in town than necessary."

Dana looked out the window. Under other circumstances, the quaint red-brick buildings of Hainesborough's small downtown would have looked charming. So would the tree-lined streets that crossed the main road and wound their way along the contours of the river. She tried to picture Remy living in one of the houses she glimpsed down the side streets, but couldn't quite manage it. "Where's River Road?" she asked.

"Why?"

"Just wondering."

"Back that way," he said, jerking his head the way they had come.

"What happened to your house when you…" She hesitated, unsure whether or not she should be bringing this up. "When you left."

"When I went to prison, my father-in-law tried to sell it, but no one wanted to buy a house where a murder took place."

"Oh. Is it still vacant?"

"It's gone. Burned to the ground last Halloween."

Dana shifted to look at him. He'd said he had built that house. Now it was gone, like everything else in his life he had valued. "How?"

"The police decided it was a Halloween prank that got out of hand. I heard Sibley handled the investigation, and I doubt if he tried too hard to find who did it. There weren't any arrests."

"Sibley? That's the policeman you said was biased against you because of your juvenile record, right?"

"Right, but it was more personal than that. Sibley is only a few years older than me. He was a rookie when he tried to arrest me the first time."

"Tried to?"

"He caught me hotwiring a car. When he was putting the handcuffs on me, he made a comment about how I was as worthless as my drunken old man. I broke his nose."

"You what?"

"I was only seventeen. He knew my father had just died in prison and I wasn't thinking straight." He hesitated. "It was the first and last time I was ever moved to violence, Dana. The judge let it go but Sibley didn't. His nose healed crooked, the woman he'd been engaged to dumped him and he's held a grudge against me ever since.''

''If he was the type of man to say cruel things like that, it was probably his character more than his appearance that his fiancée didn't like.''

''Not according to him. So now you understand why he wouldn't have cared less if my house burned down.''

''Do you think there might have been evidence in that house?''

''Maybe. At least I had an ironclad alibi for the fire, since I was behind bars at the time, so Sibley couldn't accuse me of arson.''

A broken engagement and a broken nose explained Sibley's grudge, but neither excused his failure to do his duty. A fire in an accused murderer's house couldn't have been simple vandalism. It seemed obvious to Dana that someone was deliberately targeting Remy. Couldn't Sibley put aside his personal bias long enough to realize he was persecuting an innocent man?

An innocent man? Was he?

Yet again she pushed the issue aside. Her head wasn't clear enough to deal with that question, not with the traces of adrenaline from their foray to the post office—and from Remy's smile—still elevating her heart rate.

All of a sudden Dana realized they were no longer moving. They had reached the edge of town, yet rather than following the road to the highway, Remy had pulled up beside a small park, angling the pickup into a space beside a snowbank.

Cars drove past, a group of children dragging sleds walked along the plowed sidewalk, but Remy paid no attention to them.

''What are you doing?'' Dana asked. ''I thought you wanted to get out of town.''

He didn't respond. He exhaled hard, as if he'd been

punched in the stomach. Gradually the expression on his face lost its intensity. The harsh lines of his lips softened and his cheeks relaxed into the hint of a smile.

Dana twisted around to see what had caused the change, but all she noticed was another group of people following a path that had been made through the snow in the park. There was a gentle hill on the other side. As he watched, a lone, dark-haired child slid down the hill.

"Stay here," he said, opening his door.

She jerked around. "Where are you going?"

"That looks like Chantal."

"Remy, no!" She made a grab for his arm. "Don't. It's too dangerous."

He didn't seem to hear her. He pulled out of her grasp and was outside the truck before she could say another word.

Dana flung open her door and hurried after him.

Streetlights along the edge of the road spread pools of light over the snow, but the hill on the other side of the park was blue with dusk. The dark-haired child wasn't alone—an adult stood at the top of the hill. Even from here, Dana could hear a woman call that it was time to go home.

A child's voice drifted faintly in reply. Remy walked toward her, stumbling over a chunk of frozen snow as if unaware of his surroundings.

Oh, God, Dana thought. If that really was his daughter, he likely wasn't thinking of anything other than seeing her again. She broke into a run. "Josh," she called.

Remy glanced at her but kept moving.

"Darling, I'm sorry," Dana called, quickly improvising a reason to be running after her fiancé. "Let me explain."

At that, he slowed just enough for her to catch up to him. She flung herself against him, wrapping her arms tightly around his waist. The only way he could keep moving would be to drag her with him.

He stopped, but his body quivered with impatience. "Dana—"

She bumped her forehead into his chin. She hoped that anyone watching would think they'd had a quarrel and were on the verge of making up. "Don't do this," she whispered urgently. "Stop and think for a minute, okay? That probably isn't Chantal. Bundled up in those snowsuits, all kids look alike."

"She loves to toboggan. I could never get her to stop until it was dark."

"Even if it is her, she's not alone. Who's with her?"

He muttered an oath. "That's Sylvia's mother."

"Your mother-in-law?" She grasped his arms and gave him a shake. "Of all the people in Hainesborough, she'd be the first to recognize you and turn you in. Don't do this. *Please.*"

"Chantal's hat fell off."

"I'm sure they'll find it."

"She had an ear infection last winter. She needs to wear a hat."

"It's not that cold right now. And look, they're leaving."

As she spoke, the child and the adult turned away and moved toward a gap in the trees on the opposite side of the park.

"The Haines house backs onto the park," Remy said. "That has to be her."

"Then she'll be warm soon enough. Please, come back to the truck. If not for your sake, then for hers." She gave him another shake. "You're not going to do her any good if you get caught."

Whether it was her words or his own belated sense of caution, he didn't try to go after the child. He watched until the child and adult were out of sight, then tipped back his head and breathed deeply a few times. Reason apparently had reasserted itself. He wasn't going to risk his freedom just to catch a glimpse of his daughter. The danger was over.

But Dana didn't step back. Instead, she lifted her hands to his face and guided his head downward. She gave him a light kiss, a let's-kiss-and-make-up kiss for the benefit of anyone who might have been watching her charade.

At least, that was the excuse she gave herself.

Remy stood motionless, his gaze inscrutable in the dim light. "What was that for?" he asked.

"All part of the act," she said, throwing his own words back at him.

"Fine." He braced his legs apart and wrapped his arms around her, lifting her off her feet. "Then so's this."

"Remy, you don't need to—"

"You're wrong, Dana," he muttered against her lips. "At this moment, I can't think of anything I need to do more." He brought his mouth down on hers hard. If anyone had been watching, it would have been the logical next step in their charade. There would have been no doubt that they had made up. So this was good.

Oh, yes, it was good. The shadowy hush of the evening, the cold air on her cheeks mixed with Remy's warm breath, the strength in his arms as he held her so effortlessly, all of it was better than she could have imagined. And his mouth, oh, his mouth. How could it feel so firm and yet so gentle? So commanding and yet so pleading? So...real?

To her there was nothing fake about this kiss. It was the real thing. He hadn't tried to hide the attraction he felt toward her, and now there was no mistaking the passion she tasted. Even through the layers of their coats she could feel his muscles tense, yet despite the urgency in his body, his lips moved tenderly, as if he were coaxing her, wooing her to respond.

And God help her, she did. For one stolen minute she closed her eyes and took the pleasure he was giving. If they hadn't been in a public park, if the circumstances had been different...

But they weren't, were they? When it came to circumstances, they couldn't get much worse. All too soon the minute was over. She brought her hands between them and pushed.

Chapter 10

There was something primitively satisfying about swinging an ax. The blade whistled as it sliced through the air; the honed edge glinted with purpose. The woodshed echoed with the solid thud of metal biting into maple and the clean crack of splitting wood.

It was simple. It was brutally straightforward. And it was about the only thing in the whole damn situation that was either.

Remy wiped his forehead on his shirtsleeve and placed another chunk of wood on the chopping block. Aim, swing, split, stack. He went through the motions mechanically. The neat pile of kindling he'd already made was enough to supply every fireplace in Half Moon Bay for a year, but he wasn't ready to stop.

He was accustomed to working with his hands, so he welcomed the physical exertion. His muscles were stretched and limber. His pulse was comfortably quickened. Each thud of the blade sent vibrations of power through his palms and up his arms. To a man who had been powerless for almost a year, it was unexpectedly satisfying.

A cold draft swirled past his ankles. He paused in mid-stroke as the door to the woodshed opened. Dana stepped inside, clicking off the flashlight she carried.

He waited, expecting her to say something about the phone, which he had unplugged as usual and brought with him before he'd left her alone in the cabin. Or maybe she wanted to know where he'd hidden the lodge keys.

"What are you doing?" she asked.

"What does it look like I'm doing?" he muttered, bringing the ax down. Pieces of maple clattered to the pile on the floor.

"Preparing for the next ice age?"

He retrieved the thickest piece of wood and balanced it in the middle of the block. He hefted the ax and brought it down, smoothly severing the wood into slivers.

"Remy, I'm sorry."

"What for?"

"For having to stop you." She closed the door and set her flashlight down, then moved closer. Her hair gleamed softly as she passed beneath the bare lightbulb overhead. "You know it was for the best, though."

"Yeah, I know."

"I can understand how much you must have wanted to see her."

He rested the ax on his shoulder and straightened up. She was talking about stopping him from going to Chantal. He'd thought she was talking about that kiss.

Either way she was right. There was no point tormenting himself with something he couldn't have.

"It might not even have been her," she continued.

"It was."

"But—"

"I can't explain it, Dana, but I knew she was my daughter."

She unzipped her coat, stooping down to pick up an armful of kindling. "It must be so frustrating."

Frustrating? The word didn't come close to describing the situation, especially when it came to his feelings for Dana. His gaze dropped to the opening of her coat. The loose neckline of her sweater gaped outward as she leaned over. Although he told himself not to, he couldn't stop from noticing the shadowed hint of cleavage within.

Yet another snug, warm, private place, he thought. He hadn't been able to forget how soft her skin had felt when he'd brushed his hand below her waist. He'd caressed her like that once when he'd been Becker, and he hadn't been able to forget that, either. His body was warm from exercise. His heart rate was already elevated. It wouldn't take much to channel his energy toward her instead of the firewood. "Leave it, Dana. I'll get it later."

"I don't mind."

He swung the ax in a lazy arc and embedded the tip in the chopping block. Squatting down in front of her, he plucked the wood from her hand. "Would you please let me do this myself?" he asked, phrasing his order as a request. "I need the exercise."

Her lips quirked. "Oh, I can understand that. You'd be amazed at what I find to do when one of my books is giving me trouble."

"Is that why you came outside?"

"Partly. Mortimer isn't cooperating with the scene I'm working on. He was escaping the pirate mice but he found a hole in the bottom of his boat."

"Wasn't that what you had planned?"

"No. That's what makes my work so interesting. I never really know how the story's going to end until I get there."

He tossed the wood to the floor and stood up, extending his hand to Dana. "You said that was part of your reason. What's the rest?"

"I was curious." She grasped his hand and let him tug

her to her feet. "You didn't say anything after you finished going through that mail. Did you find something?"

"Not to support my alibi, no." He looked at her hand. He knew he couldn't justify touching her now any more than he could justify kissing her earlier, but he didn't want to let her go. He wanted to haul her against his chest and kiss her again. He wanted to lose himself in her softness, surround himself with her scent, use her sweetness to drive out the despair that always hovered on the edge of his emotions.

Use her. Damn.

"Remy?"

He guided her over to sit on a bench, then returned to pick up the ax. "I did find something odd."

"What was it?"

"An insurance statement."

"Life insurance?"

"No, my company had a group plan to cover prescriptions and extra medical expenses. The annual summary of the benefits lists how much each beneficiary has claimed."

"I don't understand. What's odd about that?"

"Last year, there was more than seven hundred dollars in total claims by my wife." He brought the ax down on a hapless piece of wood. "But as far as I know, she didn't have any medical problem."

"That is odd. What could it be from?"

"Whatever it was, she kept it a secret from me."

"Could it be drugs? Do you think it might be connected to her death?"

"I don't know how, but considering my lack of progress, at this point anything odd is worth investigating."

She frowned. "And how would you do that?"

"Her doctor would probably still have files. I need to take a look at them." Another piece of wood met its doom. "Tomorrow's Saturday. The doctor's office would be closed. We'll wait until dark to make sure no one's there. It shouldn't be a problem."

She remained silent. He had expected an argument, or at least a challenging comment. Then again, after her initial resistance earlier, she had ended up helping him. No, it had gone beyond help. She had wholeheartedly participated, right down to covering for him when he had gone after Chantal.

Had he thought it would be better if Dana didn't fight him? He'd been wrong. The more cooperative she became, the more like scum he felt. She was a good person, and he was drawing her deeper and deeper into this entire mess. He slammed the ax into the chopping block with more force than was necessary. Vibrations hummed through his hands to his forearms as the shed echoed with the crack of the blow.

Dana flinched. Yet rather than looking alarmed, she looked concerned.

He studied her. She *should* have been alarmed. She was alone with a convicted murderer who was armed with an ax. The last time they had been in the woodshed together, she hadn't wanted him to touch it. She'd made some excuse about having enough kindling, but now he realized her behavior must have been due to nervousness.

When had it changed? He knew that he hadn't been able to show her any proof of his innocence, but she no longer seemed nervous around him. Was it merely because she had resigned herself to cooperating?

Or was there another reason behind her change of attitude? Could he dare to hope that she trusted him?

Part of him was afraid to find out. He'd told himself over and over that it didn't matter what she thought of him, but it did. How could it not? He was placing his life, as well as his hopes for his daughter's future, in Dana's hands.

Yet it wasn't only fear of being betrayed that kept her constantly on his mind. Was it simply a physical attraction due to their proximity and his long period of abstinence? Or was it more?

There was a soft rustle of wool against wool as Dana

stood up and started toward him. "Remy? Is something wrong?"

Something wrong? Where should he start? He shook his head and stooped down to pick up an armful of wood. He carried it to the stack of freshly split kindling and concentrated on lining up the ends.

She followed, waiting until he had finished stacking the wood before she spoke again. "Is it Chantal?" she asked, laying her fingers against his arm. "I am sorry that I wouldn't let you see her, but I thought it was for the best."

He looked into her eyes. He saw the same compassion she had shown when they had first met, when she hadn't yet known who he really was. And just for a moment he wished he could have been John Becker or Josh Lawrence or any other man who would have had a chance with a woman like Dana. If only they could have met under other circumstances...

But that was impossible. The tangle of events that had brought them together couldn't be unraveled. If he hadn't found her cabin in the storm, if he hadn't escaped prison, if he hadn't been convicted of murder, if Sylvia hadn't died in the first place, he would still be a married man.

The clinic didn't have a pharmacy, which was probably why no alarm system had been installed. With no drugs to steal there was little reason for anyone to break into the doctors' offices.

And this time there was no getting around it: they were guilty of break and enter. Compared to the other two forays they'd made into Hainesborough, this was dead serious.

"Do you ever get used to this?" Dana asked, sticking close to Remy's side as he walked silently down the dark hall.

"To what? Crime?"

She nodded, the beam from her flashlight wobbling.

"No," he responded. "Every time I did something illegal when I was a kid, I felt like throwing up."

"I can believe that."

He heard the anxiety in her voice, and again he regretted having to take her with him. He hadn't wanted to. Because it was night, and there was little chance of running into anyone, he didn't anticipate needing her to provide cover for him. He had almost told her to stay behind.

But then he reminded himself what was riding on his judgment. He couldn't afford to trust anyone.

"Why did you keep doing it?"

He understood that she wanted to keep talking. It likely helped keep her mind off what they were doing. "I've wondered that myself."

"And?"

"Maybe it was because that's what everyone expected of me, considering my old man's reputation. Maybe I enjoyed being the town bad boy. Maybe I was just a rotten kid."

"Or maybe you didn't have a chance to be anything else."

He felt a glow of pleasure at her words. But at the same time, it made him feel worse for the way he was continuing to use her. This situation was really messing with his mind.

Remy paused when they reached the main reception area. Behind the counter was a pair of large open shelves that were stuffed with rows of beige file folders. There were also two large windows. He kept his flashlight aimed at the floor and quickly closed the blinds before he turned his attention to the files.

Less than a minute later, he pulled his wife's file from the middle of one of the shelves. Wedging his light on the shelf at elbow level, he opened the folder and flipped through the contents.

Dana pressed close to his side. "Did you find anything?"

He frowned, trying to decipher the doctor's handwriting. "Prescriptions. That would account for some of the insurance claims."

"What are they for?"

"Painkillers. Antibiotics. I don't know why..." He looked at the next paper in the file. "This is a receipt from the hospital. Day surgery."

"What for?"

"I have no idea. I was out of town that week." He picked up a typed form. It took him a moment to realize it was the record of a lab test.

"What's that?"

He read the date, then focused on the box that had been checkmarked. The result had been positive.

He swore under his breath. He had thought he was beyond the reach of Sylvia's ability to inflict pain, but still, to be confronted with the facts in such an in-your-face way hurt.

"Remy?"

He gritted his teeth and handed her the form.

Dana's forehead furrowed as she read it. "This looks like a—" She went still. "Remy, this is a pregnancy test."

"That's right."

"Oh, my God. Was Sylvia pregnant?"

"The test was dated last February. She wasn't pregnant in April when she died."

"Then..." Dana drew in her breath. "Oh, no. She must have had a miscarriage."

"That would explain the prescriptions and the hospital charges." He kept looking through the file.

"Didn't you know?" Dana asked.

"No."

"Your wife was pregnant. She lost her baby, and you didn't even know?" Her voice rose. "You didn't care?"

He glanced at the date on the top of the hospital bill and tried to recall his schedule. "I wasn't here that week. There was an equipment auction in North Bay."

She backed away from him. "You left her to go through it on her own."

Her reaction was out of proportion to the situation. What was going on? "Dana, calm down."

"Didn't you think about the pain she must have been going through? She must have been trying to give you what you wanted. How could you turn your back on her like that?"

He dropped the file and grasped her shoulders to keep her from retreating further. "She hadn't told me."

"She would have felt so empty, so alone—"

"Dana," he said firmly, leaning down to bring his gaze level with hers. "Listen to me. I didn't know Sylvia was in the hospital. I hadn't even known Sylvia was pregnant until one minute ago."

"What?"

"She hadn't told me," he repeated. Were those tears in her eyes? He knew that Dana was a compassionate woman, but her distress had to be from more than that. Beneath his hands he could feel her shoulders tremble. "Dana, what's going on? Why are you so upset?"

"I…I was surprised, that's all."

"Tell me the truth, Dana."

She looked away.

"Please," he said.

"I overreacted. Sorry."

"But why?"

"I'm a little on edge, I guess. I've never been guilty of break-and-enter before."

"It's more than that." He slid his hands down her arms until he twined his fingers with hers. He could feel her tension and wished he knew what to do. He wanted to comfort her, but why should she need comfort over something that had happened to a woman she didn't know…?

All at once the pieces fell into place. Her marriage had been childless, but she loved children. She understood his pain over being away from Chantal. She had once said she hadn't been able to give her husband what he wanted. Could she have been talking about a baby?

"It happened to you, didn't it?" he asked.

She was silent for a minute before she gave a quick dip of her chin in reply.

He should let this go. He shouldn't be touching her. There was no excuse, no one to play a part for this time. He had the file, he'd gotten what he'd come for. Every minute they stayed here increased their risk.

Yet somehow he couldn't leave her like this. Would another few minutes hurt? In a motion he wasn't aware of until it was done, he pulled her into his arms.

She held herself stiffly. "I'm sorry. I really did overreact. We should get going."

"We've got time."

"It's not a big deal. It happens to plenty of women. It was two years ago, and I shouldn't—"

"Don't give me that. I know you, Dana." He rubbed her back in slow circles, urging her to lean on him. "I've read your books. I knew what you were like even before I met you. Your emotions run deep."

She shuddered.

He held her, simply held her. He expected her to pull away, but instead she sighed and pressed her face into his shoulder.

He brushed his lips over her hair. "Want to talk about it?"

She breathed deeply a few times. "It was a boy. I carried him for five months. I had already felt him move before—" She cleared her throat. "He was too small to survive. My marriage didn't survive, either. Hank left me."

He remembered the other things she had said, how she had assumed he hadn't cared and had turned his back. She must have been talking about her husband. What kind of jerk had the man been, to desert her when she needed him most?

But when it came to a man's character, Remy realized he wasn't in a position to judge anyone. "You would make a great mother," he said. "I can see it in your work. Maybe someday…" He paused, unwilling to complete the thought.

He didn't want to picture Dana remarrying and having more children. He didn't want to consider her being touched by another man. "I'm sorry, Dana," he said.

"And I'm sorry for saying those things about you. I…wasn't thinking."

"Don't worry about it." He gave her a gentle squeeze. "You okay now?"

She rubbed her forehead against his coat. "I'm okay. I don't dwell on it, really I don't. Just sometimes out of the blue it hits me."

"I understand. It's that way for me with Chantal, too. Some times are worse than others."

"I've seen that." She tipped back her head to look at him. "Like at the park."

It was the wrong thing for her to say, he thought. Instantly the memory of their kiss in the twilight flooded his mind. This embrace was supposed to be for comfort, but she felt too good in his arms. It wouldn't take much for it to change. The way she was looking up at him, with the trace of tears brightening her eyes and sympathy softening her lips, could make him forget the reason they were here.

He focused on her mouth. Another mistake. All he could think of was how she had tasted, how she had responded. He hadn't been acting. Had she?

Headlights slid across the blinds. He glanced at the window and tensed. "Dana," he began.

"Oh, God," she murmured. She pushed away. "Someone's coming."

He waited, straining to hear. "Sounds like it was just someone turning the corner." He bent down to gather the papers that had spilled out of the file folder when he'd dropped it. "But we shouldn't push our luck."

She crossed her arms. "I'm sorry, Remy. This is just awful."

"Don't worry about it."

"No, I mean I shouldn't be thinking of myself. This was

a horrible way for you to find out about your baby. Sylvia should have told you she was pregnant."

"I'm not surprised that she didn't."

"Why not?"

He braced his fingertips on the floor and looked up at her. "Because she knew she wasn't carrying my child."

"What?"

"We hadn't slept together for almost a year."

Her eyes widened as she realized the implication of what he had said.

"I had suspected she had a lover," he continued as he stretched to reach a paper that had slid under the shelf. "I told the police about it right from the start, but there wasn't any proof. My insistence made me come across as paranoid and jealous, and it ended up helping their case against me."

"Oh, Remy. I'm sorry."

"You're right, though. Sylvia should have told me about the baby. It wouldn't have been easy, but we could have tried to work it out."

"If she hadn't miscarried, you would have found out eventually. She couldn't have hidden her pregnancy forever."

He glanced at the last page of the doctor's notes, intending to slip it into the folder. He inhaled sharply as a word caught his eye.

"What is it?" Dana asked.

He pushed himself to his feet and grabbed his flashlight off the shelf to shine it directly on the handwriting. When he realized what it was that he was seeing, his hand shook.

How could he have been so wrong about the woman he'd married? Considering the state of their relationship, he could understand why she would be tempted to break her vows by having an affair. But this?

"Remy?"

"Sylvia knew I'd never find out." He closed the folder

and tucked it under his arm. "She didn't have a miscarriage."

"But—"

"She had an abortion."

Chapter 11

The fire crackled behind the spark guard, flames licking along the fresh wood—there had been more than enough kindling to build the blaze. Heat pushed outward like a firm hand, forcing Dana to slide farther back on the rug. Still, she drew her knees to her chest and wrapped her arms around her legs as if to warm herself. Lately she had been getting a lot of chills that couldn't be dispelled by a fire.

Sylvia Haines Leverette was gone. Whatever her faults, she was beyond blame. It was pointless to detest a dead woman.

Yet that's what Dana did, because even dead, Sylvia had hurt Remy.

How could any woman be unfaithful to a man like Remy? With six-foot-three of hard-muscled male in her bed each night, how could she want to look elsewhere? The proof of her unfaithfulness was in her pregnancy. Dana believed Remy completely when he had said the child couldn't have been his. The pain in his gaze had left no room for doubt.

But that wasn't the worst of it. Dana would have felt sympathy for Sylvia if she had lost the baby in a miscarriage, no matter how the baby had happened to be conceived. Yet now that she knew Remy's wife had deliberately terminated her pregnancy...

Dana pressed her eyes to her knees, swallowing hard. It wasn't fair. She would give anything to be able to bear a child of her own. Just one. Sylvia had been about to have her second, and she hadn't wanted it. Seeing that lab report had brought everything back with a vengeance. Two years had passed, but Dana vividly remembered the joy of carrying a life within her. And she would never forget the grief that had followed.

As she had told Remy, miscarriages happened all the time. Many women went through that heartache and got on with their lives, but when Dana had lost her baby, she had also lost her husband and the dreams she had held for their future. The loss that had been the worst, though, was her loss of faith in her own judgment.

A weight settled at her feet. She lifted her head to watch Morty shape himself into a loaf on her toes. Grateful for his warmth, she dropped her hand to his fur.

He did a rumbling purr, his way of letting her know that he might tolerate her attention for a while.

Remy sat down beside her. Morty looked at him expectantly, and Remy obliged him by ruffling the fur behind his ears. The cat closed his eyes to slits and purred again smugly.

"He adores you, you know," Dana said.

"He's pretty easy to please, for a celebrity." Remy stroked his palm along the cat's back until his hand met Dana's. He squeezed her fingers. "Are you all right?" he asked.

"I'm fine, but I should be asking you that."

"Why?"

She rested her cheek on her knee so she could look at him. Remy had been subdued since they had returned from the clinic, and it was little wonder. After what he had already been through, how much more pain could he take? "It had to have been a shock for you, what we found out tonight."

He withdrew his hand and gazed at the fire. "It confirmed what I already suspected about Sylvia having a lover, so that part of it wasn't surprising." He paused. "But I'm disappointed that she felt she had to rid herself of the child."

She could see by the drawn expression on his face that he was more than disappointed. The fact that his wife had had an abortion—in secret—had hit him hard. It was obvious to Dana that he loved the child he already had. How would he have dealt with this one?

He would have loved it like his own, she thought immediately. It didn't matter what he said about his background or his juvenile record. The man who had held her so patiently while she had told him about the baby she had lost wouldn't have rejected an innocent child. He wouldn't have blamed the baby for the sins of the mother. If Sylvia had wanted to mend their relationship, he would have found a way to accept her child into their family.

She smiled wryly when she realized what she was doing. She had just reminded herself of her lack of faith in her judgment, so when had she started putting her faith in Remy? He had lied to her; he was a convicted felon; he was everything any mother would warn her daughter about; yet he was the first man she had opened up to in years.

Once more she wondered how any woman could have betrayed a man like Remy. "Do you have any idea who…"

"Who her lover was?" he finished for her.

She nodded.

"No. I was too busy with my business that last year to keep a close eye on Sylvia. Any spare time I had I spent with Chantal. Sylvia had plenty of opportunity to see whoever she wanted, but I never noticed any one man paying more attention to her than usual.'' His lips thinned. ''She was good at keeping secrets.''

''I guess she was.''

''I've been through everything in her medical file, and there's nothing that gives any hints about the child's father in there, either.''

''Are you sure you want to know?''

He swung his gaze back to hers. ''Of course, I want to know. I *need* to know.''

''I mean, Sylvia's dead, so—''

''Because her lover killed her.''

''How… What makes you so sure? You told me you didn't know who did it.''

''I don't know who he is, but I know what he is. He had to be her lover. Everything points to it.''

''How?''

''The same reasoning that threw suspicion on me also implicates him. There hadn't been any sign of forced entry, and nothing had been missing, so it wouldn't have been an attempted robbery. There hadn't been any signs of a struggle, either, so Sylvia must have known her killer.''

Dana hugged her legs more tightly, feeling another chill. ''Go on.''

''It wouldn't have been a casual acquaintance, because she was in the bedroom when I found her.''

''Okay. What else?''

''According to the coroner's report, the first wound was the fatal one, but there were seven more.''

Dana made a noise in her throat.

Remy paused. ''I'm sorry. This is upsetting you.''

''No, I just—'' She pressed her lips together briefly. ''I have a vivid imagination.''

''Sorry.''

She waved her hand. ''Go on.''

''The brutality and the location of the attack point to a crime of passion,'' he said. His voice was level, mechanical, as if he were describing the puzzle in a mystery story.

"The killer had to be someone who was passionate about Sylvia. I believe it was her lover, but there's no way to prove my theory. The prosecution decided her husband was a likelier suspect."

"The medical records could help you, after all," Dana said. "They could prove that Sylvia did have a lover."

He shook his head. "From what I read in the file, there was no paternity test done on the fetus, so I still have no way of proving she was unfaithful. The fact that she wanted an abortion would only demonstrate how bad our marriage was. Unless I can prove the identity of her lover, this information about her pregnancy would hurt my case instead of helping it."

She tried to think objectively about what he had described, but it was difficult. Remy had had almost a year of practice at distancing himself from what had happened. She couldn't. This was no mystery-story puzzle, this was his life. "Remy, can I ask you something?"

"Sure. What?"

"Why did you marry Sylvia?"

He laughed. It wasn't from humor. "Along with the other question, who killed her, I've been asking myself that every day."

"From what you've told me about her, you two didn't have much in common."

"No, we didn't. If train tracks ran through Hainesborough, I would have been from the wrong side of them."

"Then how did you two meet?"

He slanted her a look. "Are you sure you want to hear this?"

"Yes."

"I met Sylvia when I was working on an addition to the country club. I liked the way she looked in her tennis whites, and she got hot seeing me sweat."

Dana could easily picture what Remy would look like in jeans and a work shirt, with his muscles flexing and damp from exertion. Oh, yes, he could raise any woman's temperature, even a tennis-playing member of a country club.

"We had an affair," he said bluntly. "She wanted to keep it secret because she knew her family wouldn't approve, and because she got an added thrill out of it that way. I didn't care where we met as long as it was private enough to do what I wanted. When she told me she was pregnant, I stopped playing along. I insisted that she marry me."

It was foolish to feel a pang at the idea of Remy being intimate with another woman, especially now that the woman was dead. It didn't surprise her that he would insist on marriage, though. Considering his own unstable childhood, he would have wanted to provide a secure home for his child. "She must have been very beautiful."

He paused. "Yes, she was that."

"What was she like?"

"Like a poor man's dream," he said. "Porcelain skin, a mouth that looked sexy when she pouted and a cloud of auburn hair. It took me too long to realize that the beauty was only on the surface."

"Did you love her?"

"I thought I did. She was the mother of my child, and I hoped we could build a decent life together, despite the differences in our backgrounds. For a while, I thought we had a chance."

"What happened?"

He lifted his shoulders. "The infatuation wore off. Sylvia realized she was stuck with a man who wore his hair too long and had calluses on his hands, and she wanted her old life back. I tried to give it to her. I went to her father for loans to expand my business, I built her a fancy house, I worked twelve-hour days to give her what she asked for. It wasn't enough. It just got worse."

"But you tried."

"I didn't love her anymore, Dana. She wasn't stupid, she realized I was just going through the motions. We became like two strangers living in the same house. The only bond left between us was Chantal.''

She thought about that for a while. "It's ironic," she said. "I had been convinced that a child would save my marriage.''

His gaze softened with sympathy. "Was it in trouble before your miscarriage?''

"Yes," she answered honestly. "Hank wanted a big family. So did I. That's why I'd married him, for the home and family and all that. There was this…emptiness inside me. I had put all my hopes on having his baby.''

"Having a child with him might not have helped." He reached out to tuck a strand of hair behind her ear, his knuckles gently grazing her cheek. "I was wrong to get married only for the sake of a child. Any relationship should be based on more than that.''

She tipped her head, unconsciously seeking more of his touch. "What do you think a relationship should be based on?''

"Depends what kind you're talking about.''

"Give me an example.''

He rubbed his thumb along the line of her jaw. "Between a man and a woman?''

"Well, yes.''

"Before I met Sylvia, I would have said sex.''

"Oh. And now?''

"I think there has to be more.''

"Like what?''

"Common interests. Respect." He paused. "Trust.''

"Yes, there would have to be trust.''

"And honesty.''

"I would have thought they sort of go together.''

"That's right." He reached for the cat, carefully lifting Morty from her feet and setting him down on the rug closer to the hearth. Morty glared at him briefly before he averted his head with feline disdain and went back to sleep. Remy watched the fire for a while, then turned to face Dana and took her hand. "It's my turn to ask you something."

"Go ahead."

"Do you think I'm a murderer?"

The question took her off guard. Her hand jerked. She started to pull away, but he hung on, curling her hand into his chest.

"I need to know," he said. "You've said it doesn't make any difference, and I've told myself it shouldn't, but it does. It makes a hell of a difference."

"Remy…"

"Please, Dana. Tell me the truth. Do you believe I killed my wife?"

It was hard for her to hold his gaze. She had danced around the question for days. She should have known she couldn't keep ducking the issue indefinitely.

Do you believe I killed my wife?

She searched for the doubts that had served her before, but they were no longer there. Somehow, when she hadn't been looking, they had crumbled and fallen away.

She had thought this would be harder, she had agonized about this for more than a week, but the answer was easy, because it had been there all along. She had just been too afraid to admit it. Although she might never be ready to trust her judgment, that didn't change the fact that the judgment had been made.

Of course she didn't believe Remy had killed his wife. She never had. Otherwise she wouldn't have lifted a finger to help him, no matter what he had threatened her with.

She'd used her suspicions the same way she had used her anger. It was a way to distance herself from him, to keep her heart safe.

It hadn't worked, had it?

"Dana?"

She blinked. In the firelight his eyes were shadowed. The planes of his face looked harsh and his expression closed. He should have looked dangerous. Instead, for all of his size and strength, in this moment he looked more vulnerable than when he'd been helpless and half-frozen on her doorstep.

"No, Remy." She splayed her fingers over his shirt. "I don't believe you could kill anyone."

He regarded her in silence for a while, his heartbeat hard beneath her palm. Slowly his lips relaxed into a smile that zinged right through to her toes. He lifted her hand to his mouth. "Thank you."

The words were quiet, yet they sounded as if they had been pulled from the depths of his soul. Her eyes misted as she tried to imagine what it must have been like for him this past year. To lose everything, to be condemned to a life without hope, it truly must have been hell.

He'd been so alone, for so long. She had been alone, too, but it had been her choice. She had been too afraid of making another mistake, of trusting the wrong man, so she hadn't wanted to try. Yes, she had her career, her family and her friends, but it had been far too long since she'd felt the simple, basic pleasure of a man's touch.

Only, there wasn't anything simple about this, was there? Nothing had changed. He was still a wanted criminal. He was still using her, and the path they were on could lead them both to disaster.

Yet everything had changed. Their relationship had irrevocably shifted, and she realized why she had fought this moment for so long.

She hadn't merely given Remy her trust.

She was on the verge of giving him her heart.

Remy pressed a kiss to each of her knuckles, then turned her hand over and rubbed his lips across her palm. "Do you have any idea how good it feels to know you believe me?"

"I can imagine."

"Can you?" He looked into her eyes, his gaze probing hers. "You saved my life when you brought me in from the storm. You made me warm again. Knowing you believe me does the same, but in here," he said, tapping his index finger against his chest. "You're like sunshine in the winter. You make me warm inside."

His words moved her. She felt them curl into her soul like a soft embrace. She made a wordless sound that to her ears seemed suspiciously like a purr.

With nipping kisses, he traced from the base of her thumb to the inside of her wrist.

She watched the corners of his lips curve as he tasted her skin, and she shuddered. His smile was hungry. Predatory. And indecently appealing.

What was it she had wanted to say?

He eased the cuff of her sweater farther up her arm, continuing his leisurely sampling. "Remember what I said two people need in a relationship?"

She was finding it difficult to concentrate. "You mean trust and honesty?"

"No, not that." He licked the inside of her elbow.

"Mmm. Common interests?"

"No." He slipped his arm behind her shoulders and slowly eased her backward until she was lying on the rug. "I mean sex."

Her stomach quivered. "You said you wouldn't want to base a relationship on it."

"No, what I said was sex shouldn't be the only basis." He stretched out beside her and hooked his foot behind her leg, rolling her hips against his. "That doesn't mean we can ignore it."

She gasped at the contact of their lower bodies. He was right, she couldn't ignore that. She could feel the length of his arousal press against her stomach. Slow, heavy heat gathered between her thighs.

He cupped her cheek, his fingers not quite steady. "I said I wouldn't lie to you again, and I won't."

"Remy…"

"I've been in prison for almost a year. Before that, it had been twelve months since I had shared my wife's bed.

I haven't had sex in so long…'' He breathed hard, his nostrils flaring. ''I'm a man with less than nothing to his name, because I don't even have a name I can use. But I'm still a man, Dana.''

Oh, yes, she thought, nestling closer. He was that.

His fingertips feathered over her eyebrows, her cheeks, her lips. ''And I want you. I've wanted you from the time we met.''

She turned her head to kiss his fingers.

His eyes glinted. ''Each night when I lie on the couch and listen to you turn over in bed, I think about all the ways we could make that mattress creak. And counting positions sure isn't a good way to get to sleep.''

Positions? Were there that many? she wondered, tantalized at the prospect of finding out.

''Did you know that when I was staying at the lodge, I would watch you through your window and I pictured myself sliding under the quilts and—''

''You watched me?''

''Derek's telescope,'' he said, no apology in his voice.

An odd thrill tickled through her at his words. What had he seen? What would she have wanted him to see?

''But it's been so damn long.'' He wrapped a lock of her hair around his fist. ''I'm afraid if we start, I won't be able to stop.''

She swallowed. He was leaving it up to her. Despite his obvious desire, he was waiting for her to make the decision. ''It's okay,'' she said. ''I trust you, Remy.''

He went still, his jaw clenching. ''I don't have any protection, Dana.''

Protection? It took her a second to realize he was talking about condoms. It took even less than a second for her to reply. ''That's okay, too.''

''If there's any chance that you might get pregnant—''

''No, Remy.''

''Wrong time of your cycle?''

She nodded an affirmative, not wanting to think about

that now, not with her blood pounding and her body humming.

"We both know I can't make any promises," he continued. "I could go back to prison tomorrow."

"No, don't say—"

"It's true, and you know it."

Yes, she did know it, but that didn't stop the response that was continuing to tingle through her body. Instead, it grew stronger. He could be wrenched from her life tomorrow, or the next day, or the day after that. There was no way to be certain that he'd ever be able to prove his innocence.

"Dana?"

"I don't want promises, Remy," she said, grasping the front of his shirt. She yanked him closer. "I just want you."

He didn't give her a chance for second thoughts. He rolled on top of her and lowered his head.

In the heartbeat before his lips met hers, Dana knew that this time, she had been the one who had lied. She *did* want promises. For her, sex had always been an expression of love. She had never had a one-night stand in her life, and she wanted to be able to have more than only one night with Remy.

But she had learned there was a big difference between what she wanted and what she could have. Even one night would be better than none at all. Shutting out thoughts of tomorrow, she closed her eyes and parted her lips.

He accepted her silent invitation and deepened the kiss with a bold, slow slide of his tongue. Despite his warning, he was deliberately holding himself in check. She could feel it in the tension that trembled through his arms and in the shallow rise and fall of his chest. He tasted her tenderly, thoroughly, as if they had all the time in the world.

Yet they didn't, did they? Dana moved her hands to the buttons on the front of his shirt. She undid the top two, then found her hands trapped against her breasts as he settled his weight more completely on top of her. Without

breaking their kiss, she arched her back and twisted, pushing him to his side so that she could reach the rest of his
buttons.

They had lain on this hearth rug before, when he was
pretending to be John. She had undressed him before, too,
she realized. Right in this spot, she had dragged off his
clothes. His body had been lax and unresisting. He wasn't
lax now. Every muscle and sinew in his incredible body
was hardened to steel. She parted his shirt and flattened her
hands on his chest, sighing in pleasure as she ran her palm
down the molded ridges of his abdomen.

Oh, but he was magnificent, she thought. A perfectly
formed male. His skin was taut and smooth and heated
beneath her touch. She stroked upward, running her fingertips over the crisp curls that stretched across the breadth of
his chest, then lowered her hand once more, following the
line of silky hair that led downward from his navel.

"Dana," he murmured against her lips.

The line of hair didn't stop at the top of his jeans, and
neither did she. Flicking open the stud at his waistband, she
dipped her fingers inside. "Mmm?"

He grasped her wrist. "I told you, it's been a long time."

"Mmm."

"If you keep that up…"

She ignored his warning. She didn't want to go slow. It
would give her too much time to think. He had said it had
been almost two years for him, but it had been longer than
that for her. And with Hank she had never felt this sense
of urgency. Was it only because of their situation?

But she didn't want to think, she reminded herself. Sliding downward she kissed the center of his chest.

He remained motionless for a trembling moment, until
suddenly his restraint snapped. He grasped her waist and
rolled her on top of him.

She lifted her head, flicking her hair from her eyes.
"Remy, what—"

"The trouble with winter," he muttered, grasping the

hem of her sweater, "is too many clothes." He tugged her sweater over her head and flung it aside. Before she could utter a word, he had his hands behind her back, unfastening her bra. He flung that aside, too, then cupped her breasts in his hands.

This was what she wanted. There was no room for thought, no time for doubts. All she could do was enjoy. She braced her hands on his chest, lifting herself more fully into his caress.

He smiled and curled upward to take her nipple in his mouth.

She cried out at the jolt of delight. Remy made a low, rough sound in his throat and rolled to his side with her as he rubbed the edge of his teeth across her nipple. She groaned and grasped his head to hold him there, loving the way he made her feel.

She barely noticed when his hands left her breasts to unzip her pants. She was only dimly aware when he shifted her from one side to the other as he eased them down her hips. So she should have been shocked when she felt his hand slip between her thighs, but she wasn't. It felt too…right, too natural to resist.

His breath was hot and fast on her stomach as he slid downward, kissing his way to her waist. With his mouth and his thumb, he started a rhythm, firm and steady, pushing her closer, lifting her higher.

Dana shuddered in disbelief as she felt the first wave hit. It was impossible. It was so fast. She had never had this happen so easily. How could—

"Let it go, Dana," he murmured. "Please. For me."

"Remy, I—"

"We need this. I need this. Now."

"Oh," she whispered. He was doing something unbelievable with his fingers. "Oh, oh, oh…" She arched upward, her body shaking with a sudden, unexpected climax. "Oh, Remy."

Before the wave receded, he rolled her to her back and

came to his knees. With quick, savage movements, he stripped her pants the rest of the way off her legs and opened the front of his jeans.

Her mouth went dry at the sight of him. His shirt hung open, his chest gloriously bare and golden in the firelight. His skin was damp, his lungs heaving. He pushed down his briefs and grasped her knees to part her thighs.

She had never seen a man more blatantly aroused. It was more than his size, more than his hardness. It was the flush on his skin, the trembling in his muscles, the rigid tendons in his neck and arms. It was the way his dark gaze burned into hers with a demand…and a plea.

Dana moistened her lips and stretched out her arms.

He came down on top of her, his entry swift and sure. His big body moved in the rhythm he had used before, and soon she felt the tingles starting all over again. It was too much, she was going too high, it wasn't possible for it to get better….

But it did, it did. She dug her nails into his back and lifted her hips to meet him, feeling reality slip away. Nothing existed, nothing mattered, except the man she held and the pleasure they were giving each other.

And just as she reached the point when she felt every nerve in her body straining, clenching, weeping for relief, he wrapped his arms around her and lifted her from the rug.

"Remy," she asked shakily. "What—"

"Open your eyes, Dana."

She hadn't realized they were closed. She blinked to bring his face into focus.

He rocked back on his heels to sit up with her, pulling her legs on either side of his hips. Locking his gaze with hers, he clamped his hands on her waist and slowly raised her up.

She felt every inch of him. And she felt him swell even more. Her eyes widened. Her breath caught.

He smiled and brought her down hard.

The world exploded in a shower of sparks. Dana screamed and clutched Remy's shoulders.

He moved her again.

She was going to die. This was too much. She couldn't possibly...

He surged upward, his entire body tensing. He shuddered, his breath escaping on a low, grating moan. The sparks turned to stars. Hot. Powerful. Too many to count.

"Dana."

The sound of her name, the need in his eyes, the sudden heat that flooded her sent her over the edge. She sobbed and collapsed against his chest.

Remy tucked the quilt around Dana's shoulders and glanced at the window. The sky was already growing light. The night was almost over.

But the night should never have happened.

What kind of man would take advantage of a woman who had saved his life? What kind of animal was he, to use her body over and over to satisfy his needs? Of all the things he'd done since he'd gone over that prison fence, what he had done to Dana last night was the worst. He should be buried in guilt right now. He should be tormented by his conscience.

Instead he felt so damned good he wanted to turn around, crawl back into her bed and do it some more.

He rubbed his face and headed for the bathroom. "You really are a bastard," he muttered to himself as he flushed the toilet and zipped up his jeans. He scowled at his reflection in the mirror over the sink. "She's a good woman. She deserves better. You managed fine for almost two years. Couldn't you keep it in your pants for another few days?"

The bastard staring back at him didn't look remorseful in the least. He looked sated.

Remy slapped shaving cream on his cheeks and grabbed the razor, removing his morning beard with quick, vicious strokes. Yet, if he'd hoped to punish himself into feeling guilty, it didn't work. He rubbed the remnants of lather off his face with a towel and braced his hands on the edge of the sink.

Maybe he'd lived with guilt for so long, he'd become immune.

Or maybe he couldn't bring himself to regret something that had felt so…inevitable. This had been building for days. They were two adults. They were unattached. They were mutually attracted. Where was the crime in letting nature take its course?

Sure, he'd used her body, but he'd made certain it hadn't been all one-sided. She hadn't resisted. She had been with him all the way. His gaze was caught by a red smear on his shoulder, and he twisted to see his back. Four sets of parallel pink scratches crisscrossed his skin.

He couldn't help it. Despite the confusion of emotions that were warring between his conscience and his body, he grinned. Oh, yeah. Dana could give as good as she got.

Before he'd married Sylvia, he hadn't been a saint. He'd enjoyed women. He'd enjoyed sex. As a matter of fact, he'd enjoyed sex so damn much that it had led to his disastrous marriage. But being with Dana had been different. She was nothing like the other women he'd known. He'd never experienced anything like what they'd shared last night. It was so good it could prove addictive. He was tempted to follow through with his threat to tie her to the bed…

His grin faded. Once they had started, there was no doubt she had been willing, yet how much choice had she actually had? He hadn't physically forced her, but she hadn't been completely free, either. From the moment last week when she had spoken his real name, he had made sure she couldn't leave. He had coerced her and he had used her.

I trust you, Remy.

And she did. She had told him she believed him. She had trusted him with her body.

The question was, could he trust her? She had lied to

him before, and she had lied well. As long as Dana believed she had as much to lose as he did if she went to the authorities, he would be safe. Why change that now? Just because they had made love? He knew better than to confuse sex with anything deeper, didn't he?

Trusting a woman, getting swept away by a sexual attraction, had gotten him into this trouble in the first place. He was still dealing with the repercussions of his mistake with Sylvia. Could he afford to be wrong this time?

But could he live with himself if he wasn't wrong?

Remy cursed under his breath and turned away from the mirror, no longer able to look his reflection in the eye.

Chapter 12

Dana woke up to the jangle of keys. She opened her eyes just as Remy moved beside the bed. There was a moment of confusion, when her sleep-fogged brain wondered what he was doing in her bedroom, but her body had no trouble remembering.

Although she lay motionless, her pulse thumped. All she needed to do was look at him and her heart came alive. He had put on his jeans and a shirt, but she knew exactly what the fabric concealed, and how his skin had gleamed in the firelight.

She had touched that skin, slid across it and felt it slide over her. She'd learned how he had tasted as the rumble of his moans tingled through her cheek. She knew the texture of his hair and the scent of his neck.

But for the life of her, she didn't know what to say to him now that it was daylight.

She lifted her gaze to his face, hating the awkwardness. "Hi."

"Good morning, Dana."

She sighed. Just the sound of his voice set off a reaction deep inside. She had always loved his voice. It was low and strong and certain, like the growl of distant thunder.

He looked at her hard, the line of his jaw sharp with tension. "Are you okay?"

"What do you mean?"

"Did I hurt you?"

Gradually she became aware of a discomfort in her thighs. It wasn't painful, it was just the stiffness that resulted from muscles unaccustomed to vigorous exercise. Her face heated. Oh, yes, it had been vigorous.

"Dana?"

She shook her head and sat up, holding the covers over her breasts. The sheet brushed her nipples, and she wasn't surprised to feel a certain amount of tenderness there, too. "I'm fine. What about you?"

He continued to look at her. Instead of replying, he tossed a ring of keys to the pillow beside her. They settled into the indentation his head had left.

She didn't make a move to pick them up. "Those look like the keys to Derek's truck."

"They are."

"Why are you giving them to me?" she asked. "You know I can't drive a stick shift."

He tossed another set of keys on top of the first. They were for her car.

The sheet crumpled in her fist as she clutched it more tightly. Something was wrong, and it wasn't simply morning-after awkwardness. "Remy…"

"I found a pump in the garage and fixed your tires," he said. "The gas tank's full."

She stared at him.

Another ring of keys clanked onto the pillow. "Here are the keys to the main lodge."

"I can see that. Why are you giving them to me now? We did the check yesterday before we went into town, remember?"

"I remember everything we did, Dana."

It wasn't what he said, it was the way he said it, with that hoarse edge to his tone. She knew he wasn't talking about checking the lodge. He was referring to what they had done together. On the hearth rug. And in her bed.

She had been sure he'd enjoyed it. Why, then, was he acting like this?

"I've left your phone plugged in," he said. "I won't be taking it away again. You can use any of the phones in the lodge, too."

"I don't understand."

"It's simple. I won't make you help me anymore, Dana."

"What?"

A muscle twitched in his cheek. "Whatever happens, I'm not going to say you were my accomplice. I'll swear I forced you. You can say the same thing."

She looked at the heap of keys on the pillow. The significance of what he was doing hit her all at once. It wasn't just transportation or phone access he was giving her. He was giving her her freedom.

She swung her gaze back to his. "I'm not going to turn you in."

"That's because you have no choice. You helped me because I threatened you."

"That's not—"

"I lied about that, too. I never would have dragged you down with me, Dana. I was bluffing."

"Remy—"

"Do whatever you have to. All I ask is that you give me a day's head start."

"Head start?" She slid to the edge of the bed, tugging the sheet free of the blankets so she could wrap it around herself. The floor was cold as she padded over to where he stood, but she barely noticed. "All right, what's going on?"

"You're free to go."

"Why now? Because I slept with you?"

He hesitated. "In part."

She flung one arm toward the keys on the pillow. "Was that supposed to be some kind of payment for services rendered?"

"No, Dana. God, no."

"Because if it is, you can take those keys and stick them sideways somewhere really uncomfortable."

He caught her hand. "You've got it all wrong."

"No, *you've* got it all wrong. Do you really think I would have let anything stop me if I'd wanted to turn you in?"

"I gave you no choice."

"That's what I'd wanted to believe, because I needed an excuse to stay with you. It took me a while to admit it, but I don't believe you're guilty. I never really did."

"That's all the more reason for you to get as far away from me as fast as you can."

"That doesn't make sense."

"You have to protect yourself before it's too late, Dana." He dropped her hand. "I'm running out of places to look for evidence. I might never prove my innocence. The police are going to catch up with me eventually and it would go better for you if you cooperated with them."

"No. You're safe here. Everyone thinks you're my fiancé."

He shook his head. "There are too many holes in that story. It's only a matter of time before it falls apart. Your cousin could return anyday."

"Derek's not due back until next month. And I'm sure if I explained everything to him, I could make him understand."

"What about when John Becker comes back from his trip? Once the police talk to him they'll realize he wasn't the person you took in from the storm. They'll know you really had seen me."

"Then I'll say that I lied, that I made up the whole story. Savard thought I was batty anyway, so—"

"No, I can't let you do that."

"You can't *let* me? Remy, let's get something straight right now. I make my own decisions. You can't force me to go now any more than you could force me to stay before."

"Then I'll leave."

"Like hell you will," she said. She grabbed his shirt and lifted herself on her toes to glare at him. "We're in this together now. That's what you said, remember?"

"Dana—"

"You're an innocent man, and neither one of us is leaving until we find a way to prove it."

He tipped back his head and exhaled slowly. "Damn, it's been a long time."

"What do you mean? It's only been a few hours."

"Not that, Dana. I meant since anyone had faith in me. I can't remember the last time." He paused, returning his gaze to her face. "No, I do remember. Your uncle believed in me."

"My uncle? Derek's father?"

"Axel Johansen. Despite my record, he hired me to help build this resort. Fifteen years ago he gave me my start."

"That's…"

"Ironic?" he asked. "That I repay his faith in me by using his resort and his niece?"

"No, it's not ironic at all. It's like…fate."

Do you believe in fate, Dana? He'd asked her that once, when he'd been John Becker. The more entwined their lives became, the more she was beginning to believe. She swayed into him, her grip on her sheet loosening. How could she have doubted Remy's innocence for one moment?

"But it's not fair to involve you any further," he persisted. "You came to the cabin to work. You have obligations of your own."

He was speaking the truth, but she didn't want to hear it. She didn't want to think about how precarious their budding relationship was, or how little time they might have left. And she knew just the way to drown those thoughts out. She rubbed her nose against the hollow at the base of his throat and reached for his buttons.

A tremor went through his frame. "Dana…"

"I can think of a better way to spend the morning besides arguing." She pushed his shirt apart and kissed his chest.

"Damn it, Dana," he murmured. "I'm trying to do what's best for you."

She stepped back, smiled and let go of the sheet altogether.

He looked down, his breath hissing out between his teeth. He skimmed the heels of his hands over her hips to her breasts and up to her shoulders until he cradled her face in his palms. Holding her steady, he covered her mouth with his.

Oh, yes, this was better than arguing. Or thinking. She wrapped her arms around his neck and smiled into his kiss as he carried her back to the bed.

Dana emptied the last of the herbal tea from the pot into her cup. The camomile was supposed to be calming, but it wasn't very effective. Considering the level of tension she felt, it might as well have been espresso.

This morning's respite from reality in her bedroom had been only temporary. She should have known distractions didn't work. When a book was giving her trouble, it never magically got better if she vacuumed the floor or shoveled the walk or fixed another pot of tea. Granted, sex with Remy was in another league of distractions altogether, but it had only postponed the problem.

All too soon she and Remy had turned their attention back to the matter that had brought him to her in the first place. For five hours straight, they had been poring over the material he'd gathered during their trips to Hainesborough. The kitchen table was covered with notes and scraps of paper, but it didn't matter how many times they looked or sorted or organized, nothing helpful appeared.

She had told Remy that neither of them were leaving until they had proved his innocence. Unless a miracle happened, her brave words would prove to be nothing but bravado.

"Are you sure you don't want any of this?" she asked, carrying her cup to the table.

Remy glanced up as she took the chair across from him. "No, thanks."

"It's no trouble. I can make a fresh pot."

He stretched his arms over his head, arching his back until it cracked. "Dana, I have a confession to make."

"What?"

"I think that herbal stuff tastes like hay."

She sputtered. "I thought you liked it."

"Sorry."

"It might help get rid of your tension."

"Is it working for you?"

"Well, not as much as it usually does." She set the mug down and sighed. "Maybe I should try warm milk. It works for Morty."

"Used to work for Chantal, too."

"Really?"

Lacing his hands together behind his neck, he tipped back his chair. "Only if I put it in her cup with the bunnies on it."

"That's sweet."

"Sweet? I've had to tear the house apart looking for that cup more than once. She liked to share it with her dolls. One time she'd had a picnic in the backyard and her bunny cup had rolled under the forsythia bush. I was out there crawling around with a flashlight until after midnight..." He paused, then brought his chair back down with a bang. "There's no point talking about this."

"No, please go on," she said quickly. "I love hearing

you talk about Chantal. What does she like besides her bunny cup?''

He thumbed through a stack of receipts from his office that he had already gone through at least a dozen times. He fingered the thin pile of doctor's notes. ''Tobogganing,'' he said finally. ''The Mortimer Books. Pyjamas with feet. Strawberry ice cream.''

Dana propped her chin on her hands as she listened to him talk. Once again she heard more in his tone than in his words. This was a man who had a great capacity for love. That alone was amazing when she considered how bleak his upbringing and his marriage had been. Add to that the hell he'd been living and it was a wonder that he hadn't turned bitter.

What would it be like to be loved by a man like that? She already knew he was a wonderful lover—the combination of passion and tenderness he had shown her had made her entire body hum with pleasure. But that was just her body. What about her heart? How would it feel to hear the words from his lips and see the promises in his eyes?

She gritted her teeth to keep her chin from trembling. He'd already warned her he wouldn't be giving her any promises, and she had accepted that. There were no guarantees that he'd even be able to give her one more night.

''She was excited about starting kindergarten in the fall,'' Remy said. ''She used to ask me to walk her to the school in the evenings so she could see where she'd be going.''

Despite the poignancy of what he was telling her, there was no self-pity in his tone. Dana marveled at his strength. How could she be worried about her own feelings when Remy was the one whose life had been stolen? She wanted to comfort him, but they both knew any assurances she made would be hollow. Wordlessly she reached across the table to cover his hand with hers.

He turned his hand palm up and squeezed her fingers.

"She won't have such a long walk now," he said. "The school is closer to the Haineses' house than it was to ours."

"Who would be taking her to school?"

"Her grandmother."

Dana thought about the woman she had glimpsed at the park. "I'm sure your mother-in-law dotes on her."

"She does. She saw more of Chantal than Sylvia did."

"How's that?"

"That was another source of arguments between us. I never liked how often Sylvia used to get her mother to baby-sit Chantal so she could go out during the day. If I'd known that she was neglecting our daughter so she could meet her lover…" He paused. "Damn, she was a real piece of work."

Dana agreed. The more she learned about Sylvia, the more she detested her. "Do you think Marjory Haines knew what her daughter was up to?"

"It's possible. Sylvia was always really close to her mother."

"Wouldn't she have tried to intervene?"

"I doubt it. The Haineses didn't approve of me. If Marjory knew about Sylvia's affair, she would have found some way to justify it. Sylvia could do no wrong in her parents' eyes. They always found excuses. They probably meant well, but their continuous indulgence might have led to her turning out the way she did. Who knows."

Dana rubbed her thumb along his. "Are you worried about the same thing happening to Chantal if she's raised by Sylvia's parents?"

"At times. I have to remind myself that she's a different person from her mother."

"She probably inherited a lot of traits from you."

He snorted. "God help her if she did."

"Seriously, Remy. You're a terrific father. I can see it in your face when you talk about your daughter, and I hear it in the tone of your voice. I might not have any children of my own, but I've had plenty of opportunities to watch other parents. You'd be surprised what I learn about families when I do one of my readings.''

"If it's anything like what happened at the post office, I wouldn't be surprised at all. That woman would have talked your ear off.''

"People who are familiar with my books don't act like strangers. They tend to think they know me.''

"In a way they do, Dana. Your personality shines right through your words and your drawings.''

She leaned forward, struck by a sudden idea. She grabbed his knee. "Remy, you said there's a possibility that Marjory Haines knows who Sylvia's lover was, right?''

"Sure, but that wouldn't do us any good. Even if I wanted to risk getting thrown back in prison to ask her, she wouldn't tell me.''

"No, but she might let it slip to someone else.''

"Like who?''

"Like D. J. Whittington, her granddaughter's favorite author.''

He went still. "And how would that happen?''

"If I struck up a friendship with her, I could nose around a bit and—''

"Dana, no. You can't involve yourself any further.''

"Why not? Think of the opportunity here. I often do readings from the Mortimer books at schools. The kids and the teachers love them. I could arrange to do one at Chantal's, and I'll make sure to meet her grandmother afterward when she comes to pick her up.''

He frowned. "Even if you did meet her, that doesn't mean you'll be able to learn anything.''

"It doesn't mean I won't. If Chantal is as big a fan of my books as you say, the Haines would be happy to have me visit them. I realize I can't come right out and ask directly who Sylvia was messing around with, but there might be clues in their house or…'' She drew in her breath. "Or maybe Chantal knows,'' she said.

"The only way she would know would be if she saw them together."

Dana nodded.

"Even Sylvia wouldn't have done anything that despicable," he muttered.

"There's one way to find out."

"It's a long shot."

"I know, but we've tried everything else." She squeezed his leg. "And even if I don't learn anything useful, I'll be able to meet your daughter and tell you how she's doing. That alone makes this idea worth trying, doesn't it?"

Dana's steps echoed down the corridor, stirring up the scent of linoleum tile, winter boots and chalk. Long bulletin boards full of construction paper masterpieces lined the walls. Banks of fluorescent lights buzzed softly overhead. The classrooms she passed were empty, but she could hear the lilt of children's voices coming from a doorway at the end of the hall.

"We're a small school, so we've assembled the students from kindergarten to grade six in the library, Miss Whittington. They're sitting on the carpet, but of course, we've given you a chair."

Dana smiled at the woman who walked beside her. Mrs. Hogan, the principal of Hainesborough Public School, was a pleasant, apple-shaped woman in her fifties. She had been virtually gushing with gratitude since Dana had contacted her yesterday, and had been only too eager to arrange an appearance for the local celebrity. "That sounds perfect, but please, call me Dana."

"And I'm Betty." She gestured toward the source of the noise. "As you can hear, everyone is thrilled you could work us into your schedule."

"It's my pleasure, Betty, and I do apologize for the short notice. I usually line these appearances up a few weeks in advance, but I met a woman at the post office the other day who gave me the idea, so I thought, 'why not?'"

"Oh, yes, that must have been Mrs. Shaunessy," she said with a laugh. "I heard little Jared brought your autograph for show and tell. It created quite a stir."

"I'm flattered."

"It's what you deserve, Dana. In these days of video games and MTV, your books are a refreshing return to real family values. You're the kind of role model the children need."

A role model? Dana thought with a twinge of guilt. Would the school principal say that if she knew Dana was willingly aiding and abetting a fugitive? Would she still be enthusiastic if she knew this entire event was being staged for the purpose of gathering information?

The people at this school were all so nice, Dana felt uneasy about using them this way. If this was what Remy felt when he had been using her, was it any wonder why his gaze had often looked haunted?

Betty Hogan beamed as she paused at the doorway. "Ready?" she asked.

Dana nodded.

The principal strode into the library and clapped her hands for silence. The children who were grouped in a loose semicircle jostled shoulders as they looked up expectantly.

"Boys and girls," she said, her tone immediately taking on the patented briskness that all school principals seemed to master as part of their job. "This afternoon we have a special visitor."

Dana forced herself to relax as she listened to the introduction. It was the same as countless other times, in other schools and libraries and bookstores. This was the real payoff of her profession, meeting the children she wrote the stories for. This was how she filled the emptiness that her own lack of children had left in her life.

Only, this time it was different. She wasn't thinking of the dozens of little faces that turned toward her. She was thinking of one particular girl with a fondness for cups with bunnies on them. She had never seen a photograph of Remy's daughter, so she wasn't sure whether she would be able to pick her out of the crowd, but there were many ways to discover which child she was. She could play a name game, or stage a draw for her books and make sure Chantal won. And after that...

The doubts she had tried to push to the back of her mind surged forward. What was she doing? This was her career, the most important thing in her life, and she was using it for what both she and Remy admitted was a long shot. Oh, God. She wasn't a detective, she was a writer. What made her think she could interrogate a murder victim's mother? She must be nuts, finally cracked up from the stress of her deadline and all the distractions that had been going on lately and—

Her gaze was snagged by a girl in the middle of the front row. Like the other children, she was sitting cross-legged, fidgeting restlessly as she waited for the story to start. She had black hair, but it wasn't as deep a black as Remy's— there were streaks of chestnut, almost auburn in it. Her features were delicate but weren't really distinctive. Her small nose, her tilted chin and rounded cheeks carried no more than a suggestion of the face she would have as an adult. There was nothing Dana could put her finger on to have attracted her notice.

But then the girl smiled, and Dana couldn't breathe. It was Remy's smile, or rather it was how Remy's smile must have looked before the world had taught him to hide it.

"Miss Whittington?"

With a start, Dana glanced at the principal. Everyone was waiting for her to be D. J. Whittington, to entertain them with the exploits of Mortimer Q. Morganbrood. Yet all she could think of was the dark-haired girl with the beautiful smile.

Her heart pounding, Dana sat in the chair that had been placed at the front of the library. Her usual routine would be to talk about Mortimer, chat with the children a while and then open up her latest book and read through the story.

This time she was going to take a different approach. "Who knows what a pirate is?" she asked.

A dozen hands shot up. "They wear black patches over their eyes," said a boy with two missing front teeth. "And they have swords."

"They have big ships," someone else said.

"Yeah, and treasure."

"They're bad. They make you walk the plank and sharks'll eat you."

The last comment had come from a chubby blond girl in a striped sweater. Instead of contradicting her, Dana nodded. "Some pirates are pretty scary, all right," she said. "But sometimes they have a good reason for the things they do. Let me tell you about the pirate mice that Mortimer meets."

And so, instead of talking about a book the children might have already read, Dana spoke about the book she had yet to finish. The plot had taken so many unexpected twists, she wasn't sure herself how it was going to end, but it seemed the most appropriate story to choose.

While she made sure to pay attention to as many children as she could, her awareness kept returning to the dark-haired girl at the front. She was no longer smiling. Her expression had taken on a touching seriousness as she listened to the story.

If this was Chantal, would she realize how the tale of the misunderstood mice paralleled Remy's story? Was she wishing that she could turn to her friends, especially that chubby blond girl in the stripes, and say, "See? I knew it all along. My father isn't really bad."

The girl's gaze met Dana's, and the dark-brown depths glistened with a hint of sadness that no child that age should know.

Once again Dana had trouble drawing a breath. Logically, she couldn't be sure who this was, but her instincts were becoming more certain by the minute. Her heart knew, and lately she was learning to listen to her heart. What else could explain this growing desire she felt to scoop the child into her arms and promise her everything was going to be all right? She wanted to tell her what a fine man her father was, and how he was strong and smart and decent, no matter what anyone else might say. She wanted to assure Remy's daughter that she loved him and would do everything in her power to help him.

Whoa. Wait a minute. She loved him? Dana cleared her throat and reached for the glass of water the principal had placed near her chair. She was in front of a roomful of strange children. This was hardly the time or the place to have a revelation like that, was it? She was just getting used to the idea of believing in Remy. It was too soon to start considering the idea of love, wasn't it?

But would there ever be a right time?

Would there be any time at all?

She chugged down the water and picked up some of the working illustrations she had brought with her to show the children. "This is the boat Mortimer builds to chase after the pirate mice," she said, holding it up to make sure everyone saw it. "And here's the leader of the mice."

The dark-haired girl took one look at the dashing, mustachioed mouse and broke into a grin. "What's his name?" she asked.

"John," Dana decided. "His name's going to be John."

Remy was gripping the steering wheel so hard his fingers had gone numb. This was the riskiest thing he'd done since he'd made the decision to go over the fence in the exercise yard. He was courting disaster. A man alone in a truck, parked near a school, could appear suspicious, no matter who he was, and he couldn't afford to draw unwelcome attention.

Yet he hadn't considered letting Dana drive into town by herself today. It wasn't entirely an issue of trust that had brought him with her. Most of it was need. If things didn't work out the way he hoped—and at this point, it didn't look as if they would—this might be his last opportunity to see his child.

His heart turned over as the door to the school pushed open. A trio of boys burst out and ran across the school yard, racing each other as they skidded across a patch of ice. A pair of minivans left the parking lot, blocking Remy's view of the door for a moment. What if she hadn't been at school today? What if she had caught a cold that evening at the park, or if her ear infection had flared up again?

A woman with a scarf around her head walked briskly past the truck toward the school. Remy didn't need to see her face to recognize her. There was no mistaking that rigid posture, or the way her nose angled into the air. He'd seen her back view often enough when she'd been walking away from him. It was his mother-in-law, Marjory Haines.

Normally the sight of his mother-in-law wouldn't make him smile. It did this time, since it meant Chantal must be here after all.

The double doors pushed open again. He saw a flash of red—Dana's parka. She was being ushered outside by a group of children who were hanging on to her hands. Several clutched what appeared to be rolled sheets of paper, probably some of Dana's sketches. She had said she was going to give some away, and she obviously had.

The activity around the doors took on a slow-motion intensity as Remy's gaze zeroed in on one of the children. She had a new coat, a pink one. Her hat was on crooked, her mittens had come off and were hanging by their strings, but she wore a wide grin as she clutched one of Dana's sketches. She started toward Marjory, then spun around and ran back to say something to Dana.

For a moment Dana looked startled. Then she leaned over and pulled the child into a firm hug.

Remy's throat swelled. He had known Chantal would be

happy to meet Mortimer's creator. He hadn't counted on how seeing them together would hit him like a fist in the gut. Dana pressed her cheek against Chantal's, her gaze darting toward the truck, and Remy knew the gesture had been for him.

He wished he could freeze the moment. He wished he could wrap them both in his arms and take them far, far away...

A cramp knifed through his rigid fingers. He whispered a curse and reminded himself once more of the reason Dana had come up with this plan. She was supposed to ingratiate herself with Sylvia's mother, but it looked as if Marjory wasn't cooperating. Moments later Marjory straightened Chantal's hat, put her mittens on and took her hand to lead her away.

Remy held his breath as they walked by. They were so close, he could hear his daughter's voice as she chattered about the new Mortimer story. But they were walking too quickly. Time had sped up once more. These few stolen glimpses couldn't possibly be enough. What would happen if he turned his head, if he opened the door...

The passenger door swung open with a burst of cold air. Remy tensed, then exhaled harshly when he saw it was Dana. To his surprise she was smiling.

"Chantal is just as wonderful as you've always told me," she said, slamming the door and clicking on her seat belt. "I knew who she was, even before I heard the teacher call her name. She's so much like you, Remy."

He looked in the rearview mirror, watching his daughter until she was out of sight. There was so much he wanted to say, to know, but where could he start? "Is she okay, Dana?" he asked finally.

"She's fine. She liked the new story."

"I thought she would." He had to swallow hard before he could continue. "You hugged her."

"I couldn't help it. She looked like she needed one."

"The kids all seemed to like you."

"I like them. It's the best part of my job."

"Is that why you looked so pleased?"

"It's more than that. She told me something just before she left." She pried his hand off the steering wheel and chafed his fingers between hers. "Remy, Chantal said she wants to write a book when she grows up, just like her mother."

"Her mother? Sylvia never wrote anything. She didn't even like to read."

"Chantal said she wrote a book. She wanted to show it to me."

"Why would she say that? It doesn't make sense."

"Chantal doesn't strike me as the type of child who would make something like that up."

"No, she isn't." Remy frowned.

"Whatever it was, Sylvia's mother changed the subject fast. She left before I could ask anything more about it."

"She did seem to be in a hurry."

Dana tugged on his hand until he turned to look at her. "There's one kind of book that Chantal might have seen her mother write in." She paused. "Remy, is it possible that Sylvia kept a diary?"

Chapter 13

"A diary," Remy muttered, pacing across the lobby floor.

"It's possible, though, isn't it?" Dana asked. She closed the main door of the lodge and toed off her boots before she followed him. "Do you think Sylvia was the type to keep a diary?"

Remy stopped by the front desk, snatched off his hat and jammed it into his jacket pocket. "I never saw one."

"From what I've learned about your late wife, she enjoyed secrets."

"Yeah. Sneaking around gave her a thrill."

"I suspect she kept many things secret from you," Dana said carefully.

"You're right." He raked both hands through his hair distractedly. "A lover, a pregnancy, an abortion. What's a diary compared to that?"

"I'm sorry if it hurts you, Remy, but we have to consider the possibility. It could be the break we need."

He scowled. "If she kept a diary, if she wrote down the

name of her lover, if she recorded something that could implicate him in her murder, and if we can get our hands on it, sure, it would be great.''

She checked the answering machine behind the desk, saw that there were no new messages, then stopped in front of Remy. She eyed his rumpled hair and reached to smooth it down. ''Where do you think it would be?''

''If it had been in our house, it would have burned up in the fire.''

''I think it must still be around. Otherwise, why would Chantal know about it, and why would your mother-in-law be in such a hurry to change the subject?''

He caught her hand and brought it to his lips, pressing an absentminded kiss to her knuckles. ''Good point.''

Encouraged, Dana continued with her line of reasoning. ''If you were right about Sylvia's mother knowing about her affair and wanting to cover it up, then she'd be doing the same thing with the diary, wouldn't she? She wouldn't have been able to bring herself to destroy it because it was her daughter's, but she wouldn't want to let anyone see it, either.'' She paused to think. ''Oh, but then how would Chantal know about it?''

''Chantal's an active, curious five-year-old. She has some kind of built-in radar when it comes to the birthday and Christmas presents I would stash around the house. If her grandmother had tried to hide something, Chantal would have found it.''

''Then she might be able to get it for us. We could give it to the police and—''

''I'd sooner break into the Haines house and look for it myself.''

''Remy, no! That's way too risky.''

''It was bad enough involving you. I don't want to involve my daughter.''

''I can be subtle about asking for it. Or now that I've met Marjory Haines, I can invite myself to her house and try to distract her so I can snoop around—''

"Dana, for God's sake, this isn't one of your stories." He tightened his grip on her fingers, squeezing almost to the point of pain. "Don't you realize what you're risking? If you're caught in the act of helping me, there's no way the police will believe you were forced. You could go to jail."

"It worked out okay this afternoon."

"You were lucky."

"We were both lucky. I'm surprised no one reported you lurking around the school yard. You shouldn't have insisted on coming with me."

"I had to come."

"Well, I have to help you."

"The door's still unlocked. You can walk away anytime."

"What's the matter with you?" she cried. "I told you I'm not leaving. Why can't you believe that?"

He dropped her hand. "It's not a matter of belief."

"Sure it is. You want me to trust you, but you don't want to trust me. You don't want to trust anyone. Not really, not deep down inside where it matters."

He didn't respond. Silence fell between them, heavy with the echo of Dana's words. She wanted to call them back. She wasn't being fair. He had already demonstrated his trust by giving her the keys. What more did she want?

She wanted the impossible. She wanted his heart. She wanted him to love her the way she loved him.

There it was again. Love. For the second time today, the word just popped into her head from nowhere. First in a classroom, now in the cavernous entrance of a deserted lodge. Not exactly the romantic moment she might have dreamed of, was it?

Okay, so she was in love with Remy. Definitely, thoroughly, hopelessly in love. There. Now what? A dramatic declaration? A tender moment of sharing?

Oh, damn. He was right. This wasn't one of her stories, and there was no guarantee of a happy ending. Blinking hard, she spun around and headed for the stairs to continue her rounds of the lodge. She had just checked the bathroom in Derek's top-floor suite when she heard Remy approach.

"Dana, I'm sorry," he said. He stood in the bedroom doorway, his gaze steady on hers.

She waved her hand. "It's okay. I'm just…stressed. I shouldn't have brought it up."

"I do trust you."

She knew he was talking about matters of the law, not of love. "Sure. I know."

"I appreciate your help."

"Right."

"I don't want to argue."

She started to brush past him to get to Derek's living room. "We're not arguing."

"You're angry with me," he said, snagging her arm before she could go by.

"No, I'm angry with myself."

"Why?"

Why? Because she had gone ahead and done something as stupid and hopeless as falling in love with a wanted criminal. "I should have tried harder to get information out of your mother-in-law," she said, seizing on an excuse. "That would have made things simpler."

He leaned back against the door frame and pulled her into his arms. "Dana, there is nothing simple about this entire situation."

She sighed. "You've got that right."

"Except for one thing."

"What?"

He dipped his head, pushed aside her sweater with his nose and lightly bit the base of her neck.

She trembled at the reaction that pulsed through her veins. "Remy…"

He pressed a line of hot, moist kisses up her throat.

"We should finish checking the lodge."

"We will." He nibbled teasingly on her earlobe. "Later."

She turned her head, breaking the contact. "Remy, we can't do this here," she said breathlessly.

He braced his legs and leaned back against the door frame, lifting her from the floor. "Why not? I thought about it, Dana. When I was staying here, I imagined how it would be."

"Uh…" She shuddered as their lower bodies fit together. "Oh!"

"Too fast?"

"It's always fast," she said.

"Not always." He cupped her bottom and slowly rotated his hips. "We can take it easy if you want."

"That's not what I meant."

"Then what did you mean, Dana?"

"Not you, me." She clutched his shoulders. "Whenever you touch me, I…it happens so easily." Her breath hitched as heat flooded her thighs.

"Are you complaining?"

"No."

"Good. Neither am I."

"But this is Derek's place. We shouldn't…"

"We shouldn't use his bed? I already have. It's firm, Dana." He moved his hips again. "And it's big."

She didn't know why she was objecting. Over the past two days they had tried out just about every other location in the resort.

"But we don't need a bed," he murmured, his thoughts paralleling hers. He lifted her higher so he could nuzzle her throat. "There are plenty of walls."

She couldn't understand it. She had been stressed out when they had arrived here, they had been talking about his case, they had been practically quarreling. Yet she wanted this, she wanted him. Too much. Too easily.

Because she was in love.

He wasn't offering love, he was offering sex. But if that's

all she could get, she was shameless enough to take it. She moved her hands from his shoulders to his head, guiding his lips to hers. Deliberately she shut out everything else and lost herself in his kiss.

She didn't care how fast it was, or how...carnal. With one purpose in mind, they opened zippers and fumbled aside clothing. Groping, sliding, clutching, she wrapped her legs around his waist. He spun around and pressed her back to the wall. As the familiar waves began to build, nothing else seemed to matter. She closed her eyes and let the passion take her.

Remy dug his fingers into the soft flesh of Dana's buttocks, unwilling to let her go even after the spasms that had shaken her had faded. He could feel her skin cooling, and he knew she couldn't be comfortable, but he didn't want to end this yet.

Sex with Dana was...spectacular. Explosive. More satisfying each time.

And each time, he felt more like the selfish person he was. She had been right. He didn't want to trust her. He had no problem using her body, but he could see that she wanted more. She deserved more. But he couldn't give it to her.

She sighed against his neck, her breath puffing warmly over his skin.

Remy felt his body stir once again. And judging by the little wriggle of Dana's hips, she had noticed it, too. He felt her lips stretch into a smile.

Summoning every fragment of his control, he lifted her off him and set her on her feet.

She staggered briefly, grabbing his forearms for balance. Her eyebrows rose in a silent question.

Remy kissed her nose, zipped up his jeans and stepped back. "Hold that thought," he murmured.

"What?"

"Don't move. I'll be right back."

She bent down to retrieve her pants, a hint of a blush staining her cheeks. "It's okay. We should—"

"Trust me, Dana," he said. "You're going to like this." He strode to Derek's closet and slid open the door. Moments later, he had found what he wanted. He returned to Dana and held out his hand.

She looked at him curiously. "Those are my cousin's ties."

"Yeah. Silk, right?"

Her blush suddenly deepened. "Uh, yes."

He trailed the end of one of the ties over her hand, then draped it around her neck. "Remember what I said I could do with these ties?"

"I remember."

He glanced behind him. "The bed isn't a four-poster like yours, but that brass headboard would work just as well."

Her eyes darkened. She moistened her lips. "Are you saying you want to tie me up?"

He shook his head, sliding the silk from her neck. He turned her hand over and placed the ties in her palm. "Not you, me."

"What?"

"They're for you to use however you want."

"You expect me…to…" She swallowed.

"As slow as you like, as often as you like. I'm leaving it up to you, Dana."

She focused on the strips of raw silk she held, and understanding finally dawned on her face. He was offering himself to her. He was giving her control. He was trusting her.

All right, he knew it wasn't the kind of trust she had meant. It was just sex, but it was all he was prepared to offer.

Her gaze moved from the ties to the bed, a shy smile curving her lips. She drew the fabric through her fingers. "Do I get to use lotion?"

His body hummed with anticipation. "If you want."

A mock frown tilted her eyebrows. "It might stain the ties."

"There are plenty more."

"Mmm."

"We could go back to the cabin if you're not all right about using your cousin's bed."

"Oh, I think this bed will be fine," she said, taking his hand. "I like things firm. And big." She looped one tie around his wrist and fastened a loose knot.

He had a moment of uneasiness when he felt the restraint. It was too close to the sensation of handcuffs. But then he concentrated on Dana's smile and forced the memory back.

Dana coiled the silk ties into two neat little spirals and set them on the night table. Just the sight of them made her hands unsteady, but she wasn't planning on returning them to Derek's closet. She'd buy her cousin some new ones, just like she'd buy him some new sheets, although she wasn't sure how she would explain either purchase.

Swinging her legs over the side of the bed, she sat on the edge of the mattress and hid her face in her hands. What had come over her last night? She couldn't believe she had accepted Remy's invitation so readily. She'd never done anything like that in her life. To her family and friends, she was divorced, solitary Dana Whittington. To her fans, she was respectable, successful D. J. Whittington. Neither one was the kind of woman who would tie a man to a bed and have her way with him.

But that's exactly what she had done.

And it had felt good. Oh, so good.

She inhaled shakily. She could still detect Remy's scent on her skin. She could still see how he had looked, with his arms stretched over his head, his muscles flexed and his eyes gleaming with desire as she had moved over him.

No, she had never experienced anything that came close. It wasn't just the silk that had bound his hands to the brass scrolls of the headboard. It wasn't just the fancy bedroom in this eagle's nest of an apartment. The lovemaking had been so intense because she really had been making *love*.

She knew what it had cost him to relinquish control. She had seen the shadows in his eyes when he had felt the silk close around his wrist. He'd done it for her, and she loved him all the more for it.

The mattress dipped as Remy rolled toward her. He rubbed his chin over her thigh, then slipped his arm around her waist and kissed her hip.

The warmth of his breath made her shudder with an echo of memory from the night before.

"Leaving already?" he asked.

"It's almost dawn," she mumbled through her fingers. "We should get back to the cabin."

"I fed Morty and built up the fire before we left to check the lodge. That would have kept him comfortable for the night. He'll be okay for a few more minutes."

Of course Remy would have provided for her cat, she thought. He might be a virile, inventive lover, but he was also kind to children and small animals. The combination was downright deadly. How could any woman keep her heart safe from a man like that?

He sat up behind her, pulling her back into the vee of his legs. "Dana?"

"Mmm?"

"Don't be embarrassed."

"I'm not. Exactly."

He tugged her hands away from her face and held them in his as he crossed his arms in front of her. "It was good, wasn't it?"

"Mmm-hmm. Each and every time."

His chuckle was deep, and from any other man would have sounded smug, but from Remy it sounded appealing enough to send more echoes through her awakening body. "That reminds me," he said. "We shouldn't keep relying on your timing. The rhythm method isn't all that reliable.

Starting tonight, we're going to have to dig into your cousin's supply of condoms.''

"His supply?"

"I checked out the drawers of those night tables when I was here before. There's enough boxes to outfit—"

"No. Spare me the details," she said quickly. She didn't really want to think about Derek's love life any more than she would want to explain hers to him.

But then she realized the rest of what Remy had said. He assumed she was relying on the rhythm method to avoid pregnancy. That's what she'd let him believe. When the subject had first come up, she hadn't wanted to explain why she wasn't concerned about contraception.

She could let this go. What harm would it do? She could dodge the issue...

No, she'd been doing far too much of that lately, dodging issues. After what they had done together last night, after what he had allowed her to do to him, didn't she owe him the whole truth? He wasn't like Hank.

Was that why she had told him everything else but had held this back? Had she been worried Remy would reject her the way her husband had? Oh, she was a fine one to talk about trust. "Remy, we're not going to need any birth control.''

"Lean back a second and I'll show you why you're wrong.''

The way he was sitting, with his legs on either side of her, she could feel exactly what he meant. She twisted in his arms to face him. "I should have explained earlier, but when you touch me, I get...distracted.''

"Dana?''

"Don't worry, I won't get pregnant.''

"Unless you're using something, we—''

"You don't understand," she said. "I *can't* get pregnant. Ever.''

"What?''

"There were complications after my miscarriage. I...''

She cleared her throat. "I'm what they call barren. Unable to conceive or bear children. Do you understand now?"

He was silent for a while. "I'm sorry, Dana," he said. "I hadn't known."

"That's because I hadn't told you. Like I said before, I don't dwell on it. It doesn't make any difference."

"The hell it doesn't. You could have told me."

"Why?"

"It's important. It's the real reason your marriage broke up, isn't it? It wasn't just the miscarriage."

"That's right. Hank wanted someone who could give him children. When he learned I couldn't, he wanted his freedom to find someone who could. I couldn't really blame him."

"He was an idiot."

She sniffed. "Morty never liked him."

"This is why you got so upset when you learned about Sylvia's abortion. That night at the doctor's office, I should have realized there was more to it."

"It didn't matter. You had your own pain to deal with."

He regarded her for another minute. "That's why your work is so important to you."

"It's all I have left, Remy. After I learned I wouldn't have a child of my own, I knew I had to fill my life some other way. Through my work, I can reach thousands of children."

"You're a natural with kids. I could tell that when I saw you outside the school yesterday with those children hanging on to your hands, and I can see it in the way your eyes light up when you talk about your work." He paused. "And I threatened to ruin your reputation. Damn it, if I had known just how much your career meant—"

"You did what you had to do," she said immediately. "I already told you, your threats wouldn't have stopped me if I'd really wanted to get away."

Emotions chased across his face. "Now I know why you always wanted to hear about Chantal."

Did he? Did he think about this, too? Dana had no husband or child; Remy had a child but no wife. Somehow they fit together too well for it to be coincidence.

Remy and Chantal, two people so much in need of love, with so much love inside them to give, *And I want to be the one to love them,* Dana thought.

Yes. She could see herself loving them both. She already loved one of them, and it would be oh, so easy to love the other. She had felt the delicate warmth in Remy's daughter's embrace, and she'd seen the loneliness in her eyes. If she had a child like Chantal…

The thought that had been buried in the depths of her subconscious, that was so precious she hadn't dared admit it was there, finally unfurled. It had taken root the first time she had seen the love on Remy's face when he'd spoken of his daughter. The dreams she'd set aside two years ago when she'd heard the doctor's verdict weren't completely dead after all. She would never carry and bear a baby of her own, but what if there was a chance she could be a mother to a child like Chantal?

Oh, God, yes. If Chantal were hers, she would paper the girl's room with pictures of lovable cats and swashbuckling mice, she would buy her a dozen bunny cups, she would be there every single day to tend all the scrapes and kiss all the bruises and make sure she wore her hat when she went out in the snow.

And if she had a husband like Remy, she would stand proudly by his side and defend him to the world. And each night in their bed she would show him her love and chase away the last of those haunted shadows in his eyes.

Brave thoughts. Easy thoughts. Especially when she was sheltered in his arms. But she couldn't stay here forever any more than he could. Sooner or later, reality was going to catch up to them, and then…

And then what?

She rubbed her temple against his cheek, feeling her hair catch in the stubble of his morning beard. It was an intimate sensation, the kind of thing married people would share. She imagined catching her hair in his beard every morning as they lingered in their bed and listened for the sound of their daughter's footsteps in the hall.

She hiccuped, and a tear welled from her eye to splash onto his shoulder. She licked it away, tasting salt and the musky tang of his skin. "Remy, why don't we ever talk about afterward?"

"Afterward? What do you mean?"

"After we find the evidence you need, after you prove your innocence, after you're reunited with Chantal, what then?"

"There's no point talking about it." His voice cooled. "It might not happen."

"But what if it does?" she persisted recklessly. "Have you given any thought to what you'll do?"

"My priority is getting my freedom back. I'll worry about what to do with it once I've got it."

"You must have thought about it." She leaned back in his arms to see his face. "Are you going to try to rebuild your business?"

"There's no point. It's been gutted. I'll have to start again from scratch."

"What about your home? Have you thought about where you'll live? Would you stay in Hainesborough?"

"No. There's nothing left for me there."

"There's lots of opportunity to start a construction business in Toronto. They're always building things."

"You live in Toronto."

Could he hear her heart beating? Could he see the pulse in her neck and the love in her eyes? "There are plenty of nice neighborhoods for children there, too."

"So I've heard." He ran his fingertip under her eyes, his gaze on the tears he caught. His throat worked as he swallowed.

"Chantal is a wonderful child."

"Yes."

"I thought she was wonderful."

"So you said."

"I'm sure we could get along."

He rubbed his thumb against his fingertip. He didn't reply.

Dana hesitated. He was an intelligent man. He had to know what she was hinting at. Why was he ignoring what she was trying to say?

He dropped his hand to his lap. "Dana, why did you wait until now to tell me you couldn't have children?"

She inhaled sharply, the question taking her off-guard. "What?"

"When I was John Becker, you encouraged me to talk about my daughter."

"Of course, I liked to hear you talk about Chantal."

"That's when you first acted friendly toward me. It changed how you felt."

It was true. She had been captivated by the way his features had softened and his voice had rung with pride and love. "Yes, that made a big difference."

"Were you thinking about the neighborhoods in Toronto that would be good for kids then, too?"

"I don't know what you mean."

"Did you see me as a lonely widower, a single father, someone who could give you an instant family?"

That's exactly how she'd seen him, but she hadn't even wanted to admit it to herself until moments ago. "Remy…"

"A relationship only for the sake of a child doesn't work, Dana. I've made that mistake before."

She heard the disappointment in his voice. It was crazy. Unreasonable. He had to know there was more to their relationship than just her desire for a child. Just as there was more to their lovemaking than sex. It seemed as if he were deliberately looking for some reason to mistrust her.

That shouldn't surprise her, should it? They had been through this yesterday when they'd arrived at the lodge and he'd yet again invited her to leave. Another argument, a different slant on the subject, but the basic problem was the same.

You don't want to trust anyone, she had said. *Not really, not deep down inside where it matters.*

The dream that had seemed so near, so bright, curled into itself and began to wither. Far more than his murder conviction was standing between them and the future that she wanted. The problem was more fundamental than she had let herself admit. Because of what Sylvia had put him through, Remy was afraid of opening himself up to the pain of loving again. He'd been running from that emotion as surely as he'd been running from the law.

Even if Remy proved his innocence, even if he got his life and his daughter back, he might never be free of those bars that were still around his heart.

"I've been honest with you, Dana," he said roughly. "I told you I couldn't give you any promises."

"I know."

"I thought you understood."

"I do understand, Remy." A fresh tear slipped down her cheek. "I understand only too well."

"Then why are you doing this now?" he asked. "Can't we enjoy what we have?"

The words were there, waiting to be spoken. Why didn't she clear up his suspicions and tell him the truth, say that she loved him? That she wanted *him?*

And then what? she asked herself again. Once the magic words were spoken, would everything suddenly change? Would she and Remy live happily ever after?

She was an idiot. A besotted, optimistic fool. She had been living in her make-believe world of books too long. Remy was right. This wasn't one of her stories. The only future she could count on was the one that happened from one moment to the next. So why spoil it by longing for more?

She caught his sexy, early-morning-stubbled cheeks in

her hands and kissed him until the familiar passion flared anew.

Then she closed her eyes and made believe she wasn't really crying.

Chapter 14

Remy knew something was wrong the instant he opened his eyes. He stretched his arm to the space beside him. He hadn't heard Dana leave the bed, but the sheets were already cold. How long had he been asleep? How could he have let himself fall asleep?

He jackknifed upright and looked around. Dana's clothes were gone. The bathroom door was open, the light was off. No sound came through the doorway to the rest of the suite. He was alone.

She had never done this before. After they made love, she was the one who usually fell into an exhausted sleep. And he was a light sleeper. She must have taken pains to ensure she got away undetected.

Got away? Was that why he felt uneasy? Had she finally taken his advice and left him?

He raked his hands through his hair and did another survey of the bedroom. There was no trace of her. She had even taken away the ties they had used. After the night they'd had, and the tender way they'd greeted the dawn, could she really have left him without saying goodbye?

He hadn't thought Dana was like that. She wasn't cold enough to simply cut her losses and walk. She had repeatedly said she wouldn't. She had probably gone back to the cabin, that's all. She must have been concerned about her cat.

On the other hand how well did he really know her? Were there other secrets she hadn't seen fit to tell him? Why would she have waited until she had met Chantal to tell him she couldn't bear children?

The suspicions that had taunted him earlier once more slinked into his mind. Dana had wanted to talk about their future. She had wanted a commitment. With her body so warm and soft in his arms, and their lovemaking still scenting the air around them, he'd been so close to giving her the promises she'd wanted…

But then he'd remembered the last time he'd committed his future to a woman. His relationship with Sylvia had been based on sex. He'd married her for the sake of their child. He'd thought that Dana was different, but he couldn't ignore those similarities. What if he was mistaken? Could he afford to be wrong again?

So he had kept silent and had given her no reason to stay. She'd asked for one. That had been as clear as the tears in her eyes, but he hadn't given her the promises she wanted. And now she was gone.

It was probably for the best if she had left him. For her own good, she should have done it days ago.

Remy rolled to his feet and retrieved his clothes, trying to ignore the prickling at the back of his neck. It was already midmorning. He couldn't afford to hang around here in the lodge. He should be making plans for his next move, whether it was to search the Haineses' house or to go after some other source of evidence. This is what happened when he let himself get involved with a woman. He didn't think straight, or at least, he wasn't thinking with his brain.

A sound drifted into the bedroom. It was low, muffled, almost stealthy. It could have been ice groaning on the lake, or a tree creaking in the breeze, or perhaps the distant roar of a snowmobile engine. Or it could be what was making his neck prickle. Remy yanked up his jeans and shrugged into his shirt, moving silently to the doorway.

Heavy, gray-bellied clouds hung low over the horizon. The daylight that filtered through the windows was an eerie shade of yellow. There would be a storm by nightfall. Was that the source of his uneasiness?

His gaze flicked around the main room. When he'd stayed here before, he'd liked the way all the glass gave him a bird's-eye view of the resort. He didn't like it today. It made him feel exposed.

He went to the telescope that was positioned in front of the south window. It was still trained on the caretaker's cabin. He looked through the eyepiece and adjusted the focus. Smoke curled lazily from the chimney, but otherwise, nothing moved. Slowly he swung the telescope toward the lane. Nothing was moving there, either, just the swaying pine boughs. The wind was picking up. A scattering of snowflakes swirled from the roof, blocking his view for a moment. When it cleared, he noticed a dark shape at the bend of the lane.

Someone was walking there. It wasn't Dana. Her coat was red, and this person was wearing dark blue. Remy focused more carefully, but the figure moved off the lane and into the concealment of the trees.

Despite the gray day, Remy felt sweat break out on his forehead. He scanned the grounds again, this time concentrating on the edges of the buildings, the shadows of the trees, places that would provide cover.

There! Someone stood to the left of the woodshed. A pair of men moved into position beside the garage.

Remy's breath hissed out between his teeth. His pulse jumped, his muscles went rigid. This was it. After two weeks of freedom, it was finally happening. They had caught up to him. Was Sibley out there? Was he laughing?

Rage at the unfairness of it all swept over him. He wouldn't go back. Not yet. He wasn't finished. What about Chantal? And what about Dana? He had to warn her. He had to make sure she saved herself before they took him down.

Suddenly he noticed the tire tracks in the snow. A car had been driven out of the garage, and judging by the width of the tracks, it had to have been Dana's subcompact. He pointed the telescope back to the lane. The lines were faint, partly drifted over, so he hadn't seen them the first time, but the tracks continued there, heading for the highway.

He gave a grunt of relief. It looked as if she had left in time after all. That was a stroke of luck.

Or had the timing of Dana's departure been more than luck?

Remy turned away from the telescope and jogged to the door. No, he wouldn't believe it. He snatched his coat from the floor. Just because he hadn't given Dana the assurances she'd wanted, she wouldn't turn him in without giving him the head start he'd asked for. She wasn't like that. She wouldn't betray him.

Then where was she? And why had she chosen this particular morning to leave?

He jammed his feet into his boots and headed for the stairs.

Sneaking off this way wasn't really cowardly, Dana told herself. She was avoiding an argument, that's all. She knew that Remy wouldn't have agreed to her plan, but as she'd once told him, she made her own decisions. He couldn't force her to leave any more than he could force her to stay.

Just as he hadn't forced her to love him.

Oh, great, she thought, slowing down to wipe her sleeve across her eyes. This was no time to get mushy again. She'd better get used to the love thing. From the way her whole heart and soul was committed to it, this love she felt for him was probably going to be around for a while. Whether or not Remy would be around as long was another matter entirely.

The street dissolved into a gray-and-white blur as another round of tears welled up. Dana brought the car to a stop beside the park and took a tissue from her pocket to blot her eyes.

She had to get ahold of herself. Tears wouldn't help anyone. It had been difficult enough to slip out of bed undetected so she could make her phone calls. She didn't want her efforts to be for nothing. Long shot or not, one way or another she was going to find the information Remy needed to prove his innocence.

That's what really mattered here, right? First he had to prove his innocence. And once he had his freedom, if he chose not to continue their relationship, well, that was the definition of freedom, wasn't it? He was free to choose. She wouldn't try to hang on to him if he wanted to go. She didn't want him to feel obligated to her. She loved him enough to want what was best for him.

She wadded up the soaked tissue and stuffed it in her purse. A quick check of her appearance in the rearview mirror made her grimace. She rolled down the window, hoping the cold air would take the puffiness away from her eyes, then smoothed her hair behind her ears and eased back into traffic.

An impatient hiss came from the back seat.

"I'm sorry, Morty," she said. "We're almost there. Only a few more minutes."

He screeched, his claws scraping the wire mesh on the front of his carrier.

"I understand," she said. "No one likes to be caged up. You've been so patient, such a good boy."

Silence. She threw a quick glance over her shoulder. Morty glared balefully at her through the mesh.

She knew that Morty hated to be shut in that carrier. He

didn't mind short trips in the car, but the distance from Half Moon Bay to Hainesborough was at the limit of his patience. She could have left him at the cabin, of course, but he would be more useful if he accompanied her. Dana felt a stab of guilt. She had used the school and that nice Principal Hogan yesterday. Now she was using her cat, and she was planning to use Remy's child.

She tamped down the guilt with a burst of resolve. The deeper involved she became, the more she understood the conflicting feelings Remy must have had. What would she do for the sake of someone she loved? *I would do anything,* she thought, hearing the echo of the words Remy had once said to her. *Whatever it takes.*

The Haines house was easy to spot. It was the largest one on the street. Made of dark, age-mellowed red brick, with old wavy glass in the bay windows and a gabled roof sheathed neatly in slate, it looked as solid and deeply rooted as the huge oak that flanked the front walk. It was stately, imposing, almost intimidating, a testament to generations of wealth and power.

Dana pulled her car to a stop and chewed her lip. It was an impressive house. It was perfectly maintained, from the sparkling windows to the ruthlessly swept walk. But a five-year-old girl lived here. Where were the little footprints that should have crisscrossed the yard? Where was the snow-man? There should have been a snow fort and snowballs and a discarded sled or two. If Chantal were her daughter, there would be whole families of snowmen on her lawn, and a skating rink in the backyard and—

She forced her thoughts away from that direction—she didn't have that many tissues. She twisted to release the catch on Morty's carrier. He sprang out and landed on her shoulder, his claws digging into her coat.

"Okay, okay," she said, stroking his back. "You did great. Now for the hard part."

Marjory Haines answered the door herself. Her expression was distantly polite, as it had been the day before when they had met at the school. But then she saw the cat Dana carried in her arms, and her face broke into a smile. "My goodness," she said. "Could this be…"

"Mortimer!" Hurried footsteps approached across the gleaming hardwood floor of the entrance hall. Seconds later Chantal bumped into her grandmother's side. "That's Mortimer, Grandma!"

Dana hadn't been sure what kind of reception she would get when she had called this morning. The excuse she had given was weak—she had said the drawing Chantal had taken from her at the school yesterday was one she hadn't meant to give away, and she wanted an opportunity to exchange it. Marjory Haines had been too well mannered to refuse, but Dana had wanted to be sure she would be invited in.

Judging by the excitement on Chantal's face over seeing Morty, and Marjory's indulgent smile, it appeared as if the plan was working.

"Behave yourself," she whispered to the cat as they were ushered into the front parlor. The inside of the house was as intimidating as the outside. It smelled of hothouse flowers and furniture polish. Everything was perfectly neat, the oil paintings on the walls aligned, the embroidered cushions on the furniture placed just so.

But where were the toys, the dolls and the skipping ropes? Where was the cup with the bunnies? What about stray socks or hair ribbons or dog-eared picture books?

Had the house been this way when Sylvia was a child? Was that why she had felt the need to seek secret amusements? And would the same thing happen to Chantal if she was raised here?

"Please sit down, Dana," Marjory said. "I'll get us some tea."

Dana chose the center of the least uncomfortable-looking couch and settled Morty on her lap.

Chantal hesitated, looking at the doorway her grandmother had gone through, then at Dana.

"Would you like to pet him?" Dana asked.

Chantal nodded quickly and came to sit beside her. She smiled her father's beautiful smile and extended her hand.

Dana held her breath, ready to intervene if Morty decided to be cranky. He lifted his head, his ears swiveling forward as he regarded the child. His whiskers twitched briefly before he touched his nose to her fingers.

Did he know? Dana wondered. He had taken so quickly to Remy, did he sense the connection to this child?

"He likes me!" Chantal said, snuggling closer to Dana's side.

That makes it unanimous, Dana thought. "Mortimer Q. Morganbrood is a special cat," she said. "He loves books. That's why I put him in all of mine."

"I like books, too. Grandma says I'm a bookworm. That's not a real worm. They're icky. I found a bunch under the rocks in the garden. They were garden worms. Do you have a garden?"

Dana drank in the sound of Chantal's chatter. She didn't want to stem the flow of words, but she wasn't sure how long Marjory would be out of the room. Gently she steered the subject back to books.

The emergency exit at the back of the kitchen was his best bet, Remy decided, bending double as he passed a window. The north side of the lodge wasn't as accessible as the south. The cops would take longer to get into position here, and the slope of the land was steeper. There would probably be a snowdrift to break through, but once he got past that, it would only be twenty yards before he reached the cover of the bush.

Remy pulled on his gloves and reached for the exit handle. He inched the door open and pressed his eye to the crack. Wind moaned past him, stinging his face with crystals of snow. The clouds were growing darker. Snow would be good. It would cover his tracks.

He squinted into the wind. There was no sign of police

yet. They were probably concentrating on the cabin. They wouldn't know he was in the main lodge.

But how had they known he was at the resort in the first place? Who had tipped them off?

And where had Dana gone?

The more he tried to push away his doubts, the more they pushed back. It would be best for Dana if she had turned him in. If the police didn't believe she was coerced, she could still bargain for immunity, or a lighter sentence in exchange for her cooperation. He should be pleased. He should be relieved. He shouldn't be feeling this chill in his chest.

He breathed deeply a few times, charging his blood with oxygen, gauging the distance between the door and the trees. Then he ducked his chin into his collar and slipped outside.

The wind ripped the door from his gloves and slammed it behind him. Remy plunged through the drift that curled around the corner of the lodge and headed for the line of spruce.

There was another bang, but this time it wasn't a door slamming. It was a shot. Something whined past his ear. Snow geysered upward to his right. He went left.

"Stop. Police."

The command came from behind him. Remy's instinct was to speed up. He was less than ten yards from the trees. He had warm clothes and good boots. He was better equipped to survive this time. If all went well, he could head straight west to the highway and then...

And then what? Keep running? Go to Alaska or Mexico? Give up the idea of clearing his name?

What about Chantal? If he left, he would never have a chance to prove his innocence. He would be deserting her for good. Dana, too. What if the police didn't believe she'd been forced to help him? Could he leave her to face the consequences alone?

Every fiber in him rebelled at the thought of surrendering. Prison was a nightmare. He couldn't willingly walk back into it. To be locked up with no privacy, no purpose, no hope…

But what hope did he have if he ran?

Could Dana have been right, should he have tried an appeal, worked with the law instead of against it? Sure, it would take time, and there were no guarantees, but the prospects if he ran were even worse.

There was no way to win. He had to choose. Could he put his trust in the legal system that had failed him before?

Trust? He didn't want to trust anyone or anything.

Maybe it was time he did.

All of this flashed through his head between one step and the next. The cover of the trees was within reach. He could disappear, start a new life.

But what good would life be without his child and the woman he loved?

The woman he loved.

The realization knocked the breath from his lungs. It had come so easily, it must have been there all along. He hadn't seen any proof, but he didn't need to. His heart knew the truth. The doubts that had clouded his vision scattered like snow on the wind.

Remy stopped.

He chose.

"Don't shoot," he called, raising his hands over his head.

For a suspended moment the air went still. He could hear car doors closing, the crackling static of a radio…and the sound of a gun being cocked.

Pain exploded in his back. And the snow-gray morning turned to night.

Dana couldn't contain her excitement. If it hadn't been snowing, if she hadn't been wearing boots, if she hadn't been carrying Morty, she might have done a jig down the walk.

Finally, finally, something had gone right. She couldn't wait to get back to Remy. She wanted to see the look on his face when she showed him what she had.

They had been right. Sylvia had kept a diary. And that inquisitive, wonderful, impulsive, adorable daughter of Remy's had known exactly where her grandmother stored it.

Grinning, Dana pressed her face to Morty's fur. "You clever, clever creature," she whispered.

He dug his claws into her sleeve. He knew they were heading back to the car and the hated carrier. That's what she had counted on. When she had first tried to leave, he had slipped out of her grasp and raced back into the house. During the ensuing search for her fugitive feline, Dana had gone straight to the closet at the top of the staircase that Chantal had described.

Dana knew she had been absolutely shameless, manipulating confidences out of Chantal that way. She would probably feel guilty for the rest of her life over taking advantage of the child's innocent eagerness to please D. J. Whittington. But if the square, tapestry-covered book that weighed down her coat pocket held what she hoped it did, it would be worth any price.

"You know that can of sardines I've been saving for you, Morty? When we get back, it's yours, and the heck with the smell."

He squirmed, but he couldn't escape this time. With drooping ears and an air of martyred dignity, he allowed her to put him in his carrier.

She was humming as she drove to the main street. Once, when Remy had been John, he'd talked about buying wine. She might do that. She felt like celebrating. This diary could mean Remy's freedom. It could mean...

It could mean he would have what he needed, his reason for staying with her would be over and he would leave.

Dana faltered for a moment, then lifted her chin and

hummed louder. It took a few moments before she heard the siren.

She flinched. Marjory couldn't have called the police already, could she? She wouldn't have discovered the diary was missing yet.

Red lights flashed in the opposite lane. A police car was speeding toward her.

Dana's palms grew damp in her gloves. Should she hit the gas? The brake? Before she could react, the police car sped past. It was followed by an ambulance, then another police car.

Shaken, Dana pulled over to the curb. It was probably some traffic accident, she told herself. None of her business. In her rearview mirror, she watched the progress of the vehicles as they went through the center of town. Her gaze was caught by activity in front of the courthouse. Through the cloud of blowing snow, she thought she saw the glare of camera lights. The ambulance and its police escort turned off at the next block, heading toward the town's hospital. The camera lights went out. Moments later a white van with a satellite dish on the roof veered away from the courthouse and turned down the street after the ambulance.

Something was going on, and it wasn't just a traffic accident. Fear clawed at Dana's heart. She didn't want to know. She wanted to pretend nothing was wrong. She wanted to make believe…

Taking a deep breath, Dana did a U-turn and followed the van.

The scene at the hospital was a nightmare, the snow-covered sidewalks and trees flickering with flashes of red. Police cars blocked the drive that led to the emergency entrance. Dana skidded to a stop behind the white van that she now saw bore the logo of a television station. She jumped from her car and ran forward through the gathering crowd just as the rear doors of the ambulance were opened.

At least half a dozen police officers flanked the stretcher that was brought out. Dana had no more than a glimpse of the dark-haired man who was handcuffed to the rail on the stretcher's side. His mouth and nose were covered with an oxygen mask, his face was dark with blood.

She stumbled forward, her body turning to ice. "Remy."

Flashbulbs glared as he was wheeled inside.

Dana broke into a run. *"Remy!"*

Before she could take more than three steps, her path was blocked by a middle-aged man in uniform. "Miss Whittington, you'll have to come with us."

She looked into the ruddy, farmer's face of Constable Savard. She saw no sympathy there, none of the amiability he'd shown before. "No," she said, moving sideways. "Not yet. I have to know if he's all right. I can't leave him—"

"Dana, stop it," a familiar voice said. Hands gripped her arms, pulling her back. "For God's sake, let him go. It's over."

She twisted to see who held her. And looked straight into the eyes of her cousin, Derek Johansen.

No, this was impossible. He was in Florida until next month. "Derek? What are you doing here? What's going on?"

Snow darkened his sun streaked hair. No humor crinkled the laugh lines around his eyes. "What's going on?" he repeated. He leaned down, his blue gaze snapping with questions. "That, my dear cousin, is precisely what I flew seven hundred miles to find out."

Chapter 15

Dana watched her cousin rub the back of his neck wearily as he held the phone to his ear. He was still wearing the tropical print shirt he'd arrived in Hainesborough with. The gaudy turquoise and yellow seemed indecently cheerful here in the cabin. Considering what he'd done, he should have worn black.

It was his fault, she thought, pressing her nails into her palms. He'd been the one to call in the police to check out the resort. He'd been the one who had set off the chain of events that had ended with the man she loved being shot.

She forced her anger down. She shouldn't blame Derek. Given his outgoing nature and his connections in Hainesborough, she should have realized that word of what was happening would get back to him, that someone would mention the escape of the notorious local murderer Remy Leverette and the sudden appearance of his cousin's fiancé. Combine that with a casual comment from her sister about the stranger Dana had rescued in the storm two weeks ago and it hadn't taken long for the keen mind behind Derek's choirboy face to connect the dots.

With an effort she relaxed her fingers and rubbed her palms over her arms. No, she shouldn't blame her cousin. He had done his best to help her. He'd taken care of Morty when Constable Savard had snapped the handcuffs on her. He'd found her a lawyer and he'd posted her bail. Then he'd placated the rest of her family, helped her avoid the press and brought her back to the privacy of her cabin.

Except the cabin no longer seemed the cozy retreat it once had been. The piles of paper she and Remy had so carefully gathered and meticulously sorted, the notes they had made, even the diary that she'd been so excited about finding meant nothing anymore without him.

She felt Remy's absence in everything she saw or touched. She felt it deep inside herself, as if something vital had been ripped away.

She had known she might lose him. She'd known it this morning when she'd slipped from his bed. But not like this, God, not like this.

A car engine sounded outside. Headlights swept past the window in the dusk, heading for the lane. It was yet another police car. Wouldn't they be finished by now? Was this much activity normal in the case of a police shooting?

Derek had said the main lodge was off-limits until the police finished taking their photographs and measurements. There would be yellow police tape cordoning off the place on the north side where the shooting had happened. Dana hadn't wanted to go there, anyway. She didn't think she would be able to handle seeing the trampled snow and the frozen blood.

Derek said a few words and finished his phone call. The receiver rattled into its cradle.

Dana turned her back on the window and studied her cousin's face, trying to guess what he had learned. She was almost afraid to ask. "What did you find out?"

Derek came over to stand in front of her, his expression

grim. "I just talked to the head nurse on the surgical ward."

Fast. Please say it fast and get it over with, Dana thought. *No, don't say anything. Let me hope for another minute.*

"Leverette's out of surgery. He's expected to recover."

The relief that washed over her made her stagger. The world tilted, then righted itself once more.

Derek caught her shoulders to steady her. "Dana, are you all right?"

She pressed her lips together hard to keep the sob inside. She nodded quickly.

"Maybe you'd better rest. It's been a long day."

Remy was out of surgery. He would recover. The weight that had been pressing down on her soul, smothering her thoughts, suddenly lifted. "I need to see him."

"You can't. He's under guard, and they're not allowing visitors." He paused. "It would be better for you if you distanced yourself from him. He's a convicted felon."

"Remy's innocent. He never should have been convicted."

Another pause, this time longer. "Dana, I know you've always had a soft spot for strays and underdogs, but don't let some misguided sense of compassion blind you to the truth."

His words were like an echo of her own doubts, the doubts she had overcome days ago. She met his gaze squarely. "I'm in love with him, Derek. And I'm not going to rest until I finish what he started."

"What do you mean?"

"I'm going to prove his innocence. And you, my dear cousin, are going to help."

"I came here to help you, not him."

"Then it's the same thing." She smiled. "Remy and I are in this together. The only way to clear my name is to clear his."

* * *

The cop on guard duty pushed open the door to Remy's room. "You've got a visitor, Leverette."

Remy concentrated hard to get the water glass on the tray table. He didn't want the cop to see his weakness. His grip was too shaky to hold the glass steady, but he could only use his left hand—his right was handcuffed to the bed.

Since he had awakened in this room three days ago, Remy hadn't been allowed any visitors. No one had come through that door except cops and hospital staff. There had been plenty of them, too, too many to count, but there were only two people he wanted to see.

Instead of a doctor or another uniformed officer, a bald man in a camel-hair overcoat entered the room, strode past the cop and walked directly to the side of the bed. "You are Remy Leverette, I presume?"

Remy started to nod, then hissed at the pain the movement caused. "Yeah."

The man placed a twenty-dollar bill on the tray table beside Remy's glass. "Would you give me that bill, please?"

What was going on? Was this some kind of sick cop joke? "Why?"

"Once I receive your payment, I will officially be your lawyer, and we can tell that beagle at the door to go polish his gun."

Remy eyed the money. A lawyer? It had been three days. He was wondering when the vultures would descend. "The last Legal Aid guy didn't play games like this."

"Sir, I am not here at the request of Legal Aid." The man removed his coat and draped it over a chair, revealing a charcoal wool suit and an elegant burgundy tie. "My name is Evan Packard. And considering what I'm charging by the hour, you would be wise to complete our transaction as quickly as possible."

"Whoever told you to come here made a mistake. I don't have any money to pay you."

"You have twenty dollars to start with, and it appears you also have generous friends."

"Who?"

Packard glanced at the policeman behind him, then looked pointedly at the bill on the table.

Remy didn't like lawyers. He didn't trust them. But lately he'd come to realize that trusting too little could be as bad as trusting too much. He put his fingertips on the bill and shoved it toward Packard.

"Very good," Packard said, slipping the money into his breast pocket. He flicked his fingers dismissively at the policeman, waited until the door had closed behind him, then pulled a chair next to the bed and sat. He spoke before Remy could form his first question. "First of all, I want your version of how you were shot."

"My version? Like I told the cops, I was surrendering."

Packard's head gleamed as he nodded. "Excellent. That agrees with Constable Savard's findings. You were shot in the back, you were unarmed, and the measurements taken at the scene suggest you had been stationary. Second," he continued with no perceptible pause for breath. "How incapacitated are you? What's your prognosis?"

"They got the bullet out. They say I'll be fine. From what I've heard, they'll be transferring me to the infirmary at the Kingston Pen as soon as I can be moved."

"Then I shall have to work quickly."

"Before we go any further, I want you to do something for me."

"Very well, what would you like?"

"I want you to find out what happened to Dana Whittington. And if she doesn't have a lawyer, I want you to forget about me and help her."

To his shock, Packard laughed. "You two must have read from the same script."

"What?"

"I'm well acquainted with Miss Whittington. It is she whom her cousin initially hired me to defend."

Despite the agony in his ribs, Remy gripped the side of the bed and sat forward. The chain at his wrist clanked noisily against the railing. "How is she? Was she charged? The cops won't tell me anything."

"Yes, she was charged with aiding a fugitive, but we hope to have the charges dismissed. That's why—"

"Where is she? Is she all right?"

"As far as I know she is in good health. She is free on bail and staying with her cousin."

Remy exhaled slowly and eased back into the pillows. So she was safe, she was free. At least temporarily. "Her cousin. That would be Derek Johansen. You said he was the one who hired you?"

"Yes. And he is continuing to pay my salary." Packard *tsked* and shook his head. "There is a certain amount of irony to the situation when one considers that Mr. Johansen was the one who instigated your arrest in the first place."

So it hadn't been Dana. Remy had already discarded that suspicion. It had dissolved along with the rest of his doubts in that shining moment of revelation.

The days since his arrival at the hospital were a blur of pain and frustration, but his memory of the instant in the snow, when he'd recognized his love for Dana, was as vivid now as it had been then.

If only he could live over their final morning together, if he could go back and tell her what she wanted to hear, what he'd been too blind to see and afraid to say…

Right. Sure. With good behavior, in another twenty-five years maybe he'd get the chance.

Packard was still talking. "Mr. Johansen quite correctly deduced that the best strategy to use to eliminate the charges against Miss Whittington would be to clear your name. While I've made considerable progress to that end already, we do have our work cut out for us."

Hope sparked, quick and vicious. He wanted to believe, but he didn't dare. "You said you made progress?" Remy asked, his voice hoarse. "How?"

The corners of Packard's mouth pinched into an impatient expression. He was obviously a man who preferred to follow his own agenda during a conversation. "Actually, you did that yourself by your actions before you were shot."

"What?"

"If you had been in the act of fleeing, the shooting would have been justified, but as you were stationary and in the act of surrendering, there was strong evidence to suggest the shooting was deliberate. That was our first break."

"Do you mean that because I chose not to run…"

"You'll obtain your freedom more quickly than if you had chosen to escape," Packard finished for him. "My goodness, this case if full of ironies, isn't it?"

Remy's head was reeling. He wanted so much to believe what he was hearing, it hurt.

"We could file a suit against the officer responsible," Packard said. "But since he is already facing far more serious charges, there may not be much point."

Remy hadn't bothered to ask. He hadn't thought it mattered who had pulled the trigger. All cops were the same—the enemy, not to be trusted. "Who was it?"

"Detective Charles Sibley."

"Sibley shot me? That son of a—"

"Please Mr. Leverette. Let's endeavor to keep on topic here. Detective Sibley has been charged with attempted murder for his unprovoked shooting of you during your surrender. Combined with the new evidence which Miss Whittington has provided—"

"Wait. What evidence? What did Dana find?"

"Why, your late wife's diary, of course. It was very, ah, explicit, shall we say?"

Remy whispered an oath. Sylvia's diary. He hadn't been sure it even existed. Dana had believed it did. She hadn't given up.

Dana. It hurt to think about her and not be able to see her, touch her, hear her voice, taste her kiss…

"The diary provided grounds to execute a search warrant at Sibley's residence," Packard said. "As a result, he has also been charged with obstructing justice for withholding evidence."

"What?"

"He was in possession of records from your home and your business that confirm your alibi for the day of your wife's murder."

The spark of hope flared so brightly, Remy couldn't breathe. He listened to the lawyer in silence.

"Sibley's animosity toward you is well known, yet apparently he withheld this evidence not only to convict you but to protect himself. He was your late wife's lover, Mr. Leverette. Once all the evidence is processed, Detective Sibley will be charged with the murder of Sylvia Haines Leverette."

Detective Charles Sibley. It all seemed so obvious, once you knew where to look, Dana thought. She had wondered more than once what was wrong with Sibley and the Hainesborough Police Department. She hadn't pursued that idea, because she had attributed the problems with Remy's trial and conviction to his influential in-laws, Sibley's personal bias against him and to a small town's collective long memory of his father's repeated problems with the law.

Remy hadn't seen it, either. Again, it would have been obvious if he'd known where to look. He'd been right about Sylvia having a lover, but he hadn't predicted she would follow the same pattern that she'd followed with him. She preferred edgy, physical men over the refined country club types. She liked secrecy. She got an added thrill from sneaking around.

And what better way to titillate her sense of adventure than to have a brazen, daylight affair with a cop? Especially one who had a personal grudge against her husband.

Except this time her affair hadn't worked out the way she had anticipated. The entries in Sylvia's diary detailed her growing uneasiness with her lover's escalating possessiveness. Sibley's hatred of Remy was irrational. He regarded stealing Remy's wife—and fathering her child—as payback. His rage when he'd learned of her abortion had frightened her. This was no longer a pleasant diversion. In her final diary entry, Sylvia had written about planning to meet Sibley one last time so she could break off their affair.

Was that why he had killed her? Probably. The diary alone made a strong case against him, but so did the material the police found at his house. It was bound to come out at Sibley's trial. Dana didn't really care about the details, as long as Remy was exonerated.

Dana kept her face averted as she walked past the policeman who was sitting outside Remy's room. According to Derek and that lawyer friend of his, she shouldn't be here. Until Remy's conviction was overturned, he was still guilty in the eyes of the law. Continuing her association with him, as Packard put it, wouldn't help her chances of having the charges against her dismissed.

But it had been three days. She had to see him, even if it was only a glimpse through his door. She had to see for herself that he was doing as well as the nurses had told Derek. She wanted to make sure he knew he'd soon be free…

Free to leave.

Her eyes filled. She reached into her pocket for a tissue— she never went anywhere these days without a good supply. Stopping at the end of the corridor, she wiped her eyes, then sat in one of the ugly orange vinyl chairs that were grouped under the window and fixed her gaze on the door of Remy's room.

The main thing was, Remy was alive. And he'd soon be happy. He'd have everything that he wanted.

And she still had a book to finish.

Well, that cabin at Half Moon Bay hadn't turned out to be such a great, distraction-free place to work after all, had it? Where would she have to go next time? Did any of her relatives own desert islands?

She wasn't sure how long she waited. She had gone through three more tissues by the time the door swung open. The policeman guarding the door sprang to his feet as Packard walked out. They had exchanged only a few words before the small man in the camel-hair coat caught sight of Dana. He pursed his lips and gestured to her with an imperious flick of his fingers.

Dana hurried forward. "How is he? Is something wrong?"

Packard sighed. "Miss Whittington, I specifically advised you not to come here. But it's just as well. This will save time."

"What happened?" she asked, glancing at the door, wishing she could see through it. "You never answered my question. Is he all right?"

"Acting as Mr. Leverette's attorney, I'm obliged to carry out his instructions. I was just informing this officer that my client has requested to be allowed a particular visitor."

The policeman smothered a yawn as he turned to look at her. "You're Dana Whittington?"

She nodded.

"Hold out your arms."

She complied immediately.

He patted the sides of her coat, then reached beneath it to pat her thighs, her hips and under her arms. He stepped back and tipped his head toward the door. "Go ahead. I'll stay right here, so just yell if you need—"

She didn't wait for the rest of what he was going to say. That was all she needed. She pushed open the door and slipped inside.

A long, thin fluorescent light fixture on the wall was the room's only illumination. Stark shadows flanked the utilitarian hospital furniture. There was only one bed.

Remy was lying against the pillows, his face almost as pale as the sheets. A blue hospital gown barely stretched across his chest. Metal gleamed at his wrist. He was hand-cuffed to the bed.

Something grabbed at her heart and squeezed. She had known he'd been in prison, but the reality of what he must have endured didn't strike her fully until right now. The sight of him alone, helpless, shackled, was obscene.

He turned his head toward the door. "And while you're at it, Packard, see what you can find out—" His words cut off as his eyes met hers. He stared. "Dana?"

She clasped her hands in front of her. They were shaking. She wasn't sure she'd be able to speak past the lump in her throat. She moved to the foot of the bed.

He grasped the rails on either side of him and levered himself up. His lips thinned as he breathed hard through his nose a few times, but his gaze didn't leave her face. "How... I only told Packard a minute ago."

"I was outside. I..." She paused, not knowing what to say now that she was here.

So she simply looked at him, feeling the void his absence had made slowly begin to fill. He was going to be all right, she told herself. Despite his pale cheeks, his gaze was bright. Despite the trembling in his arms, his muscles were still strong. And she loved him so much her knees were buckling.

"Packard told me you found the diary," Remy said.

"Yes. Morty helped."

"Thank you."

"You're welcome."

"It was Sibley."

"Yes, I know. He was arrested this morning."

"I can't believe it's over."

She wouldn't cry, she told herself. She wouldn't have him remember her that way. "Almost," she said.

"Have you seen Chantal?"

"Yes. She's fine."

"Does she..." A muscle flicked in his cheek. "Does she know about me?"

"Marjory promised she would tell her, when you're cleared."

His knuckles whitened where he gripped the rails. "I'm still trying to take it in."

"Me, too." She saw the controls for the bed on his right and realized the way he was restrained wouldn't allow him to reach them. She moved to his side and pressed the button that would raise the head of the mattress.

He leaned back slowly, then let go of the railing and held out his hand toward her as far as the chain at his wrist would allow.

With a sob she laced her fingers with his.

At the touch of his skin, a sensation of completeness blossomed in her soul. She felt the calluses on his palms, the strength in his grip...and the indefinable bond that had sparked between them the very first time she had held his hand.

What was she doing? she asked herself. What had happened to the noble sacrifice she had been willing to make for his happiness? He was alive, he was going to be free. For the past three days she'd told herself that was all that mattered. If she really loved him, she would let him go.

Like hell she would let him go.

She pressed their joined hands to her breasts and looked into his face.

His eyes were shining with an emotion that took her breath away. "Dana, I want to talk about afterward."

"Afterward?"

"After I'm exonerated, after I get my freedom and my daughter back." He swallowed. He brushed his knuckles against her breasts. "I know this isn't the best time or place, and I know I'm not in the greatest shape, but I thought I would have to wait twenty-five years to say this, and I don't plan to wait another second."

There wasn't enough air in the room. There wasn't enough space in her chest for the love that was swelling in her heart.

He lifted his free hand to her face. His fingers shook as they whispered over her cheek. "Dana, I don't want you to leave."

"You don't?"

"When I get out, I want you to stay with me. Or I'll stay with you. I don't care where, as long as you don't leave. Ever."

"Oh, Remy, I'm not going anywhere. You can't make me."

His lips curved into a smile. "Seems I've heard that before."

"Probably."

He slid his hand into her hair and cupped the back of her neck. "I love you, Dana. I can't picture my future without you in it. Will you marry me?"

The joy that burst over her was so fast, so deep, so huge, it made her gasp. She braced her hand on the pillow beside his head and leaned toward him. "I love you, Remy. You. Don't ever doubt that."

He pulled her closer, showing her his love with a kiss that left no room for doubts. Although there still was a shackle on his wrist, the bars around his heart were gone for good.

Epilogue

Remy heard the voices from the bedroom before he reached the doorway. Good, he wasn't too late. It had taken him longer than he'd figured to get back from the new job site. If work kept going this well, he'd have to hire a second shift.

It had been a challenging six months. After he had been released and the charges against Dana had been dropped, he'd begun to rebuild his life. It had been as difficult as he'd thought to establish another business, but Dana's cousin had been a big help. It had taken a while for Derek Johansen to warm to him, but once he had, Derek had been as supportive as his father had been fifteen years ago when he'd built the Half Moon Bay resort.

Sylvia's parents were another matter. They had spent more than a year believing Remy had killed their daughter, so he couldn't expect them to change overnight. They were making an effort to be fair, though, and he had no intention of keeping them away from their grandchild. He knew only too well how hard it was to trust someone again.

Thank God Dana had shown him how. He smiled, leaned a shoulder against the door frame and watched as the nightly ritual unfolded.

''And the brave leader of the pirate mice threw down his sword. His work was done.'' Dana waited while Chantal turned the page. ''The lazy rats would steal no more food. They would be too busy harvesting the corn that Mortimer planted.''

Chantal leaned forward to pet Morty. The cat curled up on the quilt, settled his head on his paws and purred smugly, as if taking credit for his namesake's deeds.

Dana chuckled, then lifted her arm so that Chantal could snuggle underneath once more. They were on Chantal's bed, their heads propped against a mound of frilly pillows that Dana had bought last week. A doll was tucked into the bed beside them and a pair of roller skates dangled from the footboard. Remy's gaze wandered to the framed prints on the walls and the overflowing bookcase, more of Dana's contributions to his and his daughter's life.

But the cheerful room, the house they had found together last month, all the positive changes she had brought couldn't compare to what she gave so freely every day.

Love. It was there in her eyes, her voice and her touch. It made the future shimmer like gold.

''And then what happened?'' Chantal asked, although she knew the story by heart.

''John and Mortimer made a promise to always be friends. They jumped into their ships and sailed to the is-land of pirate mice.'' Dana turned to the last page and leaned her cheek against the top of Chantal's head. ''The entire village was at the pier to meet the ships. There were fireworks and marching bands and ice cream and cake for everyone.''

Remy pushed away from the doorway and walked into the room, saying the last line himself. ''And then John lifted his daughter onto his shoulders and danced all the way home.''

"Hi, Daddy!" Chantal said, her face lighting up as she held out her arms.

"Hello, Remy." Dana smiled. "Welcome home."

Remy felt his chest expand. Sometimes it took him unawares, this love he felt. He put his arms around both of them, hanging on until his breathing steadied. Then he tucked his daughter into her bed and carried his wife to theirs.

And afterward, as he was drifting to sleep, he marveled yet again at the wonder of it all. Somehow this incredible woman he had married had created the best happy ending in history.

*   *   *   *   *

▼™ SILHOUETTE®
SENSATION™

AVAILABLE FROM 19TH JULY 2002

HARD TO HANDLE Kylie Brant

Charmed and Dangerous

Meghan Patterson dared not let Detective Gabe Connally get close enough to her nephew to discover his special psychic gift. Yet her burning desire made it impossible to resist Gabe's persuasive ways…

A HERO IN HER EYES Marie Ferrarella

Childfinders Inc.

Eliza Eldridge was dreaming of a missing little girl. But could Eliza convince Walker Banacek that she was the one woman who could find his daughter…and then love him with all her heart?

TAYLOR'S TEMPTATION Suzanne Brockmann

Tall, Dark & Dangerous

Bobby Taylor, protector of the innocent, found it hard watching over gorgeous redhead Colleen Skelly. She was his best friend's sister but he couldn't help wanting more than just his eye on her…

BORN OF PASSION Carla Cassidy

First-Born Sons

One stolen night of passion and Kyle Ramsey had left Joanna Morgan pregnant! Now Kyle was determined to win over Joanna and claim her—and his child—as his own…

COPS AND…LOVERS? Linda Castillo

Policewoman Erin McNeal had come to sleepy Logan Falls for a second chance, not to be chased by a killer or to be watched over by a man as infuriating—and disarmingly attractive—as Nick Ryan.

DANGEROUS ATTRACTION Susan Vaughan

Undercover agent Michael Quinn didn't trust anyone, especially Marie Claire Saint-Ange. She might be a dangerous criminal but when she trembled in his arms he longed to believe in her innocence…

MARIE FERRARELLA
BEVERLY BARTON
LINDSAY McKENNA
DANGEROUS TO LOVE
3 SENSATIONAL, SEXY ROMANCES!
On sale 21st June 2002
0702/81/SH32

SILHOUETTE INTRIGUE

presents

two stories from popular author
Sheryl Lynn
set in

McClintock Country

*High up in the Rocky Mountains is a place where
the wind blows fast and fierce, where trust is
precious and where everyone has a secret.*

TO PROTECT THEIR CHILD

July 2002

COLORADO'S FINEST

(a LAWMAN LOVERS story)
August 2002

0702/SH/LC34

2 FREE

books and a surprise gift!

We would like to take this opportunity to thank you for reading this Silhouette® book by offering you the chance to take TWO more specially selected titles from the Sensation™ series absolutely FREE! We're also making this offer to introduce you to the benefits of the Reader Service™—

★ FREE home delivery
★ FREE gifts and competitions
★ FREE monthly Newsletter
★ Exclusive Reader Service discount
★ Books available before they're in the shops

Accepting these FREE books and gift places you under no obligation to buy, you may cancel at any time, even after receiving your free shipment. Simply complete your details below and return the entire page to the address below. *You don't even need a stamp!*

YES! Please send me 2 free Sensation books and a surprise gift. I understand that unless you hear from me, I will receive 4 superb new titles every month for just £2.85 each, postage and packing free. I am under no obligation to purchase any books and may cancel my subscription at any time. The free books and gift will be mine to keep in any case.

S2ZEA

Ms/Mrs/Miss/Mr ....Initials................................
BLOCK CAPITALS PLEASE

Surname ....

Address ....

....

....Postcode............................

Send this whole page to:
UK: FREEPOST CN81, Croydon, CR9 3WZ
EIRE: PO Box 4546, Kilcock, County Kildare (stamp required)